# ORGASMIZER9000
## And other stories

Angelique Anjou
Jaide Fox
Marie Morin

Erotic Futuristic Romance

New Concepts          Georgia

Be sure to check out our website for the very best in fiction at fantastic prices!

When you visit our webpage, you can:

* Read excerpts of currently available books
* View cover art of upcoming books and current releases
* Find out more about the talented artists who capture the magic of the writer's imagination on the covers
* Order books from our backlist
* Find out the latest NCP and author news--including any upcoming book signings by your favorite NCP author
* Read author bios and reviews of our books
* Get NCP submission guidelines
* And so much more!

We offer a 20% discount on all new Trade Paperback releases ordered from our website!

Be sure to visit our webpage to find the best deals in e-books and paperbacks! To find out about our new releases as soon as they are available, please be sure to sign up for our newsletter (http://www.newconceptspublishing.com/newsletter.htm) or join our reader group (http://groups.yahoo.com/group/new_concepts_pub/join)!

The newsletter is available by double opt in only and our customer information is *never* shared!

Visit our webpage at:
www.newconceptspublishing.com

Orgasmizer9000 is an original publication of NCP. This work has never before appeared in book form. This work is a novel. Any similarity to actual persons or events is purely coincidental.

New Concepts Publishing
5202 Humphreys Rd.
Lake Park, GA 31636

ISBN 1-58608-726-6
© copyright Angelique Anjou, Jaide Fox, Marie Morin

Cover art (c) copyright Eliza Black

NCP books are available at special quantity discounts for bulk purchases for sales promotions, premiums, fund raising, or educational use. For details, write, email, or phone New Concepts Publishing, 5202 Humphreys Rd., Lake Park, GA 31636; Ph. 229-257-0367, Fax 229-219-1097; orders@newconceptspublishing.com.

First NCP Paperback Printing: 2005

4

# TABLE OF CONTENTS

# DREAM WARRIORS

By

Angelique Anjou

## Chapter One

"Mayday! Mayday! Mayday! This is the pilot of the private cruiser Laurel-Lynn M4J679. I've just passed through a micro meteor shower in quadrant LBT13009 in the Horseshoe Nebula and have experienced structural damage."

Laurel Conyers switched off the microphone while she waited to see if anyone would pick up the signal. Seeing that she'd dropped within viewing distance of the planet below her, she activated the craft's stealth mode. There was no sense in scaring the shit out of the natives.

Her radio squawked as it picked up a counter transmission. She turned it on again and started panting and gasping.

"Mayday! Mayday! This is the pilot...." She repeated the previous message.

"Laurel-Lynn M4J679--this is Station O2412 on the outer rim. What's your status?"

Laurel frowned, dropping a little lower as she saw a land mass appear in her viewing port. "Station O2412--This is Laurel-Lynn M4J679. I'm hemorrhaging air. The rudder is sluggish. Some computer malfunction. I'm going to have to set it down for repairs. Copy?"

"Laurel-Lynn M4J679, this is Station O2412. You are in restricted space. I repeat, you are in restricted space. Can you make it to the next system?"

"Negative. I'm going to have to find something closer--really close," Laurel said, panting into the microphone for a little added drama before she turned it off and leaned forward in her seat. A smile curled her lips. There was a village just below her. Pulling the cruiser in a wide turn, she headed back for another look, dropping a little lower.

"Private cruiser Laurel-Lynn M4J679, this is Station O2412. You are not authorized to land in that sector. I repeat, you are not authorized to land in that sector."

Laurel activated her microphone again. "Just what part of 'I'm fucking crashing' do you not understand, Station O2412?"

As she did her second fly by, she saw that it was a good sized city. In the center was a large building she decided was probably a temple--primitives were always big on worshipping gods. There were two smaller buildings on either side of the 'temple' which she figured must be gathering places of some sort, since they looked to be too big to be a single family dwelling. Unless they were something like apartments? The streets were laid out in a perfect grid, forming squares. Dwellings nestled shoulder to shoulder around the squares.

It looked perfect to her--not too big, but big enough to have a reasonably good sized population, she decided. She began looking for a clearing where she could land her craft.

"Laurel-Lynn M4J679 this is Station O2412, the only planet in that system with breathable air is the fourth planet from the star, NY3410--primitive society, believed to be hostile, protected species. Can you make repairs in space?"

"Negative, Station O2412. Guess I'm just going to have to take my chances with the barbarians. It shouldn't take me more than a couple of weeks, tops. I'll check back when I've had time to look everything over. Laurel-Lynn M4J679 out."

Really! All the panting and gasping and acting fearful was starting to make her head swim.

Switching off the radio, Laurel concentrated on the terrain below. It was pretty thick with vegetation--no bare spots. "Shit. I'm just going to have to make a hole."

After checking the distance from the village, she targeted a spot near a small stream of water, did a life form scan and hit it with a laser beam when she saw there was no higher life forms within the immediate vicinity. The beam cut a twenty foot diameter swath through the vegetation, clearing it to the dirt. Satisfied, she dropped her cruiser into the 'hole' she'd made.

When the onboard computer informed her that the craft had landed, she shut everything down, threw off her safety belts and moved to the viewing ports. A shiver of delight went through her. "I'm going to have *the* best damned thesis that University has ever set eyes on!" she said gleefully.

Unfortunately, she only had a couple of weeks, tops, to gather her data. Less than that if there was a confederation cruiser close enough to do a fly by and check her story out.

With that thought, Laurel drew her laser pistol from the holster and studied the interior of the cruiser carefully, trying to decide where to put the holes. Fortunately, it occurred to her before she'd done it that micro meteors would have struck outside to in, not vice versa. Sighing, she opened the hatch and lowered the gang plank.

The scent of vegetation that struck her as the door slid open was nearly overwhelming. The smell of flowers, and fruit, dead things, rotting vegetation--and burned vegetation, assaulted her in a cacophony of smells.

"This is going to take some getting used to," she muttered. "Who'd have thought plants would smell?" The plants on the space station didn't seem to have that much smell, but maybe it was because there weren't nearly so many plants so close together?

Or, maybe it was the dirt?

Or the animals?

Shrugging, she went down the gang plank and picked her way around the craft carefully, studying the ship speculatively. She really hated having to put holes in it, but the enforcers of the Confederation Policing Agency were bound to check her ship to see if she'd made up her 'emergency' landing. Sighing, she moved around to the rudder and pull a couple of half inch holes in it, scattered a couple on the fins in an artful splash and then, after studying the cockpit carefully for some time, placed two in the main cabin.

When she'd finished, she went inside to check the damage. "Well fuck! Wouldn't you know it! I hit the damned radio!"

Now they were going to be wondering how she'd managed to call for help. "Fuck it!" she muttered irritably. She could fix it later. She'd just have to tell them she'd had to patch the radio up before she radioed in her distress call, but she couldn't get the other holes plugged.

That would work.

She was probably going to have to put a few more holes in the ship before she left though.

Fortunately, she had brought plenty of supplies for repairs, just in case she met up with an accident on her trip to the Perrsons Star System, which just happened to make it necessary for her to pass right by the HS Nebula.

Shoving her pistol into her holster, she went to her locker and started pulling her instruments out and checking them.

First things first--she was going to have to get close enough to pick up speech with her translator before it could start analyzing the language. Once she had enough input, though, she'd be able to tell what they were talking about and then she could start taking notes on their social order, religious practices, mating rituals and so forth.

This was just sooooo exciting! She was going to be the first, the only, person to study the primitives of NY3410!

\* \* \* \*

Faine D'Arten narrowed his eyes as he sensed the strange disturbance in the sky above the village once more. When he focused upon it, he saw that it was almost cylindrical in shape--like a curved piece of the sky. Frowning, he followed it with his gaze until he determined the direction of its path and set off through the jungle. There he followed it by the disturbance it created in the tops of the trees. He was nearing the stream when he saw a bright light appear in the forest before him. The vegetation simply turned to ash before his eyes.

His expression hardened. He had known it must be one of the star people. They were forbidden to visit his world, but he had seen the evidence of their trespass before.

Grimly, he found a position to watch and waited to see if he could determine what the intruder had come for.

As the strange object began to settle toward the ground, it ceased to look like a piece of the sky and took on the look of the jungle surrounding it. If he had not known it was there, he might have overlooked it. It did not look just the same. The images were wavery--like when heat danced upon the horizon, but unless one were specifically searching for it, the disguise was good enough to fool most.

Of course the desecration of the forest would have been a strong indication that something was not as it should be.

When he heard a faint sound that seemed to indicate activity, he moved around the perimeter for a better look. A hole had opened in the side of the object. His heart slammed against his ribs as he saw the creature that appeared in the opening.

It was the most beautiful being he had ever set eyes upon, with hair the color of the sun and pale, golden skin. His gaze dropped to its chest. When he saw that it was female a sense of desire and possessiveness moved over him.

Mesmerized, he watched the bounce and sway of her breasts as she walked down the board that led to the ground, bringing her closer so that he could see he hadn't just imagined how beautiful she was. She wore some strange garment that covered most of her body, but it conformed to her shape and he could see that her body was as beautifully formed as her features. Her hair, drawn back tightly from her face and worn tied together high on the back of her head, swung as she walked, catching sunlight within it that sparkled like the yellow metal the women of his people were so fond of adorning themselves with.

He had no desire to adorn his body with anything but hers, he thought, stalking her as she moved around the strange object, watching curiously as she pulled a stick from a carrier along her hip. His eyes widened when light shot from the stick--straight into the object that had carried her to his world.

A smile curled her lips as she studied what she had done

and then she turned and went inside once more.

Puzzled, he settled down to wait until she came out once more, dividing half his mind between trying to understand what she had done and why she had done it, and the other half in trying to decide how best to capture her.

The weapon--it had to be a weapon--would be almost as good a prize as the female herself, but he had no desire to discover what it would do to his body when something much like it had reduced the forest to ash.

He was glad he had not ignored the strange dream vision that he had had.

He was glad he had waited to take a wife.

## Chapter Two

The sun had already begun to sink toward the tops of the trees by the time Laurel had everything organized. She hesitated on the gang plank, wondering if she should just wait until the following morning before she made her first excursion to the village. Time was something she didn't have much of, however.

It was really irritating, though, to be at the mercy of nature. She'd never thought it would be so inconvenient.

Shrugging, she went back inside and added a portable light to her bag. When she'd reached the ground, she turned and aimed the remote toward the controls for the gang plank and the door, waiting until the ship was secure, and then dropped the remote into her bag and pulled her communicator out, pulling up a map of the area, frowning in concentration as she carefully oriented her current position with the one the computer had mapped for the village.

It was only a fifteen minute walk according to the computer's calculations.

Shifting her pack to a more comfortable position on her back, she struck off through the dense jungle. Twenty minutes later, huffing for breath--sweating!--she stopped to examine the map again.

According to the map, she was only three quarters of the way there. "Computer, calculate the walk according to the current terrain," she said testily.

"Thirty minutes."

"Well, for chrissake! Couldn't you have done that in the first place?" she snapped.

"You told me to calculate on the distance."

"Explain to me why I bothered to pay extra for artificial intelligence--because if I was going to have to rely on myself anyway, I could have saved that money!"

"You should be aware that you are within hearing distance of the barbarians if you continue to speak in a loud tone of voice," the computer said warningly.

Laurel glared at the tiny viewing screen and shoved it into her pack.

There was a slight rise at the edge of the village along the tree line. As soon as Laurel began to hear sounds indicating that she was nearing it, she crouched down and began to move more cautiously. Finally, she reached the rise. Below her, she could see the natives moving about. Settling on her belly, she pulled the pack from her shoulder and dragged her translator out. When she'd adjusted it to maximum range, she set it carefully on the ground and activated her recorder.

"I have now reached the outskirts of the village of the barbarians. Currently, it appears that they are making piles with limbs of vegetation and setting fire to them. I'm not certain what the purpose of this is, but I think they might use them for light since it's late evening now and growing dark," she whispered into the tiny microphone.

Lifting slightly away from the ground, she craned her neck to see a little better. "The primitives do not appear to wear clothing of any kind--perhaps because this stinking planet feels like a fucking sauna--wait! I see a female now. Her genitals are covered by some sort of garment. It looks like some kind of woven natural fibers--so they have some manufacturing capabilities. This garment is fastened around her hips and looks like a long rectangle, which leaves her thighs bare. She has something on her breasts--a bra like thing, but that appears to be metal in nature."

"The primitives are a humanoid race, very tall from what I can see from my observation position--dark. Their skin is brown, probably because they run around naked in the sun, or half naked. But their hair is very dark, as well, so it's possible they are naturally dark anyway."

Hearing the snap of vegetation very close by, Laurel stilled, listening. When she didn't hear it again, she decided to carefully check the area to make certain none of the wildlife had grown curious of her. As she glanced around, though, she saw that there was a foot--right beside her.

Staring at it blankly for several moments, she finally followed the leg the foot was attached to, rolling onto her side when she discovered her position prevented her from seeing anything but the bottom half of the male standing over her.

"There is a very large, very angry looking primitive standing over me. He is wearing--tattoos," she said into her recorder, sliding her hand down along her thigh very slowly in search of her laser. She found the holster, but to her consternation the pistol was gone. "This particular specimen is very lean and muscular, which seems to indicate a healthy diet and rigorous lifestyle.

"He may see me as a threat and I seem to have dropped my weapon somewhere. I have not yet analyzed their speech patterns, but I will attempt to communicate via facial expressions and gestures."

She smiled at him, holding her hands out palm up to show him she didn't have a weapon.

He squatted down.

She hadn't realized until that moment that he was standing with one foot on either side of her. She tried not to notice the genitals that were hovering just above her torso, swaying slightly--the balls were swaying. The cock was looking her dead in the eye.

She swallowed with an effort. "The … uh … genitalia of the male is very much like that of a human male. The pubic hair has been shaved into some sort of pattern--it doesn't look natural, but I'm not certain if this is some sort of … uh

… fashion statement, or if it, perhaps, has mystical implications. The … uh … hooded man is at half staff, so I'm assuming that he is not attracted to … wait … it's standing at attention now. I may have been a little premature in my previous observation."

*"I am Faine D'Arten. Who are you? And what are you doing here?"*

Laurel's eyes widened in excitement. Blindly, she felt around for the translator. "The subject spoke to me. I've no clue of what the fuck he just said, but it sounded just a little bit threatening," she said into her recorder, then smiled at him again.

Finally, she found the translator and closed her fingers around it.

"Hi! My name's Laurel Conyers. I'm a grad student and I just came to do a little research for my thesis. I know you haven't got a clue of what I'm saying right now, but if you'll notice, I'm smiling and this denotes a non-threatening gesture."

He caught her wrist when she lifted the translator. Her hand went numb almost instantly. Taking the translator from her limp grip, he studied it suspiciously for several moments and finally closed his hand around it, crushing it as if it were a wad of paper.

Laurel's mouth fell open. "My translator!" she gasped in dismay. "Oh! This is good. Have you got any idea how much one of those damned things cost? *And*, I might add, now I'm not going to be able to talk to you at all!"

His brows rose at her tone. Reaching down, he grasped her upper arms and stood up, pulling her with him.

When she was on her feet, she discovered she hadn't merely imagined the primitives were big--they *were* big. She figured she could walk beneath his outstretched arm without brushing the top of her head or bending over. "The subject I am currently observing appears to be somewhere in the neighborhood of six and a half feet tall."

He studied her for several moments, his gaze zeroing in on the tiny microphone.

*"What is this?"*

He'd hardly spoken when he snatched her ear piece off. Laurel made a grab for it. He held it up, out of her reach. She leapt up, grabbing for it, but saw she couldn't snatch it back as long as he was dangling it about four feet over her head. Balling her hand into a fist, she planted it in the middle of his stomach. It felt like she'd driven her hand into the bulkhead of her ship. The impact sent painful vibrations all the way up her arm. "Shit!" she yelped, slinging her hand until the pain subsided, then glaring up at him. "Give it back!" she demanded.

He looked bemused as he stared down at her from his towering height. Apparently, he hadn't expected her to fight back.

Laurel narrowed her eyes. "I demand that you give me my recorder back right this instant! You've already trashed my translator. I *need* my recorder!"

Instead of handing it to her, he turned and tossed it into the woods. Laurel whirled to race after it. He caught her around the waist, knocking the breath out of her as he lifted her off her feet. She hung limply for several moments, trying to catch her breath. When she recovered, she saw that he was following a path that led toward the village.

Laurel balled her hand into a fist and hit him on the thigh, but she wasn't at a very good angle for packing much of a punch. There was nothing for it.

She grabbed him by his genitals.

*"Shit!"* he exclaimed.

He dropped her. She hit the ground hard enough her breath left her in a loud grunt. She didn't know what he'd said, but he sounded just a little bit pissed off. Scrambling to her hands and knees, she headed for the brush.

*"Damn it, woman!"* he growled. He caught her around the waist once more. This time, however, he slung her over his shoulder.

She grunted as his shoulder pushed the air from her lungs again. When she recovered, she started hammering against his back. "Put me down, you savage!"

His hand came down, hard, on her ass.

Her eyes widened. Rearing up, she grabbed a handful of

his long, dark hair and gave it several vicious tugs.

*"By the gods!"* he roared, dropping her to the ground once more and glaring down at her. *"You're an ill-tempered female! Dream vision or no, I'm not so sure I want you for my mate!"*

## Chapter Three

Laurel sat on the floor next to the bed, giving the alien the evil eye as he emptied her pack on the table in front of him and studied the contents curiously. He'd bound her wrists and tied her to the damned bed! She'd promptly climbed out of it again, but the rope he'd used wasn't long enough for her to get as far away from it was she wanted to.

She couldn't get her mind off of that little "howdy ma'am" his hooded man had given her in the woods.

Of course, it might have been because she was examining it and he thought that meant that *she* was interested, which she certainly wasn't! She'd only been curious. That was all, and she figured she should make notations on all of her observations. One never knew when one might discover a piece of information that fit with something else and presented a broader picture.

He picked the communicator up first, turned it over a couple of times and set it aside.

"According to my calculations, you are inside the perimeter of the primitive village, Laurel. Should you be doing this?"

"Shut up!" Laurel snapped.

The barbarian had glanced at the communicator when the computer started speaking. He transferred his gaze to her when she answered it. Picking up the device once more, he studied the map on the screen, moved it around, watching the small blinking dot. Finally, he rose and moved toward her. *"What is this thing?"* he asked, squatting down beside her and pointing to the dot.

Laurel stared at him blankly for several moments, realizing with more than a little surprise that he'd figured out that the dot was her--she thought.

He pointed to the dot again and turned the map around.

He *had* figured it out, Laurel thought in sudden excitement. This was … amazing! Everyone thought they must have a very low intelligence, but he, at least, had to be pretty bright. She pointed to the dot. "Laurel," she said slowly, and then pointed to herself and repeated it.

His dark brows rose. *"You are called La-rel?"*

Laurel nodded excitedly, repeating the name.

He pointed to himself. *"Faine D'Arten."*

It was a lot harder to repeat the words exactly the way he'd said it than she'd thought it would be. She curled her tongue around the strange sounds several times and finally managed to reproduce a close approximation.

Faine felt his lips twitch with amusement at the way she said his name. *"Clever girl!"* he said, patting her head.

Laurel blinked in surprise when he patted her head and then glared at him when she realized that the gesture was suspiciously like patting a pet that had learned a new trick. "Ass!"

He tucked a finger beneath her chin and tipped her head up, studying her face. Laurel took the opportunity examine his face, since he was so close and he was examining her.

It was an interesting face, surprisingly attractive--for a primitive, she added mentally. Actually, honesty compelled her to correct that, it was a very nice face, period. The bone structure of his face would have been enthralling even if his features put together had not really appealed--which they most definitely did. His eyes, which surprised her considering that the natives were dark skinned and had dark hair, were green. She would've expected the eyes to be pigmented much as the hair and skin was.

His mouth was very nice, especially when he smiled, but it made her belly feel trembly even when he was frowning.

She sighed. "I do *wish* you hadn't thrown my recorder away! I'll never remember all this stuff if I can't get it recorded."

A faint frown marred his brows. After a moment, he lifted his hand and placed his palm along the side of her head, spreading the tips of his fingers along her skull from her temple to a point just behind her ear.

Something ... *tickled* her mind. There was no other word to describe it. It was very light, but like a physical touch.

She jerked away from him, staring at him in surprise.

He got up after a moment and went back to the table where he'd been sitting. Lifting something from the things scattered across the surface, he returned, squatted beside her once more and dangled the object he'd picked up before her nose.

Laurel blinked, staring at it in stupefaction. It was her recorder!

"How did you do that?" she gasped, making a grab for it.

He snatched it out of her reach.

She narrowed her eyes at him as she prepared to launch another attack.

He shook his finger in her face. *"Behave yourself, you little savage, and I'll let you have it back."*

Laurel grabbed his finger and tried to bite him. He snatched the appendage away from her before she had the chance to clamp down on it. Frowning at her admonishingly, he sat back, just beyond her reach, crossing his legs and dropping his arms onto his knees. *"This will be difficult,"* he murmured.

Hers was a curious race, almost child like, despite their obvious intelligence. She had set off through the jungle as if it had never occurred to her that there was danger there for her, with nothing but that gadget she carried to take her to the village to spy upon them and then find her way back to her transport.

Perhaps it was only that she was young? Her people would have to be intelligent, he felt sure, to build the machines they were so dependent on--unless they had stolen them from others?

He supposed he shouldn't have broken her language machine.

It was going to be difficult to court her when she could neither speak his language nor communicate with her primitive mind--*that* part of her mind was undeveloped, at any rate. He should have realized that there was a reason she had brought such a thing, other than the obvious one that she was recording their language for others of her kind.

He began to think he had allowed his lust to overcome his sense. He had been so blinded by her physical beauty that he had not considered that he might not find her at all compatible otherwise.

She was like the little meanix--spitting and growling and trying to bite any time he came near her--relatively harmless because she was small and weak--but, like the meanix, she made up for the lack of size with tenacity and a very short leash on her temperament.

There would be no peace with such a one. He would enjoy a woman of fire in his bed, but not if that fire was going to be directed at removing his hide.

Perhaps he should have simply pretended he didn't know that she was there? The others would not have known that the dream crystal's foretelling had come to pass--that the golden star child that was to be his life mate had come. He could have sealed his mind from them and she would have gone away again.

But he was a leader of his people, and that included guarding their way of life as well as their lives. He could not allow her to take the knowledge of the people with her to the others of her kind. It would only bring more intruders.

He would have to see if he could pull the ability to speak her language from her while she slept. He had his doubts that it would work when she was not a creature of his world, but he could think of nothing else to try. She was destined to be his mate. He must try to make the best of it.

* * * *

Laurel decided she didn't particularly like the way he was studying her. She supposed she shouldn't have let her frustration get the best of her and tried to bite him, but as much as she hated to admit it, he was big, really big, and strong, and he scared the shit out her.

She thought, maybe, it was the tattoos that made him look so fierce. He hadn't hurt her, which had really surprised and relieved her, but he hadn't needed to to do pretty much any damned thing he wanted to--which, she reluctantly admitted was the scary part. She'd fought him tooth and nail to keep him from dragging her here. Except for that one notable moment when she'd grabbed him by his genitals, and his obvious irritation at *having* to subdue her, she couldn't see that it had put a great deal of strain on him--or at least nothing but his patience. He hadn't even broken a sweat.

She'd be willing to bet there wasn't a single soul living in his village that didn't know she'd arrived.

The confederation was going to be really pissed about that.

What made it much worse was that the natives had to know she couldn't be from anywhere around here. Her flight suit was enough to make her stick out, but the fact that she was blond was a definite giveaway. There wasn't one barbarian--man, woman or child--that hadn't come to gape at her as Faine had hauled her through the village, as if ... well, as if she was an alien.

That was going to make escape a little difficult.

It was a pity it hadn't occurred to her to disguise herself as one of the natives, but then she hadn't known what they looked like until she'd arrived. And she sure as hell hadn't expected to get captured.

She decided not to worry about that. She could figure out something to do with her glaringly bright hair. Getting loose was the problem. The bindings weren't tight enough to cut off her circulation, but it was still too tight to wiggle her hands out. She *might* be able to loosen the knot with her teeth, she supposed.

She still couldn't figure out how he'd found her, though. She'd been so careful to be quiet!

She wouldn't have minded quite so badly if he'd just let her have her recorder. Then, she could at least be doing a little research--as long as she was here anyway. She hadn't intended to get so close, but she hated giving up the opportunity that had dropped in her lap. She didn't want to trust everything she experienced to her memory. She wanted to record her impressions fresh and uncluttered by other experiences.

Deciding to ignore him, she glanced around at his abode. She assumed it was his. It didn't look like more than one person occupied it and she didn't figure he would have brought her to this place if it hadn't been his.

It was surprisingly roomy. Of course, she wasn't exactly used to single person dwellings. She'd grown up on Station Zebra375 and the university was on the Station, so she still lived with her family--which was her mother. Her sister had married and moved off with a terra farmer, so she had a bunk to herself now.

Actually, this was her first trip off Station.

The dwelling didn't look nearly as primitive as she'd expected it would. It was made out of natural materials from what she could see--the dwelling and everything in it--but the primitives she'd studied in school lived in dirt floored huts, with animal skins over the door openings and windows, if they had windows at all.

He'd brought her to what she'd thought was the temple in the center of town. It didn't look like any of the images she'd seen of other temples, though, and it seemed a good many people lived inside of it, so she thought it might be something like a primitive version of an apartment building.

His compartment had a solid door, made out of slabs of tree, if she wasn't mistaken. It also had very large windows, which almost made her uneasy since the cubicle she and her mother shared only had one porthole and it was a very small one. There was something clear over the windows--she didn't have a clue of what. Some kind of crystal-like material. But the main part of the structure seemed to be stone--the floor, the walls--there was even stone above their heads--which was unnerving--which formed another floor above them.

The bed had actually been pretty comfortable. She hadn't done much more than bounce off of it, because she didn't want him to get any ideas, but it had definitely been soft and springy.

It looked like pretty much everything was all in one room, like the apartment her and her mother shared. She didn't see a galley, though--or a head for that matter.

He didn't look dirty and he didn't stink. He had to bathe.

Actually, to be perfectly accurate, he smelled good … really good. She didn't know what that was he was wearing on his skin, but it must be some kind of aphrodisiac type chemical, because she'd gone light headed the minute she got close enough to get a really good whiff of it.

That was one of the reasons she didn't want him too close. She figured he must have bathed in something to attract females, some sort of pheromone "perfume", and she wasn't about to find out what it was like to fuck an alien--especially a primitive alien. A lot of her friends said it was a real experience, doing it with aliens, especially the less civilized ones, but she figured they just wanted to share the guilt--the old 'everybody does it so it's OK if I did too' routine.

"I really would like to have my recorder," she muttered.

Faine sighed. If she was going to talk to herself anyway, he supposed she might as well have the thing. At least she'd stopped trying to wrestle it away from him, and she seemed to have calmed down. He held it out. "My re-cord-er."

She turned to look at him in surprise. "My recorder," she said belligerently.

He nodded. "My recorder."

She snatched it out of his hand and held it close to her chest. "Mine--not yours!"

He frowned, partly from confusion, and partly because she'd gone back to being antagonistic. "La-rel."

She blushed. "Oh! I thought … never mind."

*"Hungry?"*

She stared at him blankly. He made an eating motion. She frowned at him, watching him for several moments.

"Eat what?" she asked warily, feeling very uneasy about the fact that he'd said her name and then made an eating motion.

He studied her face for several moments and finally a smile tugged at his lips. Chuckling and shaking his head, he got up and went to the door, tugging at a cord.

A female appeared at the door. Faine spoke to her. Nodding and bowing, she left. When she came back a few minutes later, she was carrying a large tray, which had a pitcher, mugs, plates, and several odd looking mounds of what she finally decided, from the smell, must be food. Faine took it, settled the tray on the table and nodded. The female bobbed up and down several times and backed out of the room.

Laurel watched the exchange curiously, wondering why the woman was behaving so strangely--not as if she was really afraid of Faine, but--almost awed.

Maybe this was supposed to be a temple after all and he'd convinced the others that he was sort of a god, or maybe a demigod? Maybe a priest?

"Subject is a male--the same male that captured me--no idea of what his age might be. It's hard to say except he looks young, not real young, but not old--or middle aged. Something like the equivalent of a thirty year old human, maybe? Which certainly isn't young, but…. I can tell by the way he keeps glancing at me that he's not sure what the recorder is for. He thinks I'm babbling to myself, I guess, but he seems to find it amusing.

"Note--the natives seem to have a strange sense of humor. This one is called Faine D'Arten. He was also amused when I tried to speak his language. He patted me on the head. The natives may not realize I'm another humanoid species."

He glanced at her. She blushed when she realized he must know she was talking about him. No doubt he was wondering what she was saying, too.

"Ha!" she muttered. "And just wouldn't you like to know? But you're not going to find out because you broke my damned translator and it cost me a whole month's pay, damn it!"

When he turned around again, she spoke a little lower. "They seem to have fairly sophisticated dwellings. They have no modern power supply that I can see. Everything they use seems to be natural. The confederation would have a field day fining them for inappropriate usage of natural resources! But they do seem to cook their food. The female that brought the food behaved strangely toward the male--as if she held him in awe, which makes me curious of his position in their social structure.

"Actually, he *is* pretty awesome looking, but I would think these people were used to looking at him."

Deciding she'd spent entirely too much time dwelling on him, she thought back over what had happened since he'd captured her. "Still haven't figured out what the fires they were building outside were for. Some kind of ritual? Or maybe I was right and it's just for light outside?"

He caught her attention when he scooped her belongings off the table and back into her pack.

Setting the pack to one side, he dragged pottery out and dropped a healthy dollop of whatever that was on the tray in the middle of each. She was still wondering if he meant to sit down and eat while she watched when he strode toward her and squatted down so that they were eye level.

*"If you'll behave, you can sit with me."*

"Subject keeps talking to me as if he thinks I'll figure out what he's saying."

After studying her a moment, he reached for the knot he'd tied in the strip of binding--which she was very much afraid had once been part of something living and didn't even want to think about the dead skin touching her skin. When she saw that he was going to untie her, she cut a surreptitious glance toward the door. It was shut, but he hadn't locked it that she could see.

Would it be better to make a break for it now and hope she could outrun him, she wondered?

She might not get another chance any time soon, and it *was* dark out. That ought to help her chances.

Of course, she was going to have to make it down the corridor and a flight of steps and another corridor before she could even get out of the temple, but she was pretty sure she remembered the way they'd come in.

Mostly, she'd seen the floor, but she still thought she could remember the direction.

He glanced at her.

She smiled.

When he'd untied her, he grasped her arm and helped her to her feet. He didn't release her, immediately. He walked her to the table and pointed toward a chair. Laurel looked at the chair, glanced at him, reached for the chair … and slung it at him, dashing for the door.

## Chapter Four

Laurel heard a growl behind her, from the chair impacting with Faine's shins, no doubt. It galvanized her into more speed. Grabbing the door, she threw it open and dashed outside. He tackled her. She managed to catch herself with her hands, but she still hit the stone floor with a bone jarring thud. He'd caught her around the waist.

His face was in her ass.

Grunting, she tried to wiggle out from under him.

He levered himself up over her and she let out an inelegant grunt as he covered her. Panting, she tried to heave upward, discovered she couldn't budge him and collapsed, defeated, panting for breath.

After a moment, he rolled off of her, dragged her up by one arm and walked her back into his compartment. When he'd locked the door, he grabbed the chair from the floor, set it upright and pushed her into it.

Laurel sent a meek look up at him, wondering just how pissed off he was. He was looking down at the dirt all over him. Sending her a warning glance, he moved to a tall pottery cistern and washed his face and hands.

When he returned to the table, he sat down across from her, eyeing her with disfavor.

Laurel sent him a placating smile. "I didn't get to wash my hands," she pointed out, showing him her hands.

He stared at her hands, met her gaze coolly for several moments and then began eating.

"They are definitely barbaric," Laurel muttered into her recorder. "He didn't even offer to let me wash *my* hands."

He sent her another hostile glare, and she turned her attention to the food before her, trying to figure out what it might be.

It was definitely not processed. It still looked like it belonged to something that had once run around on legs. She picked up the leg on the plate with her thumb and forefinger, looked it over and then sniffed it. It smelled--pungent. Whatever it was, it actually smelled rather appetizing, but maybe that was just because she'd had a lot of unaccustomed exercise and she was hungry?

She wondered if she dared eat it.

He was eating it, but then he was from this planet.

Sighing, she closed her eyes and stuck the tip of her tongue to it to test the taste before she actually tried biting into it. The moment the tip of her tongue made contact, fire shot through her, making her eyes water. She breathed on her tongue, waved her hand over it and finally grabbed the mug off the table and stuck her tongue into the cooling liquid. "Tthit!"

Her whole mouth was on fire. She took several gulps of the liquid before she realized that that was part of the source of the fire.

Digging her fingernails into the table top, she gasped for several minutes, trying to catch her breath. When she'd blinked the tears from her eyes, she saw that he'd stopped to watch her. "I don't think I'm hungry," she said hoarsely.

He tensed when she started to rise and she stopped, hovering for several moments over her chair. Finally, she sat down again, folding her hands meekly on the table in front of her and studying them while he ate. After a moment, he pushed a brown, rounded thing toward her. She looked at it, then looked at him.

Picking it up, he broke a piece off and took a bite, then broke another piece off and handed it to her. She sniffed it, but it didn't smell pungent like the other food had and she took a cautious bite, ready to spit it out and make a dive for the water if it burned like the other had.

Thankfully it had a bland taste, no fire, and a pleasing texture. It seemed to absorb some of the burning sensation that still lingered in her stomach from whatever was in the mug--which wasn't water.

When he'd finished eating, he got up and moved around

the table. She watched him warily, but he merely grabbed her arm and urged her up. To her surprise, instead of marching her back to the bed and tying her up again, he walked her out of the door and from the "temple". Crossing the open area of the village, they stepped onto a path that led through the jungle. It was dark, but the body that orbited his world shed a surprising amount of light along the path they followed.

Hope surged through her when she saw that he'd led her to a small stream. She looked around excitedly for her craft. Except for the light from the stars overhead and the risen moon, there wasn't much visibility, though. For that matter, she didn't remember there being a path anywhere near where she'd landed.

He must mean to let her go, though.

He pointed at the water and scrubbed his hands together.

She stared at him. He'd brought her all the way down here to wash her hands? She looked at the stream and turned to him again. "Confederation law prohibits willful pollution or corruption of natural resources. Penalties are jail, fines or both."

He nudged her toward the water. *"Bathe."*

She plunked her hands on her hips. "Look, you! You might be able to get away with this, but I'm not supposed to. Why don't you take me to my ship, and I'll just wash up there?" she added, pointing downstream.

He followed the direction of her finger with his gaze, frowning thoughtfully. When he glanced down at her again, his eyes were gleaming with amusement.

She scrubbed her hands together and pointed again.

Pulling her closely to him, he placed his fingers along her temple. Laurel was too startled even to think about resisting. What did he think he was doing when he put his fingers on her head, she wondered?

After several moments, he removed his hand. Turning, he began to follow the stream, dragging her behind him. "Not this way! The other way!" Laurel said impatiently as she stumbled along behind him.

He ignored her and kept moving.

Irritated, she felt silent, concentrating on trying to keep from tripping. After a few minutes, he stopped. Laurel looked around, realizing they were in a clearing--a burned clearing. She glanced around in confusion and finally enlightenment dawned. She'd been turned around, pointing in the opposite direction, but how had he known that?

She realized when she looked up at him that there was only one way he could've known exactly where she'd parked her ship. He'd been watching her when she'd landed!

She dismissed it. She'd had the ship in stealth.

But he'd walked her directly to the spot.

He pointed to the ship.

Shrugging, she turned to look at the ship, realizing belatedly that she didn't have her remote access key. She'd put it in her pack and the pack was back in his living quarters. Walking over to the hull of the ship, she tilted her head back. "Bertha! I forgot my key. Open up!"

She waited several moments for a response. When nothing happened, she pounded on the hull with the palm of her hand. "Open up, damn it! I need a change of clothes."

"Laurel. There is a barbarian standing within a three foot radius of your position," the computer said at a very low volume.

"No shit! Open the damned hatch."

"Confederation law prohibits the corruption of this protected species."

Laurel struck the hull again. "Open the damned hatch, Bertha! Or, I swear, I'll get you reprogrammed when we get back!"

"I'll have to note this violation, Laurel," the computer responded.

Laurel heard the low whir, however, of the hatch opening and the extension of the gang plank. She made an aborted attempt to snatch her arm free and race up the gang plank, but apparently he'd suspected she might try something. His fingers were curled around her arm like a manacle.

He escorted her up the gang plank and looked around curiously when they were inside.

"Lights!"

The interior of the ship flooded with light. "Close the hatch, retract the gang plank and prepare for take off," Laurel said in a singsong voice, forming her lips into a parody of a smile and trying to keep the thread of desperation from her demeanor.

"There is a barbarian onboard."

"I know. Take off anyway."

"Confederation law prohibits the removal of a protected species from their natural habitat."

"Fuck! Take off, damn it!" Laurel said through gritted teeth.

"The penalty for violating this law is ten years imprisonment."

"We'll put him back later," Laurel snapped. "Just do it!"

"You will need to remove him first."

"Just how do you propose I remove him? He's attached to my fucking arm! He weighs twice as much as I do, easily, and he's a foot taller than I am--to say nothing of the fact that he tosses me around like a rag doll any time the notion strikes him!"

The computer was silent for several moments. "He is not twice your weight. More accurately, he is...."

"Shut up! I don't want to know how much he weighs. I want him off my ship."

"The barbarian weighs 5 times your maximum lifting capacity. I do not believe that you can remove him."

"Tell me something helpful. Have you managed to analyze his speech patterns?"

"I do not have that programming."

"I *know* you don't have that programming, but can you do it?"

"Negative."

"You can at least try!"

"I have recorded the words he spoke. I can give you a list of those that I have determined the meanings of."

Laurel huffed impatiently. "Do that, then."

"In what order?"

"Any order! Alphabetically, I guess." She listened to the list of words in growing dismay. "That's all?"

"Affirmative. He doesn't seem to be very loquacious. However, this may be due to the fact that you are unable to converse with him."

Laurel ground her teeth. "Repeat them more slowly so I can pick the ones I want."

The computer complied.

"I … am … Laurel," Laurel said. "Am doing here vision savage. I want you let…." She stopped, realizing she didn't have one really critical word--go. "I want you let …" She stopped again and moved her hand up into the air.

He lifted one dark brow. *"No."*

"What did he say, Bertha?"

"Unknown."

"What do you *think* he said?"

"I'm guessing here, but 'no'?"

"That's what I thought," Laurel said glumly. She considered her options and finally gave him an 'oh well' shrug and a smile. "Guess I'll just have that bath now," she said, heading toward the cockpit.

"You're going in the wrong direction, Laurel."

"Shut up, Bertha. Manual override, please."

Faine's hand tightened on her arm, pulling her to a stop before she could reach her seat at the console. He surveyed the cockpit.

"Do you think he's figured it out?" Laurel asked anxiously.

"From the body language and the facial expression, I detect that he is highly suspicious."

After studying the room thoroughly, he pulled her around and pushed her toward the door again. Sighing, Laurel moved down the narrow corridor toward her cabin. He looked it over thoroughly, moved to the head and looked inside and finally released her.

Laurel's lips quirked wryly. Finally, deciding to ignore him, she opened a compartment and found a change of clothes, studied them and then tossed the garment over her shoulder. Ten minutes later, she'd emptied the compartment, but finally settled on a body suit that looked a little sturdier than the casual ones she generally wore. It was hard to decide what to wear as a captive, but she thought this might hold up to being dragged around better than the others.

She studied it critically and it occurred to her that it was actually a little hot to be wearing a body suit. Sifting through the pile on the floor, she finally unearthed an ankle length, flowing robe. It was white, but that couldn't be helped.

She headed for the bath.

Faine followed her. She'd already opened the jumpsuit from the neck to the crotch before she realized he was now standing in the doorway of the head. She gave him a look. Finally, she stepped toward him, placed both palms in the middle of his chest and pushed. He stood his ground. She dug her heels in and pushed a little harder. He looked the room over again and finally yielded to her determination to oust him.

Closing the door, she used the facilities and dressed.

When she emerged, he looked her over with a glance of pleased surprise. She reddened. "I'm only wearing this because it's cooler," she said tartly. "So don't get any ideas."

He lifted his brows at her tone, but merely grasped her arm and led her back down the gangplank and to the village.

She wasn't really surprised when he tied her to the bed again, but she was disappointed. She dismissed it. He would have to sleep sometime. All she had to do was to lie down, pretend to go to sleep, and once he was asleep, she could untie the binding and leave.

After several hours of tossing and turning and peering at Faine through her lashes, Laurel finally drifted off to sleep.

Almost immediately, she began to have a very strange dream.

## Chapter Five

The thing that struck Laurel first about the dream was that, unlike her dreams usually were, this dream seemed more vivid--almost "solid". She found herself on a hill, looking down at the village of the barbarians. The ground beneath her feet was covered with short grasses and flowers.

She could smell them. She could see the colors, too, and she didn't remember seeing colors in her dreams before. She certainly didn't remember ever smelling anything.

Feeling a presence beside her, she glanced to her right and saw that Faine was standing almost shoulder to shoulder with her, gazing down at the village. As if he felt her gaze, he turned to look at her. "Why have you come?"

She frowned. It was really odd, because he seemed to be speaking his own language, and yet she could understand him. "I came to study this world and the people."

"I thought as much, but I do not understand what the purpose is."

Laurel shrugged. "The pursuit of knowledge only for its own sake. To know instead of wondering why things are the way they are."

"You could not understand us in the time you have allotted for yourself."

Irritation surfaced. "It would have been easier with the translator."

He smiled faintly. "Your youth makes you impatient to sample life."

The irritation deepened. "You're so old and wise, huh?"

He turned toward her, slipping his hands around her waist and moving closer. "Old enough to know that there is much in life that should be taken slow and savored."

She felt her heart kick into high gear. She wasn't certain if it was his nearness, the look in his eyes, or the suggestion in his words. She looked at him uneasily. "Been there. Done that. Wasn't impressed."

He smiled faintly. "You have no idea of what I'm speaking."

"Sex, right?"

He frowned. "You have been with others?"

She chuckled. "Get real! I'm in college, for heaven's sake! Working on my master's thesis, I might add. If you were looking for a celestial virgin, you need to keep looking."

He didn't look at all pleased with that. "Women should be chaste until they are wed."

Laurel rolled her eyes. "If the men were being chaste, they would be. I wasn't bumping uglies with a girl."

His eyes narrowed. "You have vast experience then?"

She sighed. "I just said I wasn't impressed, didn't I? That means I tried it. I'm willing to try most anything once or twice--the good things more than that, but all that slobbering and sweating just didn't do anything for me."

"Sometimes it takes the one person you were destined to be with."

This time, she smiled indulgently. "That's sweet, really! I had no idea you were such a romantic!"

"It will be different with me."

Laurel rolled her eyes. "Why?"

"Because you and I were destined to be mated."

"Ah. This is *the* most bizarre dream I've ever had. I mean, I really think you're hot, so I can understand the sex thing. What I can't figure out is the mating thing. Unless … maybe that's because I was hoping I'd find out a little bit about the mating practices of your people?"

His brows rose. His eyes gleamed with both amusement and desire. "I am not certain what this 'hot' means."

She chuckled, lifting up on her tiptoes, she wrapped her arms around him and nuzzled his neck. "It means I like the way your skin smells. I like the way your voice sounds, but most of all, every time I look at your mouth it just makes me hot and creamy," she murmured, nipping at his chin with the edge of her teeth.

He caught her hair, tugging at it until she was looking up at him. His eyes blazed with heat as he studied her face. All traces of amusement had vanished. His face had grown taut.

When he surged toward her, her lips parted in anticipation. Her eyes slid closed as the heat of his mouth and the elixir of his scent and taste encompassed her in a web of instantaneous, fiery desire. Without quite knowing, or caring, how it had come about, she felt the earth beneath her back, the warmth and substance of his body pressing against her, felt the heat and need of his cock as he pressed it against her belly. She was intoxicated by the feel of his mouth and tongue on hers as he kissed her, and by the urgency of his possession.

His kiss felt far better than she'd imagined it could possibly feel. He made her whole body feel feverish with need.

"Is this the mating ritual?" she whispered dizzily when his lips at last parted company with hers and burned a path along her throat.

"Yes," he said huskily. "And when our bodies join, our souls unite… forever."

*  *  *  *

Laurel jerked awake as if she'd fallen off of something. Gasping for breath, disoriented, she opened her eyes and looked up at the strange view above the bed blankly.

Turning her head, she came face to face with Faine. He was lying beside her on the bed.

And he was awake.

Startled to find him in the bed with her--awake--she rolled away … and fell off the bed. When she finally regained her equilibrium, she turned her head and peered at the bed. Faine was lying flat of his back now, staring up at the ceiling. As if he sensed her gaze, however, he rolled onto his side, stared at her for a long moment, and finally reached for her, pulling her back up on the bed and rolling so that she was lying across his chest.

She braced herself with her palms. "Maybe I did something in my sleep that gave you the idea that I was OK with this, but … I'm not."

He frowned. Finally, he released her.

Laurel sat up on the edge of the bed, her back to him, cradling her head in her hands. She still felt sluggish from waking up so abruptly, and oddly jittery, as if she'd had a nightmare or something. Try though she might to recapture the dream that had wakened her, however, she couldn't seem to remember much besides the fact that Faine had been in it and she'd thought when she was dreaming it that it seemed a lot more real than her dreams usually were.

Dismissing it finally, she wondered when, and how, Faine had gotten into the bed with her. The last thing she remembered was watching him stare at her from the chair across the room and faking sleep while she waited for him to nod off. Obviously, she'd caved in first, and as soon as he'd seen she really was asleep, he'd climbed into bed with her.

It seemed unlikely she was going to get the chance to execute her escape plan. He seemed wide awake now.

She must have been moving around in her sleep … or something.

She was too tired to consider escape tonight anyway. All she really wanted to do was to lie back down and drift off again, but to her way of thinking, sleeping in the same bed with him was just asking for trouble. She didn't particularly want to sit on the floor and try to sleep with her arm over her head, though, and she didn't think he would agree to give her the bed and sleep on the floor. Finally, she compromised by lying down on the edge.

She was just dozing off when Faine grabbed her around the waist and dragged her across the bed, fitting her snugly against him and throwing an arm over her waist. It roused her, but she was too far gone to care.

When she woke, Faine was gone, and her wrist was unbound.

She woke tired. She'd dreamed all night and she was exhausted from it. She couldn't remember much about the dreams except that Faine had been in them.

"The man's giving me nightmares," she muttered, stretching, which was when she discovered he'd untied her wrist.

She jackknifed upright in bed and looked around.

She was in the compartment--alone!

Rolling out of bed, she hit the floor running. As big a hurry as she was in, though, she wasn't about to leave her belongings behind. In the first place, they were hers and she wanted them. In the second, she didn't want to be looking over her shoulder for the rest of her life wondering when a cop was going to grab her for corrupting the primitives by leaving technology lying about for them to study.

Grabbing her pack, she looked around to see if anything had been left out of it, then secured it and slung it over her shoulder. Tiptoeing over to the door, she opened it a tiny crack and peered out. A female, who was raking a bundled wad of brush back and forth over the floor, was at one end of the corridor--the end Laurel was going to have to pass.

She bit her lip indecisively, but she didn't know when she might get another chance. Finally, she simply walked out the door as calmly as she could, closed it behind her and wandered around the temple until she finally found her way out. Then, she headed for the path Faine had taken her down the night before.

Ten minutes later--she was going to send Bertha in for reprogramming for plotting her a path straight through the damn jungle when she hadn't been more than a few minutes from a well beaten path!--she'd reached the stream. She looked both ways, trying to remember which direction they'd taken the night before. All she could remember, though, was that they hadn't walked long before they came upon the site she'd cleared for landing.

Shrugging, she just chose a direction and headed out. When she'd walked for at least fifteen minutes and seen no sign of the spot, she turned around and walked in the other direction for a while. Passing the path again, she came at last to the unmistakable mess she'd made right in the middle of the untouched wilderness.

There was only one problem.

The ship wasn't there.

### Chapter Six

Laurel was totally speechless for a stretch of time that she couldn't even count because she was also struck catatonic. When it finally filtered through her mind that the ship really was gone, she still couldn't believe it. "Shit! Fuck! Damn! All right, be calm! It has to be here somewhere."

Maybe it was the stealth mode? Maybe the conditions were just particularly good today to make it work at its peak? She crisscrossed the burned circle back and forth, waving her hands in front of her for another thirty minutes before she finally had to accept that the ship really was gone.

She sat down, crossed her legs and dropped her chin on her hand, thinking.

"The intrepid explorer of the forbidden planet has just discovered that her fucking ship has disappeared," she muttered into her recorder. "The question is where did it disappear to? I don't care how. I don't particularly care when. I just want to know where."

It must have been Bertha. She'd compromised the ship when she'd taken the barbarian onboard, and Bertha had taken it into her head to move the ship so that the barbarians couldn't find it.

Dragging her pack off of her shoulder, she poured the contents on the ground and looked through them. Her communicator was missing.

That conniving, good for nothing savage! He'd taken her communicator. Now how was she supposed to find her way to the damned ship!

Had he figured that part out too?

She frowned, thinking it over. "There's something very strange about these barbarians. The subject I'm currently studying--and will probably get the chance to *thoroughly* study because I can't find my *frigging* ship!--is oddly clever for a primitive being. I could almost suspect that he might have had something to do with the disappearance of the ship, except that it took me six months to learn how to fly the damn thing and I absolutely can not frigging believe he figured it out while I was asleep!"

After a while, Laurel decided she might as well return to the village. Unless she just happened to find her ship, she was going to have to wait until the confederation sent someone to investigate her distress call. She might just as well do some research in the meanwhile.

"I have been wandering around in the woods for approximately an hour now. Note: In the future, it would probably be best to use the paths the natives have cut through the woods since I don't seem to have a very good sense of direction. If I find my way back, I'll be sure to use the path next time. I'm not certain how the natives manage to find their way out of the jungle when they go in. The path goes directly to the small stream, which they apparently use for bathing, despite confederation guidelines regarding the proper use of natural resources."

She was just beginning to get really anxious when she heard a sound that reminded her strongly of an alarm. It was shrill, piercing and continued to repeat at short intervals.

Perking up, she turned slowly around until she was pretty sure she had the direction of the sound's origin and took off through the woods. A few minutes later, to her relief, she came to the rise overlooking the village. As she reached it, however, a commotion drew her attention and she stopped, turning toward the sound. Her eyes widened. "There's a herd of barbarians stampeding this way. They're carrying some sort of stick-like things that must be a weapon of some sort. They seem to be converging on the temple in the center of town. Now, they are racing up the steps to the top of the temple walls. I see my barbarian standing at the top. Perhaps he summoned them for some reason?" She stopped, gasping in surprise. "Holy shit! They have … they dove off! No! They launched themselves into the air. They're … un-fucking-believable! They have sprouted wings. Actually, they have changed shape altogether."

Laurel fell silent as she watched the townsmen--who didn't look at all like people anymore--fly off toward the setting sun. Feeling weak kneed when they disappeared from view, she sat down, still staring toward the point on the horizon where she'd last seen them.

"Apparently I was mistaken about them being humanoid. I'll have to give this some thought. A lot of thought. What was really bizarre was that they changed into different … things … creatures. OK. The bizarre thing was that they changed at all. But the other part is equally bizarre. One would think that they would all, basically, be the same sort of … creature."

She looked around, swatting at a buzzing insect that had landed on her arm and started gnawing. "I don't think I'm asleep. They could pass for nightmare creatures, though--except, thankfully, I've never had nightmares like that.

"Some sort of hallucinogen? Maybe there's something in the water and I only thought I saw them change into strange winged beasts? But … that would mean I must not have seen anything, because otherwise they'd be piled in the dirt at the base of the temple.

"Maybe there's something in the water that made them change? Gruesome thought. I'll have to see if I can find an alternate liquid until I can study this further."

After a little while, because the insects were really starting to feed on her, she got up and made her way back into the village. She noticed the villagers were burning again. She also noticed the insects weren't gnawing on her now. Stopping, she sniffed the smoke coming off the burning vegetation and decided, maybe, the only purpose was to chase away the insects--which it seemed pretty effective at doing.

She couldn't help but notice that there didn't seem to be a lot of males around.

They really weren't in the village anymore.

She didn't *feel* like she was hallucinating. Shouldn't she feel strange if she was?

But how possible was it that it had actually happened like she thought it had happened?

Faine wasn't in his compartment.

Of course, she *thought* she'd seen him fly off into the sunset, looking like some kind of really big, scary looking beast.

Settling in the compartment, she thought the event over for a little while.

She'd heard something that sounded like an alarm and then seen the men come running, carrying things that looked like weapons.

"I may have timed my visit a little badly. The barbarians appear to be in the middle of a war," she muttered into the recorder. "I still haven't figured out the beast part, but the rest of it seemed an awful lot like soldiers responding to a threat to me."

Someone knocked on the door, interrupting her thoughts. When she opened it cautiously, she saw it was the same woman who'd brought food the night before. The woman motioned for her to follow. Shrugging, curious, she left her pack in the room and followed the woman from the temple to the building that stood next to it.

Once they were inside, she saw that the majority of the huge room was taken up by a large pool of water. Men, women and children were splashing in the water, bathing.

Why had Faine taken her to the stream? She wondered.

The woman motioned at her to remove the gown she was wearing. Shrugging, Laurel removed it and handed it to the woman a little reluctantly. The woman tugged her toward the pool, chattering at her.

It didn't take a lot of imagination to figure out that she was being urged to join the others.

Laurel didn't particularly want to. It didn't seem very hygienic to bathe in what looked like a public bath.

She wondered if that was why Faine hadn't brought her. But was that because he thought she might be reluctant? Or was it because he was reluctant for her to bathe with all of the other men and women?

From the way the men were studying her, she couldn't help but feel a little uneasy. Finally, she decided to get into the water so that she wasn't so exposed to their view.

To her surprise, the water was very warm--almost too warm. It also smelled strongly of some sort of herbs, or maybe chemical--no, she corrected that thought. It wouldn't be chemical, unless it was something that was naturally in the water.

Maybe there was something in the water that killed the germs? Otherwise, since they all seemed to use it, it looked like they would have a problem with diseases and the people looked very healthy.

Was whatever she smelled what made them change into beasts, though? Or what made her *think* they'd changed into beasts?

Shaking the worrisome thoughts, she splashed the water over herself experimentally, deciding she liked the way it felt on her skin.

The woman who'd brought her appeared beside her with a

cloth and some sort of sudsy lotion. Laurel balked at being bathed, however. Determinedly, she took the cloth and washed herself.

This was a really primitive sort of ritual.

She decided, though, that she'd record it later. The natives were already looking her over as it was. There didn't seem to be a lot of point in drawing more attention to herself.

She discovered when she got out that the woman had done something with her robe. Anger surged through her, but naturally, there was no way to express her feelings beyond yelling things at the woman she couldn't possibly understand. Resentfully, she took the skirt the woman held out to her and put it on. The woman had to help her with the top.

She didn't particularly care for it. In the first place, it didn't just look like metal. It *was* metal, and, as little as there actually was to the thing, it was stiff and uncomfortable. She didn't see much point in wearing something that spiraled around her breasts, leaving most of them exposed, and only actually covered her nipples.

When she was "dressed" the woman led her back to Faine's compartment and left her. A few minutes later, the woman returned with a tray of food. Laurel eyed it suspiciously and stuck her tongue out and waved her hand at it.

The woman looked taken aback. After a moment, however, she giggled and shook her head.

That at least seemed to answer that question. A more important one was on Laurel's mind, however. She thought it over, but nothing really came to mind. Finally, she cupped her sex and crossed her legs.

The woman really did look at her oddly then. After a little more dramatization, she managed to get it across to the woman that she desperately needed to relieve herself. Laughing and shaking her head, the woman led her across the room and drew back a curtain, revealing a short hallway. At the end was a door.

Hoping the woman really had understood, Laurel followed the hallway, opened the door and peered inside.

It was a head--not that it looked like what she was used to, but this sort of thing was pretty basic when all was said and done.

Relieved, in two ways--she really hadn't liked the idea that she might have to find a place in the woods to squat--she washed her hands in the basin, thinking how odd it was that the primitives seemed to have running water and wondering just what stage of development in civilization they really were-- she returned to the main room and sat down to eat. To her relief, the woman seemed to have understood that part too. The food didn't set her on fire.

She found when the woman had taken the tray away that she was bored.

She was also tired. She'd wandered around in the woods most of the day and the hot bath and the food combined had her ready to nod off in no time.

Trying to shake it off, she sat down and recorded everything that had happened since she'd found her way back, but finally reached the point where she simply couldn't fight it off anymore.

She removed the garments the woman had given her. They were just too uncomfortable to sleep in and it didn't look as if Faine would be coming back--not any time soon, anyway.

Almost as soon as she drifted off, she began to dream.

* * * *

"Where did you go today, princess?"

Laurel frowned, looking around. She saw she was still in the room, lying on the bed.

Faine was lying next to her, his head propped on his hand, his eyes gleaming as his gaze moved along her body.

She saw when she looked down that she was naked.

Of course! She'd gone to bed naked. She was dreaming she was lying in the bed naked--which she actually was.

Except she was dreaming Faine was with her, which he wasn't.

She stretched, then propped her head in her hand, facing him. "I went to look for my ship so I could leave. This hasn't gone at all as I'd expected, but I discovered my ship was gone."

"What did you expect?"

She frowned. "I had read that this was a very primitive place, and it does seem strange, because it's not at all what I'm used to, but it doesn't really seem primitive. The woman took me to a public bath. Even the head works. How do you do that?"

He frowned. "Shala took you to the public bath?"

"Who's Shala?"

"The woman I left to attend your needs."

"Oh--well, yes. She took my damned robe, too. I don't know what she did with it."

He said nothing for several moments. "Most likely she only took it to clean it, but you are not to go to the public bath again. I will speak to her."

"Why not? Doesn't everyone bathe there?"

"*You* are not everyone. You are to be my consort."

"What's a consort?"

"The wife of the King of Merisea."

"What's Merisea?"

He chuckled. "The land where you will live."

"Oh. Well, I can't stay. It's nice of you to offer, but I'll have to get back. They'll be looking for me soon."

His face hardened. "Who will look for you?"

Laurel was a little taken aback. He certainly was testy about something that really wasn't any of his business. "The Inner Galactic Police, probably the enforcers of the CPA, too. I faked a crash to land here. I wasn't supposed to land," she added.

He studied her for several moments. "They will go away again."

"Yeah but with me. I sure hope I can convince them I really did crash, because it would suck to have to pay a fine--especially when I've had so much trouble already."

To her surprise, Faine lifted one hand and caressed her cheek. "You will grow accustomed."

It made her feel strange in the pit of her stomach--the touch and the look in his eyes. She cast around in her mind for something to focus on besides the unsettling sensations. "I don't know. I don't have my translator, so I can't talk to anybody. Besides that, I saw something really weird. I thought I saw it, anyway. Some guy started blowing on a big animal horn and all the men in the village just raced up to the top of the temple and jumped off. I thought they were going to splatter at the bottom, but instead, they changed into these strange, winged beasts and flew off."

"We summoned the dreams spirits and leapt from the parapets of the fortress. This is no temple."

"Huh?"

"The ancient ones. In our dream walks, we summon them and join with their spirits. When we need their strength, we summon their powers and become one with them," he murmured, slipping his arms around her and dragging her closer, so that her body brushed his each time she took a breath.

The warmth in her belly became heat, spreading outward. Even in her dreams Faine had this strange effect over her!

## Chapter Seven

Laurel sighed, wondering why she bothered to talk to the dream person at all. It wasn't like it was real or she was actually finding out anything of use. Besides, the temptation to give in to his persuasion was becoming really hard to ignore.

What harm could there be in *dreaming* she'd had sex with him?

And it was her dream. She could make it as good as she could imagine.

She looked up at him. He really was handsome. Just looking at him made her pulse beat a little more quickly, made her breath catch in her throat. Merely thinking about his mouth on hers made her grow damp and jittery with nerves.

Lifting a hand, she traced the lines of the tattoo that covered one cheek. "What is this for?" she whispered.

"It is the mark of the kings of Merisea. It tells my family line."

After a moment, she dragged her finger teasingly along his neck, down his shoulder and traced the tattoo on his upper arm. "And this?"

"Before I became king, I was prince. That is the mark of the prince of Merisea."

There was a gleam in his eyes now. Laurel smiled back at him, tracing a path down his arm and along his back to the tattoo she remembered just above his buttocks. "This one?"

"The totem of my dream beast."

She remembered that the tattoo on the cheeks of his ass was a sort of swirling pattern and traced a series of circles over one buttock. "What about this?" she asked huskily.

"It symbolizes the dream dimension where my totem resides."

She settled her palm over his buttock, enjoying the feel of the taut muscle, then skated her hand up along his back. Lifting her face, she moved closer, inhaling the scent of his skin. It sizzled along her nerve endings as if she'd taken a drought of potent wine, warming her, making her pleasantly dizzy. Lightly, she brushed her lips along his throat and then his jaw. When she reached his lips, she hesitated, gazing into his eyes. Ever so lightly, she touched her lips to his, testing the sensitive flesh, tasting him, relishing the accelerated rhythm of her heart and the heat it pumped through her body.

Pressing her lips fully against his, she flicked her tongue out and traced the seam where his lips met. He sighed gustily, opening his lips over hers, dueling briefly with her tongue before he thrust past the barrier of her lips and explored the sensitive inner flesh of her mouth with his tongue.

Laurel sighed, enjoying the pleasing sensation of mingled breaths, his taste, the feel of his tongue against hers and the heady rush of dizziness that engulfed her in a heated cloud of pleasure. Lifting her hand from his back, she gripped his shoulder, moving closer to him.

He pulled her tightly against his length and then rolled,

lying half atop her, moving his hand along her body in exploration as he made love to her mouth, cupping her breast, teasing the distended peak and finally moving lower, along her waist and belly and tangling his fingers in the curling thatch of hair that covered her mound. She moaned into his mouth when he found her clit and teased it with the tip of his finger.

She lifted her leg, curling it around his, giving him better access, and he traced her cleft, pushing one large finger inside of her. She moaned again, lifting toward his hand, enjoying the feel of his finger as it slipped in and out of her wet passage.

A shudder went through him. He broke the kiss and moved downward, kissing her throat. Shifting, he nudged the leg beneath him with one of his and Laurel opened her legs for him, allowing him to settle between her thighs.

Lifting her arms, she clasped them around him as he moved down her body, kissing her breasts, building the pleasurable tension tighter and tighter inside of her as he caressed the tender, distended peaks until she found she could not be still, until she was moving restlessly against him with her need.

Relief and anticipation flooded her as he lifted slightly away from her and she felt his hard member nudging her clitoris and then moving downward along her cleft, collecting the dew of her desire on the rounded tip before his body engaged hers. She spread her legs wider, lifting up to meet him as he entered her.

Her breath left her in a rush as she felt his turgid flesh stretching her, pressing slowly but surely inside of her, deeper and deeper.

It felt so real … so wonderful.

She wrapped her arms around his neck, gazing up at him dreamily as she felt the slow, sensuous caress of his turgid flesh along her passage, sending quakes of delight through her with each thrust and retreat. "Mmm, you feel so good, Faine," she murmured, feeling her the muscles of her passage clench around him in delight.

His face went taut. He squeezed his eyes closed, hesitated

fractionally and then he lowered himself until his chest was pressing tightly against hers. His lips sought hers once more as he increased the tempo of his caress, plunging and retreating more rapidly, more forcefully. She kissed him back, wrapping her arms around him tightly and arching her hips upward to meet each hard thrust as she felt the pleasure mounting inside of her, felt her body tightening until she began to feel as if she could hold it no longer.

Abruptly, it seemed to explode, to fragment inside of her. It was almost as much the surprise as the explosion of ecstasy itself that wrung a cry of delight from her.

As if it were a signal to him or her pleasure shot his own over the top, he shuddered with his own climax and went limp against her.

Laurel stroked his back dreamily as the heated eruption of pleasure mellowed to warmth and an all over feeling of complete satisfaction. "That was … like nothing I ever felt before," she murmured on a sigh of absolute delight.

He lifted his head slightly, nuzzling her cheek and finally rolled off of her, carrying her with him. He stroked her cheek. "The next time I make love to you, my queen, it will be in fleshly form, not spirit," he murmured, kissing her lightly on the lips. "And it will be far, far better."

\* \* \* \*

Laurel jolted wide awake, clutching her chest and gasping for breath as if she'd run a mile. Sitting up quickly, she glanced down at the bed and then looked around the room.

She was alone.

Massaging her aching chest, she leaned back against the pillow again, staring up at the ceiling above her. "It was just a dream," she muttered. A shiver skated through her. What had made her dream such an outrageous thing?

Her pussy was throbbing like hell. She reached down and felt herself, shivering at the prickles of sensation that went through her … as if she really had had sex and it was still throbbing with aftershocks. After a moment, she touched her breasts and discovered that her nipples were sensitive too.

She'd never had a wet dream before. It hadn't occurred to her that it could be so real.

It had been worlds better than the real thing!

What had made her think of the other though? The "you're mine now" part?

It occurred to her abruptly that she'd dreamed that before. Sort of. She hadn't been able to remember the dream after she'd woken up, but she realized that she'd dreamed that Faine had told her that when they joined in their dreams they would join spirits … or something like that, and be together forever.

It was odd that she remembered it now. Maybe the one she'd just had had jogged the other memory? Or maybe it was the first that had made her dream the second?

She shook her head. Why would she dream such crazy dreams at all? Especially dreams about people that could go inside of dreams and … actually mated in dreams?

There must be something in the food. Or maybe the water?

Unnerved, she lay wakeful for quite some time. Finally, however, she found that she couldn't keep her eyes open any longer. Her last thought before she drifted off was that she was going to have to figure out some way to find her ship and leave before Faine came back.

She knew it had just been a dream, but all the same it made her really uneasy.

## Chapter Eight

As soon as Laurel woke the following morning, she grabbed her pack, dumping the contents in the middle of the bed and sorting through it. It didn't take more five minutes to concede that there was nothing in the pack that could conceivably be used or adjusted that might help her locate her ship or communicate with Bertha.

Her recorder patched into the onboard commuter, of course, to record the data, but it didn't actually communicate with the computer.

Stuffing everything back into the pack, she got up and

looked around the room. An hour later, she'd searched every square inch of it and begun moving across the floor, tapping on the stones to see if any might be loose and hiding a cavity where her communicator might be located.

She was still on her hands and knees, testing the flooring, when the door opened. Her head jerked up guiltily. She relaxed fractionally when she saw it was only the maid who'd brought food before.

Apparently the woman was becoming used to the fact that Laurel did some really strange things. She scarcely looked surprised at all. Nodding pleasantly, she set the tray on the table and turned to go.

Laurel wasn't really certain what prompted her to do it. The idea simply popped into her head when she thought about the dream she'd had the night before. "Shala?"

The woman stopped abruptly and turned to look at her questioningly.

Laurel felt a cold sensation flood through her.

A wave of dizziness quickly followed. Apparently she looked a little faint, too, because a look of worry gathered on the woman's face. Rushing forward, the woman got down on her knees, as well, chattering at her a mile a minute.

Laurel wouldn't have paid her any attention if she could've understood what she was saying. She was too shocked at the really unnerving coincidence that she'd *dreamed* the woman's name.

She would've liked to think she might have overheard it, but she knew better. She considered the possibility that it wasn't a name at all, that maybe it was a word she'd picked up without realizing it, but she couldn't convince herself that there was a real possibility of that.

It took some coaxing to get rid of the woman. When she finally managed to shove her from the room and close the door, she moved to the bed and sank weakly down on it.

"This place is seriously fucking with my mind," she muttered.

Glancing around, she found her recorder and placed it on her head, ordering a playback. She listened to everything she'd recorded thus far, but there was no mention of the word Shala at all.

She urgently needed to find that ship. She couldn't wait for the Confederation to come after her.

Besides, if they found her sitting in the middle of one of the primitives' cities, she'd be up shit creek for sure. It was one thing to fake a crash she had every reason to think she could convince them was real, but she didn't think they would be at all happy if they found her living among the natives. Particularly when they discovered, as they almost certainly would, the handy little gadgets she'd brought with her that were now in the possession of the primitives.

After a while, it occurred to her that, since she didn't have any sort of device to help her locate the ship, she was going to have to rely entirely on her own senses, or figure the puzzle out.

It was a staggering thought. She was so stunned by it that she spent a good deal of time trying to figure out if it was even possible to succeed without any sort of electronics at all. It occurred to her after a while, however, that the primitives seemed to cope without electronics and that it must be possible to do any number of things if one were determined enough.

This structure--in her dream Faine had said it was a fortress, and now that she thought about it, it looked a lot more like a fortress than it did a temple--was really tall. If she went up to the top of it, maybe she could see the ship?

It was certainly worth a try.

There were warriors on the battlements. She didn't know why she hadn't expected there to be, except that she'd thought pretty much all of the men had gone off to fight. They looked startled to see her. She couldn't decide whether it was because she wasn't supposed to be on the observation deck, or if it was specifically her that had surprised them.

None of them said anything to her--which would've been a waste of breath anyway--but they didn't take their eyes off of her either.

She tried to be casual about her "stroll", but she wasn't certain she was very convincing. Every time she stopped and gazed into the distance, studying every tiny clearing she spotted through narrowed eyes, she turned to discover the men closest to her were peering in the same direction intently. By the time she'd made a complete circuit of the observation deck, most of the men were looking distinctly uneasy. They'd stare hard at the land surrounding the city for long moments, then exchange questioning comments. It occurred to Laurel as she finally gave up and went downstairs once more that they might have misinterpreted her keen interest in the forest surrounding the village, but that was hardly her fault.

Shrugging it off, she returned to the room once more to ponder her lack of success and see if her mind would furnish her with an alternative. As tall as the fortress was, she'd expected to be able to see for a great distance. Unfortunately, there were a lot of really tall trees blocking her view.

She'd seen a taller structure, however. There was one at each of the four corners of the box like building. Unfortunately, she'd been so intent upon looking out over the forest she hadn't paid them much attention. As she studied over it, though, she recalled that she'd seen some sort of rungs going up the side of one of them.

The question was, would the men stationed up there allow her to climb the towers?

They must be watchers, which meant their attention should be on the area around the fortress, but she had a feeling if she went up again she'd meet the same keen interest of before, which would make it impossible to sneak up the any of the towers for a better look. If they were there to watch, it didn't seem likely that there would be a time when she could go that the place would be empty.

They probably wouldn't notice her if she slipped up after dark, but she doubted she'd be able to see much even if she managed it.

It was a damned shame they didn't wear uniforms. If they had, she could've stolen one and blended in. As it was, going up "dressed" as they were, naked, was only more likely to gain more attention, not less.

It was possible, she supposed, if she went up a couple of times a day and walked around they might get used to seeing her and stop watching her so closely, but that would take time and she really didn't feel like she had a lot of time to spare. Faine was bound to be coming back before long and once he did he would be watching her too closely for her to escape even if she did find the damned ship.

There didn't seem to be an alternative. She couldn't just wander around the woods on foot, hoping she would run into the ship. She could wander forever.

Deciding she really didn't have any other options, she waited until after Shala had brought the evening meal and went up to wander along the observation deck once more. They still glanced at her as she strolled by, but it didn't seem to her that they were as keenly interested as before. This time, she made several circuits before she went down again.

The following morning, she went up again. Unfortunately, they'd changed the guard sometime--probably during the night or first thing in the morning--and she encountered the same curious glances as she'd drawn the first time--which made it impossible to take a chance on the towers. She did take the opportunity to study them more closely, though, and saw that she'd been right. There were rungs running up the side of each for climbing to the top.

She waited until late in the evening before she went up again and was relieved to see that the men were the same as had been on the observation deck the evening before. They barely paid her any mind at all.

Just to be on the safe side, she made several circuits of the deck before she stopped beside one of the towers. Glancing around casually, she saw that the men nearest her were staring out over the forest.

Ever so casually, she sidled a little closer to the rungs and then looked around one more time. A couple of the men glanced at her, she noticed out of the corner of her eye, but she pretended to be staring off into the forest and after a few moments, they looked away. Seizing the opportunity, she grasped the rung just above her head and started climbing. She'd almost made it to the top when she heard a yell below her. Ignoring the shout, she climbed faster. She was huffing with exertion by the time she managed to hoist herself over the top edge.

Below her, she could hear the scrambling of many feet along the stone walk.

"Shit!" It sounded like the whole pack of them was heading her way.

Getting to her feet, she moved to the edge of the platform and studied the forest. She'd been right. She could see much further from this position. Her stomach did a strange little free fall as she neared the edge of the platform, however. Swallowing with an effort, she did her best to ignore the sharp drop off and scanned the forest quickly, expecting any moment that men would come pouring up the ladder, grab her and haul her down again. She'd made it halfway around the tower when a bald spot in the forest caught her attention. She stopped, staring at it intently.

The space looked big enough, and flat enough, to have landed her craft, but it was hard to tell from such a distance-- and equally hard to tell just how far away it was--or what direction.

She looked down, trying to find a landmark that would line up with the place.

It was a mistake.

The moment she looked down a wave of dizziness went through her. She felt herself sway, felt her balance shift. A strong gust of wind thwarted her attempts to right herself. Before she quite knew what was happening, she saw that the ground was rushing up toward her.

She didn't get the chance to scream. She'd just drawn in her breath to express her supreme dismay when something snagged around her waist, knocking the breath from her. For several moments, while she struggled to catch her breath and fight off the darkness threatening to consume her, she thought she'd actually hit the ground. Pain materialized, but not the sort of pain she'd expected.

And as the darkness began to recede, she realized that she was still falling.

Or floating.

Not floating. Something hard was against her back and banded around her, like a great claw.

She did scream when she saw it actually was a great claw, her head whipping around to see what had her.

It was a monster. She squeezed her eyes closed. "If you're ever going to faint, Laurel, now's the time," she muttered.

The landing jolted her from her concentration on summoning a faint and she opened her eyes. When she did, she discovered the monster had vanished.

Faine was holding her and he didn't look at all happy.

She smiled at him a little weakly. "Oh. It's you! When did you get back?"

He made a sound that was a lot like a growl. Grabbing her by one arm, he began dragging her along the observation deck where they'd landed toward the stairs. Laurel discovered very quickly, however, that the fright had taken the starch out of her knees. She only managed a couple of steps before her legs crumpled beneath her.

Uttering another sound of anger, Faine hauled her to her feet and tossed her over his shoulder. She was too weak in the aftermath of her near death experience to do more than hang limply over his broad shoulder as he stalked down the stairs, heading for the room they shared.

She knew she was in trouble the moment he set her on her feet and slammed the door behind him.

## Chapter Nine

The torrent of words that spilled from Faine's mouth were completely incomprehensible, but Laurel could tell by the scowl on his face and the way he forced the words through clenched teeth that he was really pissed off about something.

She stared at him blankly until he paused for breath. "Guess you're mad, huh?"

His eyes narrowed.

Laurel forced a look of innocence onto her features. "I wasn't supposed to go up on the tower?"

He took a step toward her. She took a step back. She really

didn't like the look of intent on his face at all.

"I didn't know," she lied uneasily. "I only went up to have a look around." She mimed her actions by shielding her eyes and pretending to look around.

Something flickered in his eyes, comprehension, but he didn't look the least appeased by her explanation. His lips tightened.

Feeling her own anger surface, she planted her hands on her hips belligerently. "Well! It's my damned ship! You didn't have any business hiding it from me to start with! And don't try to look innocent. I know it was you. I don't know how you did it, but I don't believe for one minute that Bertha just decided to relocate!"

Faine glared at her furiously. *So what you're saying is you didn't take the hair brained notion that you could shift like we do and go up to the tower to see if you could fly? You risked taking a header off the tower knowing full well you were going to splatter at the bottom if you fell off?*" he demanded, pointing angrily in the direction of the tower.

*"If we hadn't returned when we did, you'd be dead now-- or wishing you were!"*

Laurel folded her arms over her chest. Watching his sharp, angry gestures, she had a fair idea of what he was accusing her of--stupidity. As *if* she'd fallen off on purpose! "It's all your fault, anyway!" she snapped huffily.

Turning, she stalked to the bed to sulk.

Faine caught up to her as she reached it. Plunking himself down on the bed, he grabbed her, dragging her across his lap. They wrestled for several moments, but Laurel knew it was a lost cause. She had a fair idea of his intentions even before he rolled her onto her belly and tossed her skirt over her head.

Cool air wafted across her bare buttocks. She squeezed her eyes shut, expecting to feel his palm on her ass any minute. When nothing happened, she reared up and twisted to look at him.

He was staring at her ass with a vacant look on his face, his hand suspended mid-air. Her movement distracted him and he turned to look at her, their eyes meeting for one long heartbeat. Abruptly the angry intent on his face altered to an entirely different purposefulness and he shifted her onto the bed, sprawling on top of her.

As Laurel opened her mouth to protest, he covered it with his own and she forgot all about her fear and indignation as an electric current of fire suffused every pore and molecule of her body with the first touch of his mouth on hers. Without stopping to consider the wisdom of it, Laurel kissed him back with a fervor that matched his, so enthralled by the riotous sensations pouring through her as her body registered the weight, and strength and heat of the body pressed so tightly against hers, the aphrodisiac of his scent and taste, rational thought fled. She wrapped her arms around him as she dueled with his tongue in intimate swordplay, twining her tongue along his, stroking it.

He eased slightly away from her so that he could stroke his hand over her body. Reaching her waist, he snapped the fragile tie of her skirt and pushed the fabric aside, stroking her hip and the side of her thigh before he moved his hand upward along her inner thigh and cupped her mound. He paused only momentarily, however, to her great disappointment, and then slipped his hand upward again. Catching the tiny chain that linked her bra in the front, he parted the links and pushed the stiff cups aside, catching first one breast in the palm of his hand and then the other, massaging them and sending shafts of delight through her.

Laurel broke the kiss, releasing her grip on him just long enough to toss the uncomfortable garment aside, then pressed tightly against him once more, flattening her breasts against the hard muscles of his chest as she lifted her face to nuzzle along his neck. Vaguely, she was aware of a sense of familiarity about his taste and scent and touch, the feel of his body along hers, but, as delightful as the dreams had been, the sensations flooding her now were far more intense than when she'd dreamed of making love to him and infinitely more devastating to her senses.

Within minutes, she was moving restlessly beneath him, encouraging him to possess her fully. One leg was pinned beneath the weight of his, but she lifted the other, twining it around his leg sinuously as she pressed her mound against his lower belly.

Bending his head, he possessed her mouth once more as he skated a hand down her back and cupped one cheek of her ass, squeezing it in a massaging motion before he slipped his fingers into the cleft and followed it, carefully parting the fragile layers of flesh surrounding her sex and delving all too briefly into the hot, moist cavern.

Lifting slightly, he dragged her leg from beneath him, settling between her thighs and rolling until he lay atop her. Laurel moaned in pleasure as she felt his rigid cock settle against her cleft, nudging her clit.

The abrupt pounding on the door of the apartment sent a shock wave through both of them. Faine lifted his head and glared at the stout panel for several moments. Finally, reluctantly, he untangled his body from hers, rose from the bed and stalked across the room, jerking the door open.

Still more than a little disoriented, Laurel grabbed the coverlet, flipping it over herself as he jerked the door open and bellowed at the man on the other side. A low voiced conversation ensued. Faine glanced toward Laurel several times during the course of it and she wondered if the conversation had anything to do with her.

Finally, Faine closed the door once more. Turning, he studied her for a long moment with an unreadable expression. Laurel sat up as he moved toward her once more, wondering if he meant to finish what he had started.

Apparently, he didn't. He merely leaned down and kissed her briefly on the lips.

When he drew away, he gave her a look filled with both promise and threat.

*"You scared me out of ten years of my life with that stunt. If you pull anything like that again, I swear by my ancestors I'll beat your ass till you can't sit on it for a week!"* he growled.

Laurel was still watching him with her jaw at half mast when he straightened, turned and stalked from the room.

She stared in disbelief at the vibrating door for several moments after he'd left and finally let out a growl of frustration. "You asshole! You did that on purpose! Just *see* if I let you finish later, damn you!"

\* \* \* \*

Faine was still furious as he strode down the hallway to his own chambers. His second in command, who was waiting near his door, bowed low at his approach. "Your pardon for disturbing you, sire, but I was certain you would wish to know of the visitors immediately."

Faine waved the apology aside. "Where are they?"

"Your houseman placed them in the waiting chamber."

Faine's eyes narrowed thoughtfully. "It will do them no harm to keep them cooling their heels for a bit." He turned to look down the hallway toward Laurel's room. "Have two guards posted outside her door … see to it our visitors do not leave the waiting chamber. You may relay the message to them that I will grant them an audience."

His second in command nodded and saluted.

"And, Captain Millenue, assemble your men. Make certain they understand that I am aware that my bride is a very resourceful young woman, but if she endangers herself again, I will have the skin flogged from their backs. If she comes to harm, they die."

"Yes, Sire," Captain Millenue responded sharply. Saluting once more, he departed as Faine turned away and entered his own quarters.

When he'd closed his chamber door, Faine rubbed his painfully throbbing balls absently. His member stood erect at once, however, and he sighed irritably and strode toward the bath.

It seemed likely that the guards on the walls would have stopped Laurel before she even reached the top of the tower if they had not been distracted by his return, but they lacked discipline or they would not have allowed even that to so distract them that they had failed to watch her.

As badly as he had wanted to order them flogged on the spot, he'd thought it best to allow himself time to cool his temper before he did something he might later regret. He decided, when he'd settled into his bath, that he would merely order five days intensive training to teach them the error of their ways, but they would find that he was not nearly so merciful if they failed him again.

Part of the fault was his own, he knew. He should have ordered a guard to shadow her from the first. He had not wanted to make her feel a prisoner, however. As aware as he was that she did feel that she was a captive, and that she spent her days trying to figure out a way to escape, he'd wanted her to come to accept her situation and had thought it would be best to allow her as much freedom as he dared.

He still felt that he'd not erred in his judgment of her character. She was accustomed to making decisions on her own. He would have to woo her and bind her with affection to have what he wanted of her. If he was forced to openly disclose her captivity, she would be far more difficult to woo, if not impossible.

He thrust those thoughts aside and concentrated on his bath, but he found his mind kept returning to the moments of intimacy they'd shared before they were so rudely interrupted. He'd expected her to struggle, or at least offer a token resistance. The fact that she'd welcomed him with heated passion had completely disarmed him.

Very likely she was as angry about the interruption as he was, but she could not understand why he'd left so abruptly … which meant she was probably furious with him now, he thought wryly. And he would probably find that she wasn't nearly so welcoming the next time.

He frowned. Laurel had warned him that her people would come for her, but he had not expected that they would when they had taken so much care in the past to keep their distance. He had certainly not expected that they would arrive at such an inconvenient moment.

He had been sorely tempted to merely have them sent packing, but the strength of their determination to retrieve her had disturbed him. If they wanted her badly enough to approach him, then they would only await an opportunity to snatch her, he knew. He rather thought he preferred having them close enough that he could watch them.

The hot water of his bath did nothing to cool the fire in his blood, but it did soothe the ache in his muscles from the two battles he'd engaged in to oust the invaders at his borders.

Still brooding over the intrusion and pondering the best way to handle the three very different problems presently plaguing him, Faine allowed his manservant to help him into the deep red robes of his office and left his chamber once more, striding quickly toward his reception chamber.

## Chapter Ten

Laurel fumed for a good fifteen minutes over Faine's inequity before it occurred to her that she'd allowed herself to be completely distracted from her purpose. Abruptly, she left the bed and grabbed up her clothing from the floor, then stared at the damaged garments in dismay.

She'd forgotten Faine hadn't bothered to remove them.

As eager as she'd been at the time for him to tear them off of her, anger surged through her now. She couldn't go looking for her ship naked!

She fiddled with the skirt for a time and finally managed to knot it around her waist but quickly discovered the bra was hopeless. Irritated, she threw it down again and looked around the room.

That was when she spotted her robe, neatly folded, and lying on a trunk in one corner of the room.

Grinning triumphantly, she discarded the wrecked skirt and dashed over to her robe, pulling it on over her head and settling it around her.

She discovered as soon as she opened the door, however, that she wasn't going anywhere any time soon. The moment she cracked the door to peer outside, two arms wielding two pointed pikes crossed before the threshold. She stared at the barricade blankly for a moment and finally poked her head far enough through the door to see that a guard stood on either side of it.

Uttering an irritated hiss, she slammed the door again and stalked across the room, settling on the bed to sulk and to consider if there was any possibility that she could thwart Faine's determination to keep her a prisoner in the room.

\* \* \* \*

Faine propped an arm on the arm of his throne and dropped his chin onto his balled fist, studying the visitors through narrowed eyes, torn between firmly tamped amusement at their attempts to blend with the natives and irritation at having to deal with them at all.

There were four of them--all male. The clothing they wore was a reasonable facsimile of those his people wore when they were not on alert in battle readiness as they had been for the past two months. Even from a distance, however, he could see that the cloth they were made from was nothing like anything that could be found on his world, however. Moreover, their skin, their eyes, and even their hair, was pale … and they were far more attractive than he liked when he considered that they had come believing they would fetch his woman and take her away with them.

Three, he was certain, were warriors. They were not as heavily muscled as his own warriors, but he could tell from their build and stance that they were trained in the art of battle.

The fourth was older, thinner. He decided this man must be of some political office, or perhaps a scholar since he seemed to speak for the group. His grasp of their language was adequate … which infuriated Faine since it meant that they had been intruding far more than he'd believed.

When he signaled that they might approach, the foursome detached themselves from the others crowding the audience chamber and strode confidently toward him, the older man in the lead. They stopped when they were told to do so and bowed respectfully.

"Your highness, I am Wilhem Johanson. My fellow travelers and I have come a great distance … uh … from across the great sea in search of…."

"From what kingdom?" Faine interrupted.

The man gaped at him a moment, glanced a little nervously at the man to his right and began stammering. "Uh … the horse … shoe. That is to say, Horsham."

Faine lifted his dark brows. "I have not heard of this kingdom. Across the great sea, you say?"

The man reddened but managed a deprecating smile. "It is a very small kingdom, sire."

"Since I have never heard of it, it must also be a new kingdom," Faine said dryly. "By what name is your king known?"

The man gaped at him stupidly for several moments. "Uh … name? King Stanley Holms, sire."

Faine's eyes narrowed. He sat back in his chair, studying the man thoughtfully for several moments. Obviously, he was no diplomat or he would be capable of lying more easily. As tempting as it was to toy with him a little longer and watch him squirm while he thought of lies to cover the questions, Faine had no intention of allowing him to state his business and the longer he allowed the audience to continue the more danger there was that the man would ask him point blank about Laurel. He forced a faint smile. "We welcome our visitors from across the sea."

He lifted a hand, summoning his houseman. "See that our visitors are given comfortable accommodations."

Returning his attention to the visitors, he nodded pleasantly. "We are preparing a celebration in honor of my bride. You are welcome to attend," he said dismissingly.

"Sire! If I might have only a moment more of your time?"

"You can arrange for another audience at a later time. At the moment, I have matters regarding the kingdom that require my attention," Faine responded coolly.

The visitors exchanged meaningful glances, but finally bowed and turned to go.

Faine watched them until they'd been escorted from the room. When the doors had closed behind them, he stood abruptly and left the receiving room, returning to his private chambers to pace and consider the situation.

He did not delude himself that all his resources put together were any match for the forces the visitors could wield. His kingdom was a powerful one on his own world, and his army a formidable one, but he suspected Laurel's people filled many worlds among the stars and he had seen enough of the devises they carried to know he could not hope to fight them and win.

The question was, would they be willing to fight to regain her?

Did he dare risk all to keep her, gambling that they would not call his bluff?

Almost as if he'd summoned her, Laurel's image rose in his mind's eye and with it a coldness and a terrible sense of loss at the thought of watching her leave with those who had come for her. He had bonded with her. He could no more yield her willingly than he could offer his limbs to be hacked from his body.

He would have to think of a way.

\* \* \* \*

Very likely due to the fact that Laurel had spent her entire life on a space station, it didn't occur to her to consider the window as a possible avenue of escape. Otherwise, she would have been long since gone when the men arrived the following morning to install bars in it. As it was, she could only grind her teeth in frustration for the opportunity missed.

After two days of impotent fury and abject boredom, Shala arrived late in the afternoon practically dancing with excitement. Laurel would've given a great deal to know just what the excitement was all about, but unfortunately she had only managed to pick up a few words in the time she'd spent on Faine's world and those were not enough to really communicate.

She felt a momentary rise of excitement herself when she realized that Shala was taking her from her 'prison'. It fell when she discovered two guards and a half a dozen women waited in the corridor. With great solemnity, the group bowed almost in sync and then surrounded her and escorted her, to her surprise, down the corridor in the opposite direction from which she usually went.

The group practically hummed with suppressed excitement and Laurel found that it was contagious. By the time they halted before the huge door at the end of the corridor, she was burning with curiosity to know what was afoot.

One of the two guards who stood on either side of the door

tapped on the panel. After a moment, an older man, dressed in the garb of a servant, opened it and held it wide and the procession urged her forward once more.

Surrounded as she was, it was difficult to see as much of the room as she would've liked, particularly since the group herded her across it immediately, heading for a wide doorway. She could see that it was an enormous chamber, however, and opulently furnished. Thick carpets with intricate designs woven into them covered most of the stone floor. A massive bed, situated near the center of the room, dominated the space. Deep red fabric hung from a frame above it and was pulled back and tied at each of four elaborately carved corner posts that held up the frame above the bed. Along the far wall was a huge fireplace, the mantel above it supported by two winged beasts carved from stone. On either side of the fireplace stood two large, heavily padded chairs. Four tall windows were set into the wall on either side of the bed, but these were draped with the same heavy, deep red fabric as the bed and little light filtered through them.

The light in the room was provided by dozens of small flickering tapers which gleamed off of the surfaces of the assortment of glossy wooden furniture about the room.

Laurel was delighted when she discovered that the room she'd been escorted to was an enormous bath. Although built on a far smaller scale than the public bath she'd been taken to before, the pool in the center of the room was easily big enough to swim in.

She was less pleased when she discovered the women who'd escorted her expected to attend her. Shrugging mentally, she yielded to their insistent tugging and pulling and allowed them to undress her and escort her into the pool. When she had been bathed and her hair scrubbed, they led her out again and urged her to lie down on a bench. There they rubbed oils into her skin.

Laurel was so relaxed by the time they'd finished massaging the oils into her skin and buffing her with thick cloths she would almost have welcomed the opportunity to climb into the huge bed in the next room and nap for a while.

She discovered when she was escorted back to the main room, however, that Faine was sprawled in one of the chairs near the hearth.

This was a Faine such as she'd never seen him before, though, and it was several moments before recognition kicked in.

His deep black hair had been combed back from his forehead and was held in place by a band wrought of gold that encircled the top of his head. A large red stone was set into the front of the band. It twinkled like captured fire as the light from the tapers glanced off of it.

He was clad in black, loose legged breeches and a white vest that revealed almost as much of his chest as it concealed and only seemed to accentuate his bare, muscular arms and chest.

Laurel felt her mouth go dry as she stared at him. Every foul thing she'd promised herself she would call him the very next time she set eyes on him vanished from her mind along with every other thought. The heated gaze he trained upon her set her body to humming like a revving engine.

She was distracted from her fascinated examination by the women who surrounded her once more, this time helping her into a gown that was much the same color as the fabrics that decorated the room. She saw when they had settled it and twitched it into place, however, that the fabric was far more fine. It was simply made, in much the same fashion as the loose fitting robe that she'd taken from her own wardrobe on the ship, but more form fitting. The sleeves of the gown fit snugly to her arms to a point just above the elbow and then flared. The gown, once the maids had tightened the lacing at the back, fitted closely to her body from shoulder to hip, then, as with the sleeves, flared to her ankles.

When they had finished fitting the gown, she was escorted to a short bench set before a table that held a large framed material that reflected her image back at her. To her surprise, instead of urging her to sit facing the mirror, the women indicated that she was to sit on one end. Once she had settled on the bench, two of the women knelt at her feet and laced a pair of sandals on each foot, tying the lacing at her knees. She was turned to face the mirror then and her hair was rubbed with cloths, combed and then rubbed again until it was dry and then combed once more until it gleamed. When they were satisfied that all the tangles had been removed, her hair was parted into three segments and carefully woven together behind her head into a single plait and tied with ribbons. Lastly, a sheer piece of fabric of the same color as the gown was draped over her head and secured in place with some sort of metallic clips and then she was helped to rise.

Faine, she discovered when she turned away from the table, had crossed the room. He studied her for several moments from the top of her head to the toes of her sandals, an appreciative gleam in his eyes. Finally, he moved to stand directly before her.

She saw when he lifted his hands that he held a band similar to the one he wore on his head. With great care, he settled it on her head, then caught her chin and tipped her face up.

His expression was solemn as he studied her. "From the moment that I first saw you I thought that you were the most beautiful being that I had ever beheld. Whatever fate has in store for us, I am more grateful than I can say that it brought you to me."

Laurel's lips parted in surprise as she realized she had understood every word that he'd spoken. His accent was still thick with his own language and many of the words in need of deciphering by her mind, but she'd understood him.

Before she could utter a single word, Faine drove every thought from her head by covering her mouth with his own.

Chapter Eleven

Heat cascaded through Laurel like a flow of liquid fire as the warmth of Faine's mouth enveloped hers, setting off sparks of keen awareness throughout her entire body. She made an unconscious sound of pleasure and moved closer to him until she felt the brush of his hard body against hers with each labored breath she drew. A shudder went through him. His arms slipped around her, tightening until she was molded against him from chest to hip. His erection dug into her belly, making her passage flood with liquid warmth and the muscles low in her belly clench with anticipation and need.

To her disappointment, he withdrew just about the time she reached the melting point. Briefly, he molded his lips to hers once more in a kiss of apology before he lifted his head.

"We will be late." Lifting one corner of the veil that covered her head, he tucked it into one of the pins so that the entire lower part of her face was covered. "You must wear this so for now. It is tradition."

Laurel frowned at him uncomprehendingly, her brain too fogged with heat still to identify his thickly accented words for many moments. Before she'd entirely digested the comments, he caught her hand, lacing his fingers through hers, and led her from the room.

In the corridor outside, an entourage of similarly dressed men and women awaited. They bowed as Faine and Laurel stepped from the room and then fell into step behind them as Faine strode past them down the wide hall.

Bemused, Laurel followed without protest, feeling curiosity begin to filter through the heated haze of thwarted passion that lingered in her brain. From somewhere close by, she heard strains of music and the confusing chatter of many voices. The noise grew more pronounced as they progressed. Turning at the intersection of another corridor, Laurel saw before them at the end of the corridor a pair of doors. As they approached, the men standing on either side of the doors snapped to attention, then reached for the door handles and pulled them wide.

Laurel's heart leapt in pleased surprise as she saw the gathering that thronged the great room beyond the doors. She glanced up at Faine as they crossed the threshold, smiling. "A party! Kewl!"

He chuckled at her enthusiasm, but tightened his hold on her hand when she would have hurried forward. As they entered the room, almost as if a signal had been given, it began to fall silent. A man, dressed in a vest and loose legged breeches similar to those Faine wore, ascended the two steps to reach the raised walk where Laurel and Faine stood. In his hand, he held a bright red ribbon. Faine lifted their laced hands and the man very solemnly wrapped the ribbon around their wrists, then laced it between their interlocking fingers. When he'd finished, he stepped back and turned to the assemblage below them.

*"Behold! His royal highness, King Faine D'Arten and his queen, La-rel!"*

Laurel glanced up at Faine as everyone shouted an enthusiastic hurrah at once. "What did he say?"

Faine lifted the hand laced with his and kissed her knuckles. "We must dance."

"Oh … OH!" Laurel nearly stumbled as he led her down the stairs. "I don't think I can do this!" she whispered frantically as he led her to the center of the room and she saw that the two of them were, evidently, expected to dance alone.

Faine pulled her closely to him and bent his head low. "Only do as I do."

To Laurel's great relief, when the music began, the melody they played had a slow beat. With even greater relief she discovered the dance was really very simple and she managed to follow his lead, only stepping on his toes two or three times within the first few minutes. Slowly, as she got the hang of it, she began to relax and move more fluidly.

Faine smiled down at her encouragingly. "You see."

She chuckled wryly. "Yes. A few more and I might be able to get through one without walking all over your feet."

To her delight, Faine chuckled, as well.

"When did you learn to speak my language … and how?" she asked after a moment.

He shrugged slightly. "I still learn. The box with the images teaches me."

Laurel frowned in confusion for several moments. Finally,

enlightenment dawned. When it did, both surprise and irritation surfaced. She managed to tamp the latter. "My communicator?" she asked in a voice threaded with disbelief.

His brows rose. "The box you used to find your way to my city."

She could hardly credit it, but there was no getting around the fact that he had certainly learned her language somehow. If she hadn't known better, she would've suspected that he'd known her language all along, but she found it almost as difficult to believe that he would have purposefully deceived her as she did that he'd not only figured out how to use the devise, but learned a good grasp of English.

The knowledge stunned her to silence for a time. Finally, she collected her scattered thoughts. "Why?"

"For you."

Laurel felt a blush of pleasure creep into her cheeks. "Really?"

He smiled wryly. "I had thought it would be easier."

Laurel grimaced. "You're doing far better than I am. I've only managed to learn a few words in your language … and not very useful ones at that."

He lifted his brows. "What words have you learned?"

When she told him, he chuckled.

Embarrassment filled her. "That bad, huh?"

He shook his head. "Very good. I enjoy to hear you speak my language. I will teach you."

Laurel's own enjoyment took a nose dive at that comment. She wasn't going to be around long enough to learn his language, and she was dismayed to realize how much regret filled her at the realization.

How was it, she wondered, that she had become so focused on getting away that she'd failed to realize that she wasn't actually desperate to escape … in fact, in no great hurry to leave at all?

She was fascinated by his culture, of course, but it was far more than that. Somehow Faine had caught her completely off guard and burrowed so deeply under her skin that she felt a terrible sense of loss only to consider leaving.

Swallowing against the knot of misery in her throat, she leaned closer to him, resting her head on his shoulder and breathing in his scent as she moved with him in the dance. Before she was entirely ready for it, the dance ended. Gently, Faine disengaged himself from her and led her from the floor. The man who'd laced their hands together with the ribbon removed it and tied it around Faine's upper arm.

Laurel watched curiously, wondering at the ritualistic, almost symbolic tying of the ribbon. The moment the ribbon had been tied, however, another shout went up from the assemblage and the great chamber immediately began to fill with the noise of happy celebration.

Faine led her to a raised platform at the opposite end of the room, up four steps, and to a pair of ornate, high backed chairs. When they'd seated themselves, he lifted one hand and the musicians immediately began a rousing tune. Within moments, the dance floor was full of men and women twirling and dipping and stomping their feet in time to the music.

Fascinated, Laurel watched the dancers, wishing she had her recording device with her so that she could record her impressions of the celebration, tapping her foot in time to the tune.

"You wish to dance?"

Laurel glanced at Faine in surprise, but chuckled, shaking her head. "I wish I could. It looks like such fun."

He stood, taking her hand and helping her from her chair. "Then come. There is a dance I wish to teach you … and we have stayed long enough."

Laurel lifted her brows questioningly, but there was a look of promise in his eyes that sent a shaft of anticipation through her. Without a word, she followed him as he descended the stairs and left the room.

To her surprise, he led her to the room where she'd bathed and dressed earlier.

"Should we be in here?" she whispered when he pulled her inside and closed the door.

"It is ours now," he murmured, pulling her close and tugging the veil from her face.

"Really?"

He kissed the tip of her nose. "Really," he assured her. Reaching up, he pulled the golden circlet from her head and strode across the room to a tall chest. Opening the narrow doors, he set the circlet inside carefully, then removed his own from his head and set it beside the one that she'd worn. Raking his fingers through his hair to loosen it, he turned to look at her once more, a faint smile on his lips. "As beautiful as you are in that gown I believe I like what's beneath it far more."

Laurel stared at him a moment while his comment slowly sank in. Her heart seemed to trip over itself when the full meaning hit her. She moved toward him then, turning as she reached him and presenting her back. He removed the veil first, tossing it in the general direction of a nearby chest, then tugged at the tie laced through the back of the gown. She felt the heat of his breath along her back a moment before she felt his lips.

Prickles of sensation instantly erupted all over her body at his touch, her nipples puckering and standing erect, hooking briefly on the fabric as it began to slide from her shoulders and down her arms. A sigh of pleasure escaped her as he followed the widening gap in her gown with a trail of kisses until he reached her buttocks. He turned her to face him then, pushing the gown from her hips and covering the mound of her sex with his mouth. She gasped, grabbing at his shoulders to steady herself as she felt the flick of his tongue against her clitoris and a knee weakening jolt of pleasure shot through her.

She was shaking with the effort to stand upright when he rose at last. Shrugging the vest from his shoulders, he pulled the tie of his breeches, releasing them. When they fell to his feet, he stepped out of them, lifted her against his chest and strode toward the bed. Settling her on the edge of the mattress, he pulled the ties of her sandals and pushed them from her feet before turning his attention to his own.

Laurel moved further up on the bed, propping her head in her hand as she watched the play of muscles in his back and arms. When he'd discarded his sandals and turned to look at her, she leaned back against the pillows, lifting one hand in invitation. He caught her hand, placing a kiss in the center of her palm and then pressing her palm against his chest over his heart as he moved closer, bending his head to nibble a trail of kisses from her belly up to her breasts.

Without pausing, he caressed each in turn, thoroughly, with his mouth and his hands until Laurel was on fire for his possession. She shifted, spreading her thighs in invitation. He accepted, pushing her thighs wider and settling between them as he shifted higher and covered her mouth in a kiss that told of his own impatient need. She slipped a hand between them, grasping his rock hard erection and guiding him along her cleft until she felt the head of his cock pressing against her opening.

He broke the kiss, lifting slightly away from her so that he could watch their joining as he pressed inexorably deeper until he was fully sheathed within her passage. Laurel felt her breath catch at the exquisite pleasure of fullness as her body adjusted to him, accepted his possession, wept with the pleasure of it.

He caught her gaze and held it as he began to stroke the length of her channel with his cock, sending one shock wave of pleasure after another through her with each slow caress until Laurel felt her body winding tighter and tighter with a tension that needed release. She dug her fingers into his back, lifting to meet him, urging him to move faster, moaning as he complied and the jolts of pleasure built higher and more quickly until she found herself hovering, fighting desperately to reach the peak.

When it caught her, it exploded shatteringly through her, dragging a sharp gasp of ecstasy from her throat. He groaned, shuddered, and began to thrust faster still until his own climax caught him, wringing a hoarse cry of satisfaction from him as his cock spasmed, spilling his hot seed inside of her.

His head fell forward on his shoulders as he gasped for breath. His arms trembled with the effort to hold himself above her. Finally, he shifted, pulling his expended cock from her and collapsing beside her.

Laurel rolled onto her side and kissed his chest, just above his pounding heart. "You were right," she murmured huskily.

He opened one eye a crack and gathered her close, stroking her back in a leisurely caress. "About what?"

"This was even better than when you came to me in my dreams."

## Chapter Twelve

Faine paused. After a moment, he moved away from her and pulled on a cord that hung on the wall near the head of the bed. Dragging the coverlet loose, he spread it over the two of them once Laurel had rolled off the coverlet and onto the sheets.

"You remember the dreams?" he asked after he'd gathered her close against him again.

"Some things. They weren't really dreams, were they?"

"It is hard to explain."

Laurel pulled away and propped her head on one arm, looking at him expectantly.

"It is another plane of existence. A world that exists beside the one your conscious mind knows."

Laurel was still studying over it when someone tapped on the door and entered. Clutching the sheets, she sat up and watched as servants carrying trays entered the room. Without once glancing in the direction of the bed, they laid out a banquet on the large table opposite the fireplace. When they'd finished, they moved back to the door, bowed, and departed, closing the door behind them.

"Hungry?"

Laurel chuckled. "There's enough food there to feed an army. But, yes."

"Stay," Faine ordered. Rolling from the bed, he gathered up an assortment on two plates and returned. Setting the plates on the narrow table nearest that side of the bed, he went back to gather up a bottled beverage and two glasses.

Laurel looked at him questioningly when he climbed into the bed again, but took the plate he offered her. "The bed will be full of crumbs."

He shrugged. "The servants will clean it."

Settling the plates on the bed between them, Faine stretched out on his side and propped on one arm. After a moment, Laurel followed suit, frowning thoughtfully as she ate. "So what you're saying is that even though I thought of them only as dreams, they were a different reality?"

Faine eyed her speculatively for several moments. "Yes."

"It really freaked me out when I called Shala by name and she answered," Laurel said noncommittally.

Faine frowned. "I do not understand."

"Slang. Unnerved me."

He nodded comprehension. "This is when you began to realize that it was more than 'only' a dream?"

Laurel frowned. "I think I had begun to realize it before that. I just hadn't really accepted it until then." She thought that over for a minute. "Actually, I wasn't really ready to accept it then, but I had to. Before, I'd thought it was just a strange kind of coincidence that you had explained so many things to me that I didn't understand. I suppose I thought it was only that I'd puzzled over them and my subconscious mind had figured it out."

Sitting up, Faine turned, opened the bottle and filled the two glasses. Laurel looked the clear liquid over suspiciously and finally took a cautious sip. As she'd suspected, it was some sort of fermented juices. From the first sip, heat settled in her belly and a pleasant sensation of floating began to spread through her body. It was good. Before she'd quite realized it, she discovered she had drank half the glass.

She frowned, realizing her thoughts were wandering. "You said, in one dream, that you were the ruler?"

"I am," Faine said, removing the remains of their meal and setting the plates on the table once more. When he turned toward her once more, he placed a tiny rounded fruit on Laurel's hip, then leaned forward and caught it with his teeth. It popped and a trickle of cool juices ran down her hip and belly. Laurel drew in a shaky breath as he carefully licked the juices from her skin, feeling a different warm glow settle in her belly.

After a moment, he lifted his head, gazing into her slumberous eyes. Laurel rolled onto her back, inviting him to continue. Taking her glass, he set it on the table as well, gathered a couple of tidbits and, with great care, balanced them on strategic positions of her body. She held her breath as he tipped his glass, pouring the last few drops of the liquid into the hollow of her belly. Reaching behind him blindly, he dropped the glass on the floor as he leaned down to suck and lick the liquid from her stomach.

Laurel held perfectly still, hardly daring to breathe as he nibbled the tidbits from her one by one. By the time he'd finished, her entire body felt as if it was a mass of exposed, throbbing nerve endings. Heat flashed along the sensors, gathering in her sex and so that the inner walls quaked with expectation.

When he raised up to study her, she sat up. Sliding her arms around his neck, she moved onto his lap, straddling him as she lifted her lips to nipple his teasingly. In a moment, he seized the initiative, covering her mouth and kissing her deeply, hungrily. She shifted, sliding a hand between them and lifting slightly away so that she could align the head his engorged cock with her body and then bear down to engulf his flesh within her body.

He let out a muffled sound of pleasure, grasping her hips to steady and guide her as she began to move so that the throat of her sex massaged the length of his cock, eliciting tremors of delight in both of them. When he broke the kiss and lay back, she leaned forward. Propping her palms on the bed on either side of his chest, she moved until she found the stride that produced the most exquisite sensation, increasing the rhythm as she felt her body soaring upward toward its peak, watching his face as she gave him pleasure.

Suddenly, she felt her muscles clench, spasm as her body orgasmed. She faltered, squeezing her eyes tightly, so caught up in the throes of release every other consideration vanished from her mind. He caught her hips, lunging upward in hard, jolting thrusts that brought him to his own culmination.

Weakly, Laurel sprawled on top of him when their bodies had ceased to convulse in pleasure, laying her cheek over his pounding heart while she struggled to catch her breath. A poignant warmth spread through her as the passion flowed from her body and mind and her focus turned to the feel of his body beneath hers. It was more than release, more than satisfaction. It was a sense of belonging, of security.

She was half asleep when he shifted, tipping her head up and placing a lingering kiss on her lips.

"You are sticking to me."

Laurel chuckled. "Not my fault you're a sloppy eater."

He slapped a palm against her buttocks. "Up, wench! We must bathe."

Reluctantly, Laurel slid off of him. "The bed's full of crumbs too."

He rolled to the side of the bed and pulled the cord again. Catching her hand, he tugged until she climbed from the bed and followed him to the bath.

The bath took a little longer than Laurel had expected. They bathed each other, made love, then bathed again. When they returned to the room at last, it had been cleaned. Grateful, Laurel climbed into the bed and collapsed, completely sated in every way. She was asleep almost before Faine had rolled her under the covers, gathered her against him and tucked the covers around them.

* * * *

There were a number of questions that hovered on the tip of Laurel's tongue over the two glorious days she spent cuddling with Faine in his bed and making love, but she discovered a great reluctance to voice them. Somehow, in the back of her mind, she feared that the answers might rupture the fragile bubble of happiness and she realized she was extremely reluctant to let go of it.

Regardless, she knew it couldn't last forever. She was disappointed when she woke on the third day and saw that Faine had risen and dressed, but not really surprised.

Yawning, she stretched all over, and finally sat up. Faine, she saw when she returned from the facilities, was standing at one window, staring out at the view. Two women waited to help her dress and arrange her hair.

When they had finished her toilet and departed, Faine turned from the window, his face grim.

"We have … visitors."

Laurel's heart skipped several beats. She knew just from the look on his face who the visitors must be. She swallowed with an effort, nodding slightly. After a moment, he approached her and offered his hand. She took it, allowing him to lead her.

The chamber he took her to was one she had never seen. It was perhaps twice or three times the size of his bed chamber, but not nearly so large as the great hall where they had danced … where, she had finally realized they had wed in the strange little ritual that had played out before his people.

A number of people were standing on either side of the room, leaving a center aisle clear, waiting expectantly. As she and Faine entered, they bowed.

The floor where they entered the room formed a raised platform. In the center, two high backed chairs much like those they'd been seated in at the party faced the chamber.

Leading her to them, Faine guided her to one and took the other.

Laurel glanced around a little nervously. Minutes passed. Finally, the doors at the opposite end opened and a group of men entered. They made their way up the aisle, stopping a few yards from where Faine and Laurel sat and bowed respectfully if a little stiffly. Laurel studied them, her heart thundering so hard in her ears she could barely hear anything else.

The eyes of all four men were trained on her when they lifted their heads once more.

The older of the four men addressed Faine. "Sire, we have come in search of a young woman lost to us."

Faine's brows rose. *"Why do you search here, in Merisea? Surely, if you lost her and you have not been here before, then you could not have lost her here?"*

Laurel bit her lip as the man reddened, wondering what the two men were saying to one another. She could see the visitors were wearing translators. Despite the fact that they were dressed as the people of this world, they stuck out as aliens even without the translators. She knew they must be representatives of the Confederation, and that they'd come for her. An awful sense of impending loss filled her. As hard as she'd tried not to think about it, she'd known in the back of her mind that she must expect it.

She glanced at Faine uneasily and saw that he'd turned to study her. He held his hand out to her, palm up. She frowned in confusion, but laid her hand in his trustingly. His fingers closed around hers and he tugged slightly, urging her to come to him. Flushing, she rose from her chair and looked at him questioningly.

He pulled her onto his lap, settling her against his chest, then placed the fingers of one hand along her skull, just above her ear.

*Do you wish to know what is being said?*

Laurel glanced at him sharply. There'd been no strange tickling sensation this time. She'd heard him as clearly as if he'd spoken aloud. For a moment, she thought he *had* spoken aloud.

He had said that they would bond.

*Yes.*

Nodding ever so slightly, Faine turned his attention to the men below them. "You may continue."

The man looked flustered for several moments. "She was traveling … uh … with her companion and was lost."

"This companion told you that she had been lost in Merisea?"

"Yes! It was the companion who told us."

"How did it come about that the two were separated from one another?"

The man simply stared at him miserably for several moments. Finally, he turned to the other men and consulted with them. Laurel sat forward slightly, straining to hear their low voiced conversation, but, to her disappointment, she couldn't make out enough to tell what they were saying.

"There was a storm, sire. A great storm, and the … uh … ship was damaged."

"And, somehow, this woman you seek was tossed from the ship while the companion managed to take the ship back across the sea?"

"Yes! Well, I'm not entirely certain, sire, but it must have been something like that."

"How do you know the woman still lives? Perhaps she perished?"

The man blanched. "I don't think that's at all possible. In fact, we are convinced that she was stranded here and … we must take her back. Our pres … our king insists upon it. For it is forbidden for her to leave the boundaries of our … uh … land."

Faine was silent for a long time. "Why?"

"Why?" the man echoed in dismay. "I … uh … its a law!" he managed finally, mopping the sweat from his brow.

Laurel heard Faine swallow audibly and turned to look at him. He held her gaze.

"By what name is this woman known?"

She could tell from the look in his eyes that he knew it was her they'd come for. There was pain there, as well, and it made her ache to see it.

"Laurel Conyers, sire."

"Describe her," Faine said after a long moment.

"She is twenty three years old, with blond hair, blue eyes. Weight around one hundred fifteen pounds. Height five feet six inches."

Faine dragged his gaze from Laurel and turned to study the man speculatively for several moments. "Much like my queen?"

This time, Laurel heard the visitor swallow. "Exact … uh … yes. A very great deal like your queen."

"There is no other like my queen in all of Merisea," Faine said coldly. "Or in all this world," he added after a moment.

"I'm entirely certain you're right," the man said incautiously, reddening profusely when Faine's eyes narrowed challengingly.

Faine turned his attention to Laurel once more. "La-rel is the woman my dream vision promised me. I have bonded with her, allowed my soul to unite with hers. Without her, I would no longer be whole." He paused for several moments. "But my love for her is boundless. If she wishes to go, I could not make her stay."

Laurel felt her chin wobble. Tears filled her eyes. "The laws," she whispered hesitantly.

"I am the law giver here. The laws of their world mean nothing to me."

Laurel blinked the tears from her eyes. "You don't know how powerful they are!" she said in a frightened whisper. "They could … do terrible things."

"I know."

"I couldn't let you take the risk."

He shook his head slightly. "They must know that you stay of your own free will. *I* must know it."

Laurel studied him for a long moment and finally turned to the representatives of the confederation. "I am La-rel D'Arten, wife of Faine. I may look a great deal like the woman you came for, but I'm not her."

The older man frowned. "The Confederation laws.…"

"Prohibit the interaction of people of your world with this world. I am Queen La-rel, of Merisea, wife of Faine, and … I love him. I couldn't bear to leave him. You must go back and tell them that the woman you came to find is no more."

The man frowned and turned to speak with the others. Finally, he turned to her again. "You are certain? You are not … being coerced?"

Laurel shook her head, smiling as she turned to gaze up at Faine. "I am bound by nothing but the hold he has upon my heart."


The End

# THE SEXDROID

By

Jaide Fox

## Chapter One

*Earth, AD 2193*

Sabin Grey had gone undercover before, many times. In fact, he was damn good at his job ... but he'd never gone under as an android, and he entertained a good deal of reservations about whether or not he could pull it off.

"Well? Are you going to answer me or not, Grey?" Assistant Director Hartley asked as he lounged behind his desk, an unfamiliar smile tugging at his lips as if he was trying very hard to repress it.

Sabin grunted in response. If he hadn't known better, he'd suspect Hartley was setting him up for some sort of practical joke, but Hartley wasn't exactly the type to play juvenile games with his people, even off duty. Considering the case his boss had just dumped in his lap, it seemed even less likely that there was some sort of prank in the offing. It wasn't every day one of their top scientist's came under review for treason.

All the same, something was up. Hartley was the kind of guy that could watch the Stooges with a poker face and at the moment he looked as if he was going to explode if he didn't laugh. Sabin wasn't sure he wanted to find out what it was, but he was afraid he was about to.

Wondering if there was something about the case itself that Hartley thought he was going to find particularly unpleasant, he punched the button on the case file once more, using the stylus to go through the file and surveillance photos. Emily Shue. Loner. Work and lab at home. Animal lover. He clicked to the next file and studied the image that popped up; Lips turned up at the corners, almost smiling as she chewed her pen. Pert nose with a dust of freckles and long, curly hair climbing down her shoulders. Blonde.

Trouble. Definite Trouble. Maybe that was what Hartley found so humorous--the idea of throwing Sabin in with a babe that looked like this when he was going to have to nail her if it turned out she was a traitor.

It wasn't the sort of thing he'd find amusing, but who knew what an undertaker like Hartley would find funny?

"She doesn't look like a traitor, she looks like--"

"The girl next door?"

Sabin nodded. "Yes, exactly."

"Don't let her appearance fool you. She's been evading our surveillance for weeks. Head office wanted to go ahead and bring her in for the treatment, and then we found out her grandmother had ordered her a sex--I mean, a companion droid."

Sabin leveled a dark look at Hartley, who chuckled and ignored him.

Well, there it was, the funny part, and it hadn't taken nearly as long to get to the punch line as he'd thought it would. Strange thing was, he still didn't see the damned humor in it. "What if I say no?"

"You like your job here, correct?"

Sabin sighed and shut down the case file. No wonder Hartley had been wearing that cat-that-ate-the-canary smile. "I don't have any choice in this, do I?"

"No." Hartley straightened, his aged face solemn now. "Jokes aside, this is serious. *Someone's* been leaking our dimensional jump technology to the UAN. You know as well as I do we can't afford to let this get out. Emily Shue is the keystone to the project. The breach has to be stopped, Grey, and you're my best man."

Hartley was right. Far too much valuable information had been stolen already and it was beginning to look like they were going to loose their edge on this project if they couldn't find the leak and plug it. Despite his reservations, he knew it was his duty to the country to find out if she was passing information to the other side.

"When does the droid arrive?"

"She's expecting it this afternoon."

Sabin was accustomed to the unexpected, but this knocked the wind out of him. Nothing like giving him *no* time to think it over and spot potential problems. "That doesn't leave me much time to prepare." Sabin stood as did Hartley.

"You'll manage," he said as he ushered Sabin from the office. "We all do."

\* \* \* \*

The incessant knocking had been going on for some time when it finally stopped and roused Emily Shue into consciousness.

She sat up at her desk, startled and groggy, blinking back the blur obscuring her vision. When had she fallen asleep? And who was at her door? She never had visitors.

Rising weakly from her chair, she stumbled through the room into the hall beyond to the foyer.

As if sensing her approach, the person on the other side of the door began knocking again.

More than a little annoyed at being woken, she called, "Coming! I'm comin'." She grumbled to herself, rubbed her face and discovered she had a note stuck to her cheek. She'd undoubtedly picked it up when she'd lain her head on her desk. Peeling it off, she glanced at it, saw it was important and stuffed it into her pocket as she cautiously opened the front door a crack and peered through the narrow opening.

A beaming, bright eyed youth greeted her, leaning forward to peer back at her through the slender crack. "Ms. Shue?"

"Yes," Emily croaked.

"I have your delivery here. You just need to sign for it."

Delivery? What delivery? She hadn't ordered anything since last week's pizza--still sitting at the bottom of her fridge. Or perhaps that was the week before last? Anyway, it was nearly dark. Companies had stopped delivering this close to dark years ago.

As she stood contemplating the matter, not budging, 'bright eyes' smile dimmed to headlights in her eyes. "Your companion android, Ms. Shue?"

She was still too absorbed in trying to remember what she might have ordered to really pay him any attention--until he mentioned android. Her eyes focused on him for several moments as the key word jogged something in her memory and then she slapped her forehead with her palm. She'd forgotten all about Gramma's early birthday present. Or it could have been late? She wasn't entirely sure what day of the week it was.

Emily opened the door and pressed her thumb to the delivery confirmation pad, affirming her receipt of the delivery. "What are you doing making deliveries so late? I thought they were only doing automated deliveries now."

"It is automated, Ms. Shue. I'm an android, as well." He smiled brighter.

That would explain the peachy keen disposition, she thought and wondered what she was getting in to now ... or rather what Gramma had gotten her in to.

"I'll be right back with your package, Ms. Shue."

"Hope he comes fully assembled," she murmured, chuckling as she left the door open and wandered into the living room to have a seat while she waited. She was still more than a little groggy from being awakened so abruptly. Or maybe it was just that she hadn't slept nearly long enough?

Before she could rest her cheeks on the cushions of the couch, a deep male voice called her name from the foyer.

It arrested her, mid sit, her jaw going slack.

The 'man' caught sight of her and strode into the living room, his hand extended. "I'm Sabin. I will be your new companion android," he said with a smile that turned her knees to water so that she collapsed abruptly onto the couch. She gaped at him, at his sensual, utterly kissable lips, the smoky bedroom eyes that met her own stunned gaze with a gleam that banish all thought from her brain. He towered above her. She came upright as if the couch had ejected her, and realized he still towered over her.

She ran a disbelieving stare up and down his body. He had the lean look of an athlete, muscles well defined and bulging on his bared arms, and she wondered idly if the rest of him was so ... detailed. A strand of dark hair curled over his forehead. It looked so natural, it made her palms itch to run her fingers through the thick mass.

Her brain kicked into gear as her physical reaction ran it's course, and still she stared at him, unblinking, marveling at the advances in technology that never ceased to amaze her-- to create a perfect simulation of a human being ... and a damned sexy one at that. Was he supposed to be so ... so sexy?

What in the world was she going to *do* with him?

The frightening thought provided resuscitation to the steaming pile of mush her brain had been reduced to. Or, perhaps it was only an animal reaction to fear that finally gave her a kick in the ass. Whatever the case, the moment it occurred to her that she was going to be trapped in her home with him, she dashed past him and out the front door.

The delivery boy, she saw when she ran out of the house, had loaded up and was backing down the drive.

"Wait!" she called, hailing him down before he could escape. He stopped and she caught up to him breathlessly.

"Yes, Ms. Shue?" He regarded her questioningly.

"Are you sure he's supposed to ... um ... be this way? Did you deliver the right one to me?" She hadn't expected something like this. What had Gramma been thinking?

"Of course, ma'am. He comes with award winning technical support and a manual built in to his memory capacitor. Have a nice day." The boy waved and drove off, leaving Emily staring after him in the gathering dark.

With a feeling not unlike dread, she trudged slowly back up her overgrown walkway to her new "live in."

What was she to do now?

She kept repeating the question in her mind numbly until she reached the door. Uneasiness assailed her at the thought of facing her 'companion' once more. She stepped quietly into the house, closing the door with the barest whisper of sound, then crept across the foyer and peered cautiously around the door frame of the living room.

It was empty.

Where had he gone off to?

She looked around the room blankly for several moments before she moved inside. She'd checked under all of the tables in the room before it occurred to her that he wasn't an animal, scampering about, exploring his new territory. Even if he could've managed to fit himself under her tables, there was no reason why he would. She got up and went to check the closet, wondering if it would be best just to ignore the droid and go about her routine as usual. It wasn't like he was a living thing and would keel over dead if she forgot to feed him, or water him. In general, she worked all day on her equations, occasionally remembering to feed herself and her pets--when she had them--snatching sleep when she could.

She frowned thoughtfully and realized that wasn't going to work. She had a ... person wandering around the house. She was bound to bump into him and that would be downright unnerving since she wasn't used to having another person around. She was accustomed to living alone. Even her independent minded pets avoided her most of the time.

"Hello?" she called softly as she left the living room and continued her search through the house, examining every room. It wasn't a very large house. There were only so many places he could be. He was a droid, she reminded herself. What interest would he have in exploring anyway? But as she searched each room with no sign of him, she soon found the choices of hiding places had dried up to only one remaining room.

Her bedroom.

The door was closed. She never closed her bedroom door unless she was sleeping in there--and she fell asleep at her desk more often than not. *Please, please don't let him be in there*. Emily had never had a man in her room--ever.

Reaching out, she turned the handle and let the door slowly open on its own.

She gasped as her bed came in to view, covering her eyes with her hands before it occurred to her how absurd it was to 'hide' from an android. Peeling her fingers loose, she looked at her bed again.

The android was in it.

And he was naked.

## Chapter Two

"Oh my god. Please tell me you're not really naked under there." Emily hovered in the door way, torn between horror and curiosity, not daring to step inside, unable to look away.

The place where her fantasies played out only in her dreams, the bed that had never held a man's body--all the fresh scrubbed innocence of her bedroom was completely swept away by the current occupant lounging in her bed as if he belonged there. As if he'd been invited.

Sensible scientist that she was, she shouldn't have been so disturbed. She was twenty five after all, and she'd never thought of herself as a child, even when she had been. Besides that, he wasn't even a real ... well....

He met her gaze steadily, his lush mouth curved in a welcoming smile. That mouth looked like it was made for doing things she'd only dared dream about. Slowly, as if her eyes had a mind of their own, they scanned downward, brushing her over the muscled expanse of his chest, noting the dark hair whirling over the supple muscles, the happy trail of dark hair that furrowed in a line like an arrow down his rippled stomach to disappear beneath her comforter.

Why couldn't real men look this good?

"Come to bed, Emily." He patted the mattress beside him, oh so polite, his voice a benign, non-threatening, monotone.

Emily shook her head to break the stupor holding her in thrall. Scientists did not fall into stupors, least of all while looking at naked men in their bed. "It's too early for sleep."

A subtle change moved over his face, and the friendly, welcoming smile became one of seduction. "I didn't have sleeping in mind."

Emily felt her heart flip flop in her chest. Her eyes widened. "Good god!" Whirling abruptly, she rushed from the room to the kitchen and the phone console in there.

Punching the memory button, she waited impatiently for the phone to be activated on the other end. After five rings, the video display came on, revealing the pleased face of her grandmother.

"Happy Birthday, honey. Did you like my present?" Gramma said as she eased herself down in a recliner facing the phone console.

Emily took a deep breath, forcing herself to calm down before she spoke. "Gramma, why did you order me a ... uh...." Heat rose to her cheeks at the very thought of what had gone through Gramma's head when she'd ordered *him*.

"I prefer to call him a sexdroid, dear. They're all the rage right now."

"Gramma!"

Gramma chuckled. "Now don't be a wet blanket, dear. That's what he's for, after all."

Emily spluttered. That Gramma would know such things. "I can't keep him. He's sitting in my bed! Naked! He wants to jump my bones!"

Gramma chuckled gleefully. "Really? How delightful! Stop being such a prude, dear. That's his purpose. Really, I thought you'd be more thrilled. I so despair of you ever finding a mate."

Emily rolled her eyes. It was one of the reasons she never went out anymore. Everyone always wanted to know when she was going to get a man, when she was going to settle down. In an age when enlightened minds realized marriage was obsolete, she was still constantly harangued by all and sundry on the benefits of being a Mrs.

"I'd hoped he could help you in the man department. You don't have much experience with men."

That was certainly true. She'd had the grand number of one relationship in her life, and it had been so abhorrent, she'd not thought much more on the matter. She was happy being single and free, truly. She had her work, a few pets that she'd never gotten around to naming, and ... well....

Maybe she did need to brush up on her man skills.

Gramma sniffled, catching Emily's attention. "You don't remember reading the brochures a few months ago? That's what gave me the idea. Are you sure you won't keep him, honey? I only wanted to get you something that would make you happy. I get so worried about you being alone out there."

She was putting a guilt trip on her. And dammit, it was working. "Oh, all right. I'll keep him. On a trial basis only."

She beamed. "I'm so glad. This was a lovely talk, but I really must be getting to bed. Where *did* the time go?"

They said their good-byes and Emily closed down the connection. She'd been guilted into keeping the droid, but she didn't have to like it.

Checking the time, she was surprised to see that it was late, then she wondered when her life had become so skewed as to consider 8:00 late.

Just the same, all the excitement of the day had tired her out, and she was looking forward to getting some extra shut eye.

It wasn't until she'd reached her bedroom and spotted the droid still lounging in her bed that she remembered she had a problem.

Emily stopped in front of him, hands on hips, ignoring the way his close proximity made her blood pound. "You can't sleep there--here ... in my bed."

He sat up straighter and the lip of the comforter dipped low on his hips. Emily refused to look more than a minute at the spot of attraction.

"My name is Sabin. You have yet to call me by my name."

"Okay. Sabin. You can't sleep here ... err ... stay here. I expect this matter to be resolved by the time I'm finished in the bathroom." Emily turned on her heel and went into the bathroom, firmly locking the door. She checked it twice before removing her clothes and getting into the shower.

After she finished the arduous task of shaving her legs--which she'd skipped a few too many times--Emily poured shampoo into her hands and scrubbed her scalp to work up a lather before ducking under the shower head to rinse. A cool breeze wafted across her butt cheeks at just that moment. Emily squinted through the water running down her face to check the shower curtain just as a hard object pressed into the cleft of her buttocks.

Yelping, she made an abortive attempt to turn. Two large hands grasped her shoulders firmly, preventing movement, and the hardness nudged more deeply between the cheeks of her ass, spreading her wide.

She turned her head and blew water out of her eyes, scrambling against the shower wall for purchase. But she didn't need to see to know it was him… Sabin, the sexdroid.

How the hell had he gotten inside?

What the hell did he think he was doing?

He smiled at her and thrust against her again, slipping his hands from her shoulders to her ribcage beneath her breasts.

"How ... how did you get ... in here?" she asked, breathless to feel that alien hardness tucked so close to her femininity.

"I opened the door," he said simply, and nipped the curve of her neck, sending a jolt of awareness through her. "I thought you would enjoy the company."

"You ... thought ... wrong ... oh my god...." she breathed as he moved forward, his hard shaft pressing closer.

Her knees turned to water at the feel of his cock slipping up and down her cleft, and she trembled as he reached up and cupped her breasts under the warm spray of water. He squeezed them, kneading until all thought of sending him away vanished.

Emily leaned forward, resting her cheek against the shower wall, letting the liquid heat stream down her back between them. He pinched her nipples, slipping easily in the redolent shampoo trailing down her body.

"Oh," she gasped as he probed further, parting her folds from behind even as he glided one hand down her stomach. Emily propped her hands on the wall for support, feeling herself melt under the water. He moved further, pushing one hand down her body to her cleft, fingers rubbing the top of her slit, teasing.

"Oh ... oh my," she breathed, past caring or wondering how he'd managed to get inside when she thought she'd locked the door. Just a little further and he could touch her just like she wanted....

As if reading her mind, he slipped his finger into her shallow cleft and rubbed her clit. Emily jerked against his hand, gasping as he stroked his cock against her passage and his fingers worked her moisture into her nub. He kissed her shoulder and neck as he rubbed her lightly, increasing pressure the more she pushed back against him. Her skin felt scalded by his mouth and the press of his tight muscles against her cheeks, the glide of his satiny member teasing her with its nearness.

The water heightened her awareness, until it felt like he climbed all over her skin, his hot mouth everywhere, torturing her. Her clit throbbed, painfully sensitive, reaching, reaching for that ultimate bliss, and then the climax rushed through her body like lava through her veins. Emily cried out and collapsed against the wall, breathing hoarsely, her muscles as substantial as jelly.

He trapped her against the wall, supporting her until she pushed weakly away and climbed out of the shower.

Dear god, she'd just had her first real climax with a man-- no, not a man. Emily shook her head and grabbed two towels, rushing out of the bathroom without looking back. He *wasn't* a man. She'd just ... she'd just.... She'd enjoyed herself with a--the thought was too much for her to even mentally speak.

Emily flipped her hair up in a towel and wrapped the second around her body and rushed to the video console in the kitchen. She speed dialed Gramma's, not caring if she woke her up.

Gramma answered the phone almost immediately. "Yes? Oh! Hi, honey!"

Emily clutched the towel to her chest with one arm and pointed to her bedroom. "Gramma, that ... that machine just molested me in the shower!"

Gramma's face brightened with a smile. "Oooh! Shower sex! Wait! Don't tell me yet. Let me get my toys and then you can tell me all the little details."

Emily looked at her, horrified, turning beet red. "No! I'm not going to talk to you while you--"

Gramma frowned and sat back down. She perked up after a few seconds. "Wait! Before you start … Can I record it for later?"

Emily glared at her. "NO! I've got no intention of relating the … sordid details. Really, you're supposed to at least try to act mature and be on my side."

"Spoilsport," Gramma muttered, but then spoiled the effect by giggling. "At least someone's having a good time."

"Have you nothing to say?"

"Did you enjoy yourself?"

That wasn't exactly what Emily had had in mind. If anything, she blushed more fierily. "Maybe," she hedged.

Gramma smirked. "I knew you'd like him. Just don't wear him out. And I want a report on his performance. I just may have to get me one."

"Gramma!" Emily said, scandalized but grinning despite herself.

Gramma arched one white brow, returning the smile. "Goodnight--again!"

"Night."

Emily switched off the connection. Gramma seemed thrilled she'd *gotten some*, but Emily wasn't so sure playing with toys was going to help her in the long run. She still quivered inside, just thinking about the brazen way he'd touched her and made her come. Her last boyfriend had never been able to accomplish that, and Sabin, well…. He hadn't asked permission or anything!

And maybe she liked that … but only just a little. She most certainly wouldn't admit that out loud.

Dear god, how was she going to face him after what he'd done? She thought suddenly, but then frowned. What was she thinking? He wasn't another person, someone she had to worry about would be amused, or teasing, or … anything like that.

Anyway, that was what he was made for. It wasn't like he'd be recording deviant behavior with an object *not* designed for sex.

She still couldn't get over how real he seemed. It was very hard *not* to react to him as if he was a living, breathing, red blooded male.

Emily nervously tightened her towel and went back into her room.

She hadn't really expected to find he would be sitting in her bed yet again. Or maybe she had. She didn't feel the jolt of surprise she'd felt the first time she'd found him in her bed.

He smiled at her, and she narrowed her eyes. If she hadn't known better, she'd suspect he was pleased with himself. His hair clung damply to his skin and water droplets pooled in his clavicle, just begging to be tasted with her tongue.

Good grief, just looking at him put sex on her brain and wiped out rational thought. She was never going to get any work done now, and her deadline had passed a month ago. It didn't help matters that he'd claimed her bed like it was his own. Why was he back in her bed anyway?

Weren't androids supposed to obey their masters? She frowned, trying to remember what she'd said, exactly. Maybe he hadn't understood what she'd meant? It occurred to her though, that not only was she not very familiar with androids in general, she wasn't familiar with companion droids in particular. Perhaps he was one of those new models William had been telling her about that were nearly indistinguishable from human beings--stemming from our desire to recreate our own image. William was an expert in android technology, worked on the same project she was involved in, and she trusted the things he told her.

Maybe he was actually programmed to behave this way? For realism?

For a moment, she felt an almost overwhelming sense of defeatism. Sabin was a bit much for a novice like her to handle.

Shaking off the sense of helplessness, she tried again. "Why are you still here?"

"You did not specify a destination for me to go to earlier."

She stared at him, feeling like an idiot. Of course, how silly she was. But then, she also hadn't invited him in to take a shower with her. Her skin flushed just thinking about it, and she knew she'd never look at the shower the same way again.

Groaning at the thought, she went to the closet and grabbed panties and a nightgown from the shelves. She had already bent over to put a foot through one hole when she caught sight of Sabin watching her in the mirror.

She straightened up abruptly. No way was she going to risk losing her towel with him sitting there, watching her every move. It was hot and steamy in the bathroom. She didn't want to retreat there to dress--her clothes would stick to her skin.

No, there was no choice but to get rid of him. And she was not about to be run out of her bedroom.

She refused to think of the shower incident and the fact that he had seen her naked and touched her intimately. She had to stop thinking about him as having feelings and emotions. He was an android.

"C'mon." Emily motioned him forth, but he didn't move, just watched her steadily. If she couldn't get *him* to listen, how would she ever deal with real men?

"Where would you have me go?"

"I'll think of something," she said as she approached the bed and pulled at his arm. Suddenly, he pulled her down to the bed. She gasped, too busy clutching her towel to her breasts to fight him as he maneuvered her onto his lap.

"Are you ready to play now?" he asked softly.

"Didn't we just do that?" she asked, looking up at him breathlessly.

Sabin cradled her in his arms, pulling the loosened towel covering her head from her hair. He leaned down, his mouth inches from her own, close enough she could feel the teasing breath heated by his artificial lungs.

"I would be remiss in my duties as your companion if I did not stay," he said softly, his expression serious.

"Please." She guffawed. An act. All an act. And she did *not* want a repeat of what happened just a few minutes ago. She didn't, really. Emily kept telling herself that as she shook her head and pushed against his very hard, very muscular chest. He released her without a fight, revealing no disappointment.

Emily stood over him with her hands propped on her hips. "Get up. Wait, are you ... uh ... still naked?"

He shook his head, and she breathed a sigh of relief. Slipping the covers back, she saw he wore boxer briefs that snugly fit his muscular thighs and a large bulge betwixt his legs. *Jesus*! Emily did a double take, then firmly looked away as he stood.

Where was she going to put him? The closet door still stood open, and it seemed the best spot. Taking his warm hand, she led him to the closet and directed him inside. He turned to look at her, a frown on his face as she turned out the light and closed the door.

Finishing drying off, Emily slipped her nightgown and panties on and crawled into bed, determined to put Sabin out of her mind.

## Chapter Three

Sabin stood looking at the black rectangle that was the door to the closet, a feeling not unlike flabbergast overcoming him. She'd locked ... him ... in ... the ... closet. Like he was some toy she'd enjoyed and discarded.

He chuckled inside just thinking about that and began wondering just what sort of traitor would act this way. One minute she seemed confident and capable and the next ... a blonde ditz. It often happened that brilliant scientists often lacked a certain amount of logic. But he'd never encountered one so tempting. Hell, nine times out of ten, they were old men.

His cock ached just thinking about her tight little ass and how she'd pressed it against him, urging him to take her. He sighed and forced the image from his mind, wondering what insanity had possessed him to break into the bathroom. Her reaction to him had been so amusing from the first though, that he couldn't help but press and see how far his role would allow him to go. Apparently, all the way if he so chose it--which only increased the unfulfilled ache in his groin.

He rubbed himself to ease the pressure and groaned, then pulled his hand away. Playing with himself wasn't going to help matters. He needed to get his mind off her tempting little body and focus on the assignment, not that he could do anything locked in here.

Sighing, he leaned against the back wall, resigned to a long night. Hell, there wasn't even any room on the floor to sit down with all the shoes and junk piled around his feet, and he couldn't risk shuffling them around to clear a spot without rousing her suspicion.

He'd just gotten semi-comfortable when he heard the door handle turn.

\* \* \* \*

Try as she might, Emily could not sleep thinking about some man standing in the closet. It didn't matter that he was an android, she still couldn't leave him in there--not and get any sleep.

Groaning, Emily got out of bed and threw the door open, flipping the switch on. She blinked from the light and took his hand, leading him out of her room and down the hall.

She thought about leaving him in the kitchen, but then she didn't want to give herself a heart attack if she got up in the night and found him in there. She was always so weak and helpless when first awakened. Finally, after much debate, she led him to the living room and sat him in a chair.

"Stay here," she said and patted him on the head before leaving him.

Tomorrow she'd try to remember to think of some better place to put him. And a better task than being her ... her lover.

\* \* \* \*

It wasn't a hell of a lot better, but at least he was free to roam the house. He waited until she shut her bedroom door, then another thirty minutes or so to be safe. Certain she was asleep, Sabin got up and stretched and crept to the hallway, listening.

Satisfied, he moved through the house until he found her laboratory. She had to have a computer in there somewhere, and possibly records of misdeeds also.

As he opened the door, a furry object darted from the room, startling him. His heart leapt into his throat, before he realized it was only a ferret leaving her lab with a crumpled piece of paper clutched in its mouth. Damned little beast. Probably building a rat's nest somewhere. He'd already been startled once by a cat on his wanderings through the hallways.

Sabin flipped the light switch on and was stunned at the sight that greeted him. The office was full of hard bound books, discarded paper pads, and sticky notes scattered randomly along the floor, pasted onto the walls, and lying on every possible surface. There was a small trail of carpet leading to one of those heavy, old fashioned desks. A slim computer sat atop it. A sense of triumph settled over him.

Sabin picked his way carefully to the desk and sat down, pulling up the prompt screen on the computer. The cursor blinked, demanding a password. He stared at it, thinking, but not overly concerned. He was a fair hand at hacking.

He attempted several likely possibilities, none of which actually did the trick. Finally, he resorted to scrounging through the papers on her desk. There were numeric formulas scrawled in incomplete pieces on scraps of paper, notes to feed the cats, pick up the laundry, call William. He couldn't find any hint of what her password could be.

Sabin rubbed his eyes. He had no idea how long he'd been at it, but weariness had caught up with him and he was having trouble concentrating. He decided to catch a few hours of sleep and try again once he was a little more rested and alert. He went back to the living room and settled in for the night.

Sabin awoke sometime later, a crick in his neck from sleeping on the short couch. His head locked against his shoulder, and it took some effort to straighten out. He sat up and stretched, groaning, then padded into the kitchen in search of sustenance.

Weak light slipped through the blinds. As he ducked his head under the faucet and drank his fill of water, a sense of ill usage swept over him. She should have at least made sure he was fed and watered. Androids required fuel to keep running. Modern models had been designed to process food with gastro metabolic chambers much they same way humans did. Everyone knew that, even if they didn't own one.

He supposed, irritably, that he would be forced to fend for himself like her other 'pets'.

Opening the fridge hopefully, the scent of old food greeted him. He frowned. No wonder she was such a scrawny little thing. She didn't have a damned thing to eat that hadn't spoiled. He searched valiantly and finally managed to find some old pizza in the bottom, wrapped in a paper towel.

The woman had more paper products than he'd used in a year--than anyone else he knew would use in a year. Hadn't she heard that was a no-no these days? Shrugging, he took the pizza and went back to her lab. It was early enough he didn't think she'd awake any time soon.

Inside, he caught the ferret playing with a ball of paper and chased it off. It disappeared under the desk with its treasure.

Sabin sat at her desk and unwrapped his breakfast, grimacing as he bit into the rock hard slice. He munched it absently while he tried more codes, even backtracking into the mainframe--still no luck. Soft footfalls reached his ears, and he jerked his head up, listening. He must have awakened her roaming about the house.

Sabin stood up abruptly and looked around. There was no place to hide and no time to escape. He looked down. The knee space beneath the immense old desk would have been his last choice, but it was his only option. He ducked beneath the desk just as the handle turned and Emily came inside.

He listened to the patter of her bare feet as she walked across the thin carpet and finally sat down in her office chair. Right in front of him.

He swallowed hard, his discomfort about crouching ignobly beneath her desk completely forgotten as his gaze went as surely to her crouch as if it was a heat seeking missile. The white robe she was wearing parted as she sat, revealing the pale skin of her thighs. Blood throbbed in his brain, and in his groin, annihilating rational thought. Riveted, he watched as she settled back in her chair and parted her legs, lifting her bare feet and placing them on the two front pedestal legs of the chair. Her panties were pink, the fabric thin enough he could discern the darker crevice that was her sex.

He swallowed, the sound so loud in his ears he wondered, briefly, if she could hear it.

The blood pounding in his ears fled to his cock, bringing it erect and so hard he couldn't think of much beyond its throbbing demand and the darkened crevice that beckoned.

Distantly, he heard the scratch of a pen on paper. The aroma of life giving coffee drifted down to him, and she tapped her foot, but he couldn't take his eyes off that pale triangle, couldn't seem to focus his mind on anything else. The phone rang, but he was barely aware of anything more than a distant drone of voices as she answered it.

The ferret squirmed against his bent leg. He shooed it away absently, drawn so inexorably toward the object of his desire, he was scarcely aware of moving toward it.

\* \* \* \*

Emily jumped as she felt something tickle her foot. She glanced down from the video screen on the wall to the floor just in time to catch the dark striped shape of her ferret darting away.

"What is it?" William asked, his high nasal voice touched with curiosity and mild concern.

She looked back up, shrugging as she took a sip of her coffee and set it back down again. "Just Snoopy. You know how she gets in to everything. The lab's her favorite hiding place."

Emily scribbled on her notepad, working at the equation that would enable the aeronautical tech department to develop safe dimensional jumping as she listened absently to William.

"When are you going to start using your computer again?"

"Whenever I can remember my password, I suppose." She'd lost the long access code almost as soon as they'd sent her computer over. Not that it mattered. She'd found doodling with pen and paper worked better for her.

William nodded, settling back into his monologue face. "Anyway, as I was saying, head office is in talks about shutting down the android division of the project completely, but I know if you and I both go before the board...."

Emily heard nothing after that. She was suddenly grabbed from beneath the desk. She looked down at the hands on her knees, so horrified she was stunned into silence and immobility. Her eyes widened as the hands pushed her legs abruptly apart. Remembering William was still on the video phone and could see her, she looked up quickly, surreptitiously slapping at Sabin's hands.

He didn't take the hint. Instead, he slid his hands along her thighs in a caress that made her jerk as her nerve endings leapt to life. She stared fixedly at William's image, watching his lips move but unaware of anything he was saying, unaware of anything beyond the blood pounding in her ears and the effort it took to keep from gasping out loud.

"Snoopy again?" William asked, pushing his glasses up on his nose and giving her an impatient look.

Emily clamped her lips together to keep from yelping as the hands roughly pulled her panties off her butt and down her legs. She slammed her knees together. It was a useless, last ditch effort. He peeled the panties down anyway, grasped her knees and forced them apart again. "Mmm hmmm." She nodded vigorously, squirming in her seat to avoid him. Reaching behind her, he grasped her ass and snatched her forward until she was clinging to the edge of her seat. She dared a glance down just as Sabin's head moved between her thighs. It was an erotic image that immediately set her pulse to racing.

She made an abortive move to rise, but realized that William was looking straight at her. Her robe was gaping and Sabin had snatched her panties off.

She didn't particularly want to give William a thrill.

Subsiding, she released her frantic grip on the arms of the chair and reached to grasp a handhold on his hair, tugging backward.

Hot lips pulled at the sensitive flesh of her thighs in sucking kisses that tightened her nerves like a plucked cord. He massaged the tops of her thighs, holding her possessively, spreading her as far as the sides of the desk would allow. Nestled between her legs, his kissed his way up until she could feel his breath singing the exposed lips of her sex.

Emily bit her lip, squirming her hips, no longer sure whether she wanted to evade him or smother his face. Good lord, he was driving her crazy!

William cut into her thoughts like a dash of cold water. "Are you all right, Emily? You look like you're in pain."

Emily opened her eyes like she'd been shot, unaware she'd even closed them. Sabin parted her moist folds, teasing his fingers up and down her cleft as he lathed the crease of her thigh.

"Yes ... yes ... oh. I ... uh ... have to ... go," she managed breathlessly, strained even to utter so little. Without another word, Emily switched off the connection and ignored the angry ring back, gasping as Sabin's hot mouth latched onto her aching clit.

He brushed his tongue roughly against her. Emily's hips jerked as he flicked back and forth in a steady rhythm, suckling, slipping his fingers down to her passage.

Emily clawed the arms of her chair as he pushed one thick finger inside her and curled it, stroking her G-spot with the precision of a master artist. She groaned loudly and tilted her hips unconsciously toward him, arching her head back as she wrapped her legs around his chest, urging him close. Closer.

He pushed his finger in deeper, then worked a second inside, stretching her to near pain ... but what glorious pain it was. She spasmed around him as though she were milking him, pulling him deeper with her muscles. He nipped her clit, grazing her with his teeth, then sucked the sting away, until she was mindless to anything but the feel of his mouth locked on her nub and the dull thrust of his fingers moving faster and faster inside her.

She flooded with moisture, her heart beating erratic and thunderous as the orgasm hit like a drum beat, reverberating through her core.

She gasped and clutched his head in her hands, riding the crest of the wave, reveling in the feel of his silky hair and the erotic sight of him nestled between her legs. Her nerve endings danced with exquisite pleasure to the rhythm, until he'd milked all she had to give.

He pulled out as her inner muscles jerkily relaxed, and she collapsed in her chair, weak.

He straightened from his crouch, resting on his knees and propping his arms on her lap, looking up at her. "Did I please you, Emily?"

She was damn near catatonic, looking down at him. Her eyelids felt heavy, her body sated. "Uh huh ... wow...." she said, barely able to nod. If sexdroids were all this damn good, the human race was doomed because she sure as hell had no interest in going back to the "real thing" at that moment.


## Chapter Four

Damn but she was infuriating, in a completely sexual way. He wanted her too badly--too much, but he sure as hell wasn't going to screw this assignment up now. As Emily left to take a shower and get dressed, Sabin stayed in her office/lab.

He kept an ear out, listening for when she was finished. The noise of the pipes traveled surprisingly well through the tunnel of the hall.

Recalling what he'd overheard of the conversation between her and William, he realized with a good deal of disgust that the computer was out. Obviously she was an old fashioned girl, oddly technically challenged, and didn't use it for her work. Which left the mounds of notes and pads scattered through her office. He'd never been gifted mathematically, so he couldn't make sense of her formulas and whether they were correct or not, but it occurred to him there could be some connection with one of the UAN through the phone line.

All efforts to tap her lines had failed, mainly because no one had been able to get inside. She never left the house, and using W.A.V. only captured her side of any given call, which had teased them more than it had told them. Now was his chance to check her call history to see if she'd gotten any unusual calls.

Once more, he came up against a brick wall. After scrolling through her messages, he was obliged to admit there didn't seem to be anything that looked the least bit suspicious. All of her calls were exclusive to her grandmother and one other scientist on the project, William Forsythe.

Forsythe, as head developer of androids for the mission, had little bearing on Emily's division, and her grandmother certainly wasn't suspect.

Stumped, he made his way back to her room as he heard the sounds of rushing water cease abruptly and hopped into the bed before she could come out. It wouldn't do to allow her to catch him snooping. No android would and therefore it could not possibly be explained away and still maintain his cover.

\* \* \* \*

Emily stopped abruptly as she came out of the bathroom and found him in her bed. Again.

He smiled at her invitingly.

"Uh, thanks, but I think I'm fine now. I think that'll hold me for a while."

She was just glad he hadn't cornered her in the bathroom again. "That your favorite spot?" she asked, eyeing him with disfavor, uncomfortable with everything that had happened.

And she damn well shouldn't be.

She went to her closet and pulled out some clothes. She couldn't help but notice he was following her every move. It might be no more intrusive than if a doll, or even a dog, were looking at her, but it made her excruciatingly uncomfortable. "Cover your face. And no peeking," she said, then kept an eye on him as she quickly dressed.

She shouldn't have worried. He was supposed to obey. Of course, he'd been particularly troublesome to her, but then, she didn't have much experience with all this developing technology. Maybe she needed to pay closer attention to the way she worded her commands? Maybe she was leaving too much room for other interpretations?

Irritated for some reason she couldn't quite put her finger on, Emily left the room and went down to her office to work. As she sat down behind her desk, she caught movement and looked up to see him standing in the doorway, watching her, still smiling.

Emily, stared at him for several moments and then resolutely ignored him, focusing her attention on the jumble of notes she jotted down the day before and trying to put them in some sort of order that made sense. Despite her efforts to immerse herself in her work, however, her gaze kept creeping away from her yellow pad and returning to him, over and over. Did he have to look so damn sexy?

Finally, Emily groaned and threw her pen and pad down, giving him a stern look.

"You are distracting me," she said, crossing her arms over her chest, leaning back in her chair.

"Would you have me entertain you?" he asked, coming forward.

Emily sat up abruptly, startled, holding her hand up to ward him off. "NO! I--" Visions assailed her of his idea of entertaining, but she resolutely pushed them away. She had work to do. She couldn't afford to loose any more time, not now, not when she knew she was on the verge of cracking the problem.

What *could* she do with him? she wondered a little desperately.

Her stomach rumbled, and she remembered she hadn't had anything but the last bit of coffee--oh hell! "I'm supposed to give you fuel, aren't I?"

He nodded.

Androids needed it just as badly as people. Damn, she'd completely forgotten that. She was amazed he hadn't shut down, but then, he probably had reserve fuel cells. "Do you have enough reserves to last you for a while?"

He smiled, nodding, and she felt her stomach flutter looking at those dimples creasing his cheeks. She cleared her throat. "Mmmhhmmm. Okay, I can send you on errands, right? I mean, you can do more than just ... well ... than ... uh...." She felt her skin burn with embarrassment. She couldn't remember everything she'd read in the brochures. At the time, all she'd concentrated on were the sexual aspects and even then it was more in the nature of a juvenile reading 'forbidden' material. She had never thought she'd actually own one. It hadn't seemed important to retain what she'd read.

"I am capable of performing any deed you require of me."

"Great. I'll need you to go shopping then. God knows there's nothing here to eat. It's been a while since I left the house." She was babbling, but she couldn't stop herself. She pulled a credit card from the desk and gave it to him, mouthing off a list of things she liked, with permission to buy anything else he saw--just so long as it was edible and would make enough meals to last a week.

He nodded and left her, closing the door behind him.

Emily sighed in relief, the tension knotting her insides dissipating almost immediately. He could get her worked up in a sweat just smiling at her, and she didn't like that one bit.

* * * *

Sabin shifted Emily's sedan out of auto-drive as he commanded it to turn off the metalway and turned into parking lot of the main office. He might not get another chance to report in for some time. Using the phone at her house was too risky.

Hartley was at his desk when Sabin came in, wearing his usual frown. "Well, you turn up anything yet, Grey? This sexdroid bit seem to be working out okay?"

Sabin sighed and collapsed into a chair opposite the desk, ignoring the sexdroid comment. "Yes and no, Sir. She seems to buy into me being a droid, but this Shue is totally disorganized. She's got paper everywhere, and from what I can see, she hasn't used her computer the entire time she's been with the project. I heard her admit as much to one of her colleagues.. told him she'd lost the password and couldn't access it."

Hartley perked up with interest. "What position allowed you to access that knowledge? I wouldn't have thought she'd openly share secrets in front of anyone or any*thing*, even a droid. That's not been her MO."

Sabin coughed, choking as he thought about exactly how he'd managed that one. "Just the training, Sir."

Hartley waved it away, hiding a smile. "You're not giving me what I need. How deep have you searched, Grey?"

About two fingers' worth ... and not nearly far enough as far as his dick was concerned. An uncomfortable heat flared across his face. He'd gone a little beyond the call of duty.

Hartley gave him a knowing look.

Sabin cleared his throat, shifting uncomfortably under Hartley's stare. He couldn't, and wouldn't, know all that had happened. And in any case, there was a reason he'd been assigned to this case--he was one of the few single agents in the office under forty. "This assignment could take me months to sort it all out, and I'm not so sure my cover would last that long. I think I've covered myself as far as the companion aspect goes, but there's been some kinks. And my gut is telling me she's innocent, despite what head office says--"

"Just get your ass out of here and get the job done, Grey. No more excuses." Hartley ushered Sabin out and scowled at the mild throng hovering outside his office door.

Sabin ignored the subtle smirks on his way out. Their business might be secrets, but, when all was said and done, office gossip was the same the world over. Someone had leaked the particulars about his undercover assignment--his role, if nothing else. He wasn't surprised, but he was more determined than before to get the case finished. The woman was playing serious havoc with his libid--*pride*. Havoc with his *pride*.

It was near dark when he finally finished shopping for groceries-- a more ferocious gathering of people could not be found anywhere else in the world but at the Super Plus Center. He'd rammed and maneuvered his cart through treacherous aisles clotted with people staring dumbly at credit tags, and he wondered why advancing technology hadn't righted some of the worst plagues on the world--like grocery shopping. Emily was too far out for delivery, obviously, or her cabinets wouldn't be on starvation level.

He pulled into the drive and toted the groceries inside, overloading his arms. She didn't come out to help him. As he brought the third armload in, he decided that she undoubtedly had no interest in seeing what he brought--that or she was upset he'd been gone so long.

He put the cold stuffs up and then the canned food, keeping an eye out for her arrival. He even went so far as to clean out the fridge and wipe the shelves down. What the hell was keeping her? The nagging thought that he'd somehow blown his cover kept at him through the arduous process until he finished and wandered over to her office.

He quietly opened the door and allowed it to swing open. She was sitting at her desk, chewing the top of a pen, scribbling furiously on a notepad. She didn't look up at his entry.

He stood there several minutes, waiting for her to look up. Finally, giving up on the waiting game, he said, "I've brought food as you asked."

She didn't look up. "Hmm? Oh! Great! I forgot you'd gone to the store." She glanced at him, smiling briefly before looking back at her work. "Go on and put them up then."

Sabin left, resisting the urge to slam the door behind him. Hell, she hadn't even noticed he'd been gone for hours and hours. He should be relieved, of course. He'd been anxious that he might have to field some pretty piercing questions about his prolonged absence.

He hadn't considered that she'd forget she'd sent him out.

Or that she wouldn't even notice how long he'd been gone.

He supposed he was going to have to stop patting himself on the back for the impressive work he'd been doing in convincing her he was a sexdroid.

Frowning darkly, he stopped in the kitchen, rubbing his stomach. He was hungry, and despite the fact that he'd gone out and bought the food, brought it in, and put it up, it didn't look likely that she'd come in and cook. Judging by the previous state of her kitchen, he'd more likely starve before she set foot inside it. Her thinness and disinterest in eating led him to believe he couldn't trust the quality of her cooking anyway.

Sabin noisily hunted pots and pans, glancing back now and then to see if he'd aroused her curiosity enough to bring her into the kitchen, but she ignored all hints. He pulled out the raw shrimp and began removing the veins and shells, ignoring the burn of ice on his fingers.

All the while he worked-- boiling the pasta, stirring the alfredo sauce-- he watched the doorway, thinking perhaps the scents flowing through the house would draw her. She didn't show.

After he'd finished and set the table, he returned to her lab. He saw, when he poked his head in the door that she was still in the same bent over position, her fine brows drawn down, creasing the skin between her eyes as she concentrated.

He almost chuckled, watching her, his irritation at being ignored forgotten. "I've made dinner, Emily."

She looked up, a bright smile on her face. "Really?" She hopped out of her chair and followed him out to the dining room.

"Oh! It smells delicious. I had no idea you could cook. I never even thought about you being programmed for domestic use, but it makes sense. I hadn't had a chance to go over everything you can do. This is wonderful! I haven't had home cooking in ... hmmm ... well, I never much cared for my cooking. It's fantastic you know how to." She chatted on as she sat and began eating. "It's delicious. Thank you."

Sabin watched her, worried as he ate his own portion. She'd confirmed his worst fears. Dear god, she couldn't cook, and the way she carried on wound his nerves tight. He had no interest in being her housekeeper and cook. What the hell was he going to do? He already had his hands full searching in the few night hours when he wasn't sleeping. If she put him to cooking every meal and other domestic activities like cleaning that deranged mess in her office.... He shuddered just thinking about it.

There was an old saying about the way to a man's heart.... He had never considered it before, but he began to suspect it worked in reverse, too. Emily glanced up at him, smiling sweetly. This was not the absent, polite smile that curled her lips but never touched her eyes. This smile was almost flirtatious and there was a definite gleam in her eye as she measured him with her gaze that hadn't been there before.

A man could never be sure, but he didn't think it was just the food he'd cooked.

He wasn't quite sure why, but he had the unnerving feeling she'd decided to embrace her new toy.

He quashed the thought. It didn't bear thinking on. If she decided she wanted to take up nocturnal activities, he damn well might have lost his one chance to continue his search of her office.

It occurred to him, abruptly, that he just might have outsmarted himself when he'd decided he might as well enjoy his role, and he had no idea how to undo the damage he'd done.

He felt sure, though, that something would come to him. It usually did.

\* \* \* \*

Sabin knew he'd succeeded in outsmarting himself when she insisted he join her for bed. She'd led him to her room and taken a shower, made ready as she usually did, but this time Sabin stood near the door instead of hopping into bed. All amusement at her response to his antics had vanished. No longer did she look like the girl next door, but a temptress bent on getting what she wanted. She was finally ready to play, much to his dismay.

Unfortunately, nothing had come to him to dissuade her. Hell, he was *supposed* to want to sleep with her, and do *anything* she asked. What's more, the night on the couch had left him stiff all day. He wasn't entirely sure he was up to a night of hot monkey sex. His body said yes very tiredly, but his mind said no. Not for any such noble reason like preserving his judgment but because there was no way he could slip out of her room without being caught.

Emily slipped under the covers and pulled her nightgown off. Sabin swallowed hard, watching it hit the floor in a puddle. He could hardly tear his eyes away from the silky shift to look back at her. Her curly hair was damp from the shower and tousled around her bare shoulders and face, the covers tucked across her breasts under her arms. His mouth went dry. She looked as sweet and delicious as honey and cream, and he was suddenly famished.

She patted the mattress, a beguiling smile turning up her lips. "Come to bed, Sabin."

Legs leaden, he trudged around the bed to the left side, heaving a heavy breath as he stopped before the bed.

Her gaze touched on his groin, lingered, then traveled up to his face.

"Take off your clothes," she said.

## Chapter Five

Emily had never felt so brazen in all her life. She was finally going to do everything she'd always wanted to try, with a lover guaranteed to perform her every desire. He was the most wonderful package she'd ever encountered--he could cook, entertain her, knew when to be quiet, was respectful of her wishes, and he was beautifully, harshly male with a body that made her breath catch in her throat. She felt as excited as a kid at Christmas.

His face remained impassive as he bent and removed his shoes and socks, one by one, then reached for the hem of his shirt and drew it up over his head.

His muscles played under his bronze skin as he unbuttoned the fly of his jeans, stomach rippling as he bent and pushed them down his hips and dropped them to the floor. He kicked them aside, then straightened, awaiting her inspection.

They should never have made a machine so utterly delectable. He had muscles in all the right places--not too big, not too lean--and she couldn't wait to run her fingers over them. A fierce ache spread low in her belly just looking at him and thinking of all he had done ... and had yet to do. She was determined to overcome her reservations tonight--if it killed her.

"Everything, Sabin. Take everything off," she said, moistening her lips with her tongue. Holding her gaze, he hooked his thumb in the waistband of his knit boxers and pushed them off. Her eyes dropped down, drawn by his movement. Freed, his erection jutted forth from the dark thatch on his groin, his shaft thick and swollen. Heat washed over her, pooling between her thighs, sheening her skin with faint moisture. She was shocked seeing so much naked flesh ... shocked and anticipatory.

She held her arms out, beckoning him forward, eager to begin. "Lights dim to eighty percent," she whispered, and the room dimmed to near darkness.

Sabin had stumbled upon a plan--if he had the strength to follow through with it. Unfortunately, given the way she was looking at him, he suffered some doubts about whether or not he could pull it off.

Sabin dropped to the bed, ducking beneath the covers. She closed her arms around him, flattening her small breasts against his chest. He stifled the groan that welled from deep inside him. Emily leaned back, pulling him with her, on top. She looked up at him, expectant, waiting, her breath fast and shallow as she glanced down at his mouth and back to his eyes.

His cock throbbed at the lush feel of her trapped against him, the tease of her breasts against his chest, her thigh nudging his cock. She tilted her mouth up, an invitation he could not ignore.

Why should he deny himself?

He couldn't seem to remember.

"Kiss me," she murmured, gripping the back of his head, pulling him down.

Need surged through his veins like boiling water, banishing reason. Sabin descended, crushing his lips against hers. She parted her lips on a sigh and touched her tongue to him. He groaned and slipped his tongue deep into her mouth, sweeping the tight, moist space, enjoying the taste of her and the small, whimpering noises she made. A fog of lust blinded him, and he momentarily forgot his plan.

Emily broke away, gasping. His reason returned ... and it damned well was going to kill him.

"Why do you not touch me, Sabin?" she asked, clinging to him, kissing his jaw, sucking his earlobe.

He buried his face against her neck, smelling her hair and the fresh scent of wildberries on her skin. "You must command me, Emily," he managed to breathe, barely.

"Touch my breasts. Love me," she said, stroking a hand down his arm, guiding him to her chest. He lifted up, propped on an elbow, one leg splayed across her thighs. He traced his fingers up the curve of her waist, enjoying the way she shivered at his touch. Moving past her ribcage, he rounded the curve of one breast, drawing a tightening circle around the peak, closing in on her nipple. He watched as the small bud puckered in anticipation, and his mouth watered thinking of sucking that drop into his mouth.

To hell with it! He was past fighting. He'd give her what she wanted until she was exhausted---then he would do what he needed to do. He imagined it would only take one good round to knock her out.

He bent and took her nipple into his mouth, sucking hard at her erect flesh. She gasped and clutched his head, digging her other hand into the bedding. He smiled mentally, savoring the clean taste of her and the building inferno in his groin.

He slipped a free hand down, pushing her panties away. She helped mindlessly, begging for more, parting her legs as her panties were removed. Sabin released her breast and moved over her, settling between her legs. She wrapped them around his waist, closing her wet heat to his hips. She was soaked already for him. The knowledge clouded his mind to all else.

He lathed her other nipple, shifting his hips to slide his cock against her slick core, groaning at the satiny feel of her skin.

"Please, Sabin, I need you inside me," she said, pulling him from her breast. "I can't wait any longer."

Far be it from him not to oblige. He kissed his way up the valley of her breasts, licking and kissing a moist trail to the hollow of her throat. She arched, and he slipped a hand between them, guiding his shaft to her opening.

Damn she was tight. He pushed forward, couldn't make any headway. Had he missed? Sabin touched her, found he'd rung her hole, then propped on his arms, working inside her. Sweat beaded on his skin as she tightened around him. He nearly came as he fitted himself deep inside, her muscles clenching around him, so blissfully tight and hot.

He panted against her neck, his arms shaking with the effort to control himself and not hurt her. Slowly, he withdrew, coating his cock with her juices to thrust inside again, easing his way.

She squirmed as he pulled out and plunged in again, building a stroking rhythm that had them both gasping for breath. Hooking her legs around his hips, she arched with each thrust, clutched his shoulders, digging her fingers into his back. "Yes ... that feels so good, Sabin. Oh ... you even pant and groan and sweat like a real man."

Sabin ignored her, quickened his strokes, breathing raggedly against her neck. He felt like he was going to explode. It had been too long since he'd been with a woman.

Muscles screamed from disuse, his cock throbbed from her clenching tightness, burning with pleasure.

"Faster. Yes ... like that ... no, too fast ... ooh ... just ... right."

Sabin gritted his teeth, trying to concentrate on not coming and keeping a steady rhythm. She was making it difficult. She continued giving directions, and finally, he had to shut her up. He kissed her, muffling further commentary, shoving his tongue into her mouth. She sucked him greedily, tightening her legs around his hips. He felt the spasm of her sex, the jerk of her hips as she came, and it sent him over the edge. He pumped a final time, draining himself, her body milking him to the last drop.

He collapsed on top of her, breaking from her mouth to breathe raggedly, then rolled and pulled her with him. Emily cuddled against him, her own heart pounding against him, her hair tickling his chest. He wrapped a weak arm around her, holding her close. Sabin thought he could die happy in that moment.

"I never thought I cared for that position, but you've changed my mind," she said, squirming closer, and he felt her smile against his chest. She traced a lazy trail on his skin, relaxing.

He'd just started drifting off to sleep when she spoke up, startling him. "I'm ready to try something else now."

She sat up, and he kept his eyes closed, hoping she'd think he was reserving fuel cells or something. "C'mon. I want to try it doggie style now."

He nearly strangled on his own saliva. His eyes watered with the effort not to cough. He was grateful the room was so dim, or he would've blown his cover. Could he do it again, so soon?

She rubbed her hand against his belly, traveling south, and despite what he thought, his cock started growing hard again. He groaned, and not completely from pleasure.

She jumped up to her knees, regarding him. "I love how real you feel. Now, you'll have to show me how to do this." She turned in the bed and propped on her elbows. "Like this?"

He wanted to get done as quickly as possible. But as soon as she bent on all fours, his brains ran down to his cock.

"Just like that," he growled and moved behind her, aching to be inside her again. He'd had no idea what a wild woman hid beneath her girlish innocence. Seeing the true Emily Shue was deeply arousing, almost addictive.

Emily squirmed as he leaned over her, pulling her hair back to bite the back of her neck. She moaned softly as he nipped her, pressing his hardness against her exposed, swollen cleft. The moisture from before had dried, but she felt herself getting wet again, her juices flowing as he sucked hard on her neck, leaving a brand of possession.

He reached around and dipped his fingers into her slit from the front, stroking her aching nub. It blossomed under his touch, hardening as blood rushed through her veins. She felt weak, dizzy with wanting him inside her. "Talk dirty to me," she whispered, feeling unbelievably naughty, loving the weight of him on her back.

He stilled the circling stroke of his fingers. She wanted to cry out in frustration. She squirmed and rubbed herself against his cock, needing to come. His hips jerked against her in response.

"How dirty?" he asked.

"Don't ask. Just do it. I know you have the programming." She'd read about it in the brochure and been so excited.

He stroked her clit roughly, smoothing her juices over her lips. "Do you want my cock inside you?"

She nodded. "Yes."

He bent close to her ear, his breath hot, causing chill bumps to race across her skin. "I'm going fuck you until your pussy is shaped to my cock ... until you drop from exhaustion." He nudged her opening with his huge cock head, emphasizing his intent. "And then I'm going to fuck you again."

Emily quivered at the rough hue of his voice, the possessive feel of his hand on her womanhood and the heat of his chest on her back. She felt like she'd not had an orgasm in years. Her body hungered for it, for the thick length of him inside her.

"I want you to scream when I make you come," he ground out.

He straightened off her, grabbed her hips roughly and thrust his cock into her core with one stroke. Emily cried out as he plunged into her depths, stretching her to the limit. He was so thick and hard, her delicate nerves burned with a trembling mix of pleasure and pain.

He pulled out, then drove into her again and again, his hips slapping against her buttocks with force, driving her forward with each thrust. Her womb tightened, reaching toward release. Emily reached down and stroked her clit, slipping in her juices, building the tempo, urgently needing to come. She moaned, panted, whimpered as he thrust into her harder, holding her hips to keep her steady.

An explosive tremor rippled through her core, blinding her with a wave of ecstasy. She cried out, groaning as the climax seized her in its blissful grip, felt the last jerky thrust of him and then grief of him pulling out of her. She felt hollow, achy and sated. She dropped to the bed, her body quivering all over. Her fingers and toes tingled, even her hair felt electrified.

Sabin dropped beside her, breathing heavily. "That was wonderful," she said, marveling at his skillful range and realism. She couldn't tell him apart from a real man, other than the small bar-code printed on his chest. Bless Gramma's heart. She was loving her new man.

She frowned at that, thinking about it. He wasn't a man, never would be. She knew she shouldn't get so attached, but she couldn't seem to help herself. At any rate, what real harm could there be in enjoying what she had? She'd worked hard. She deserved it.

Emily scooted close to him, draping herself over his body. The sweat from her exertion quickly evaporated in the cool air conditioning. Rather than feeling tired, she felt invigorated, eager to try something else. Sleeping could come later.

"I think in the shower this time," she murmured, brushing her lips across one of his nipples. It hardened and she flicked her tongue over it, grinning at his minute response. The wonders of him never ceased to amaze her.

He tensed imperceptibly. "In the shower?"

She chuckled and sat up. If she hadn't known better, she'd would have thought he was 'tired'. But she'd seen what he put away at dinner. He'd had fuel enough to keep running as long as she wanted. "A promise is a promise. You said you'd do it again when you were being so dirty. Speaking of which, I'm a mess." Her thighs were sticky all the way down, nearly to her knees, and her skin felt dusty from all the sweating she'd been doing.

"Lights on," she said as she hopped out of bed and trotted into the bathroom. The bath didn't have voice command convenience. She flipped the light switch on and readied the water.

Steam rose from the shower stall like thick fog, and she pulled Sabin in behind her. She picked up a puff and squirted body wash on it, then began rubbing it over his body. She moved up each arm in turn, then swept across his broad chest. His nipples puckered beneath her hands, and despite being thoroughly sated, she felt herself warming to him again. He closed his eyes as she traveled down his belly to his groin, and his cock rose almost immediately.

He pulled the puff from her hand, giving her a look that made her squirm in excitement. She grinned as he rubbed the soapy surface along her body, rounding her breasts until her nipples stood erect, then bent to move down her stomach and between her legs. He rubbed it across her sensitive nether lips, teasing her unbearably.

She moaned and reached for him, and he dropped the puff, flattening her against the shower wall as he crushed his mouth against hers in a hungry kiss. *Mmm.* He was so good. Real men could never kiss like this. His lips moved over hers, ravenous, hurried and greedy, building her excitement until she felt it down to her toes. He cupped her ass cheeks, kneading them, tightening her to his body, his hard shaft trapped between them, pressing into the taut flesh of her stomach.

Hot water streamed down them both, washing the soap away, seductive as fingers slipping over her skin. He broke away from her mouth, breathing hard, kissing along her jaw to her ear. He sucked the tender lobe into his mouth, lifting her ass as he pressed her into the corner, spreading her legs wide open with his hips.

She was exposed to him, could feel his cock head against her tender nether lips. Her sex quivered, near to climax from so much stimulation this night. She hooked her legs around his hips, digging her heels into his firm ass cheeks, hugging her arms around his neck and shoulders. His body was tense, gloriously strained as he held her pinned to the wall.

"Please," she begged, wanting him so much.

"Anything you ask," he ground out hoarsely, and rammed his cock into her in one smooth, liquid glide. She rose up as he thrust inside, slick and wet, steam drifting around their bodies, driving the temperature higher until she thought she'd melt.

Emily closed her eyes and buried her face against his neck, feeling the flex of his muscles as he stroked her, hard and swift, building the climax to a burning crescendo. It claimed her as he pulled out and pushed back inside, driving her up the wall with near bruising force. She screamed at its intensity, black stars dancing before her closed lids.

He groaned and pumped into her, once, twice, a third shuddering time that thoroughly swept the blissful tide through her every fiber. He released her ass, letting her slide down his body as he pulled his limp cock from her core.

Her breasts tingled from the abrasion of hard muscles and crisp, wet hair, and she clung weakly to him, her appetite for experimentation sated for the night.

Her eyelids were heavy as her muscles were tired, and she could barely drag through the remainder of their shower. They dried off, called the lights off, and climbed into bed, drawing the cool sheets over their bodies. Her body ached pleasurably, her womanhood sore from his loving. Never in her life had she been so thoroughly pleasured, so thoroughly happy and free. Emily draped herself over him, listening to the steady beat of his electronic heart. She was in heaven.

## CHAPTER SIX

Sabin was in hell. Every muscle screamed in pain, and he was so exhausted, he thought he was going to die. The only thing that didn't hurt too badly was his cock, and she'd damn near worn it down to a nub. He smiled in spite of his agony. Damn, she was a wildcat.

Never in his life had he done it *three* times in a row--not in the space of an hour or so--and he was thirty, too damned old to be performing acrobatics. Hartley damn well better have a citation waiting for him when he got done with this case.

At least safe sex wasn't an issue. All government agents were inoculated against every known virus, and he was on the pill to prevent pregnancy. She didn't know how good she had it. He frowned. He still couldn't fathom her being a traitor to her country. It just didn't sit right with him. Which brought him back to the case.

Minutes felt like hours, hours like days. He'd damn near fallen asleep half a dozen times waiting for her to finally nod off, and he thought perhaps he *had* dozed at least once. He had no idea how much time had passed, perhaps only an hour. His fatigue only seemed to distort his reality.

He looked down at her. It was dark, but the soft glow from outside the window allowed enough light he could see her. She was thoroughly tangled on his body--had both of his legs trapped beneath one of her lithe limbs; her head pressed into the crook of his arm; her right hand wound in his hair; and her left arm held his waist possessively.

He listened for a while to her even breathing, certain she was fast asleep. The problem lay in getting out from under her. Muscles complaining, he slowly moved one leg around the edge of the bed until his foot rested on the floor. Her foot dropped between his knees with a soft thud. He stilled, holding his breath, listening to her, waiting for her reaction. She slept on.

He sighed in relief and used his leg to pull himself, ever so slowly from her grasp. He was panting with the incremental movement, with the effort not to disturb her. He'd nearly freed his other leg when she shifted, moaning softly in her sleep. The flutter of her lashes tickled his chest hair.

Sabin broke out in an instant sweat, freezing. She rubbed her face on his chest, stroked her fingers down his belly, tickling the hairs on his happy trail all the way down to his groin. His cock spasmed as she touched it, stroked her fingers down to his cock head. It hardened beneath her feathery touch, ignoring his mental command to stay down. He stifled a groan, unable to believe that she was ready to go again and that his body was willing to accommodate her. And he knew by now he'd thoroughly awakened her with his subtle movements.

"Mmmm," she hummed when she grasped his hard shaft.

Did the woman never stop? He hovered between a mix of pride, that she enjoyed his lovemaking so much, and horror that she couldn't get enough. He would never be able to recuperate at this rate.

She kissed and lathed his nipple, sleepily lazy, slowly pumping his cock and teasing the tender head with her thumb, making it harder than he ever thought possible. She released him and climbed on top. Her moist folds pressed against his belly, tightening his nerves. In the darkness, he could barely see her, but she was naked, with nothing to impede her from taking him as many times as she wanted.

*No, no, no.* He wanted to groan in protest but couldn't. His mind fought the desire she aroused so easily, but already he ached to be inside her ... knew he could not deny her anything she wanted--for he wanted it as well.

She leaned over and kissed him, and he cupped her breasts, kneading her flesh as she nibbled his lips and slid her tongue into his mouth. She moaned as he pinched and pulled her nipples, and he felt the flow of her juices increase on his pubic bone.

She straightened and lifted off his hips on her knees, high enough to guide his cock to her opening. Slowly, she slid down his length, and he groaned at her wet heat blending with his raw, aching flesh.

She rocked, spreading her palms over his chest, arching her head back, moving faster and faster as the pleasure built, rising off him to plumb her core again and again. She fairly hopped above him, driving down, hard, harder, soaking him with the flood of her desire, enveloping him with her heat.

She was driving him crazy, teasing. He fought the need to control her movements as long as he could, then grasped her, intent on tipping her onto her back so that he could control the speed and angle of his thrust. As he pushed himself up, however, a stab of pain shot through him, centered in his groin, burning like a thousand fires. He jerked, gritting his teeth to stop himself from groaning at the sudden pain. She stopped, touching him worriedly, feeling his erection die.

"What is it?" she asked anxiously, lifting off of him.

Sabin collapsed back, mortified heat spreading over him. What could he tell her? He searched his brain, trying to think of an excuse. After several frantic seconds, he latched onto one. "I have a malfunction," he managed to say without growling in pain.

Jesus, he must've pulled a muscle. A groin muscle.

"Oh no!" She lay back down beside him. "That was promising to be a really good one." She sighed and settled against him. "You'll have to go get repaired tomorrow."

Sabin gritted his teeth and refrained from rubbing himself. He felt a little better laying there, but he knew snooping was out tonight. And tomorrow he'd have to go get "repaired." He almost laughed at that one. Christ! He hoped it was just a cramp.

\* \* \* \*

It took all Sabin could do not to creep like an old man from the house the following morning. Not that it mattered. Emily seemed to be dancing on air, and after breakfast--which he managed to cook without too much difficulty--she closed herself up in her office, leaving instructions for him to get repaired at the manufacturer.

His first stop was to a convenience store to pick up a bag of ice. He held it on his groin the whole way over to report in to Hartley. The cold felt good on his inflamed muscles, making him want to sink into a tub filled with the cubes to soothe his entire body, and by the time he pulled to a stop in front of the ugly, gray building, it almost didn't hurt.

Until he got out of the car. His muscles quivered like a plucked string, and his legs felt like they'd give out from under him. He looked at the bag of ice, then shrugged tiredly. What the hell, he'd bring it in anyway. They were professionals--it wouldn't matter to them if he'd sustained injury in the line of duty. No one need ever know exactly what had happened.

His thumbprint granted him access inside past the security guards, and he crept down the hall, heading to Hartley's office. Agents stopped and stared as he passed. He ignored their rude stares and chuckles behind his back. Emily would have given any one of them a heart attack, he was sure.

After some effort and a generous helping of humiliation, he reached his destination, knocking briefly on the office door before the command to enter was called.

Sabin opened the door and stepped inside, carefully closing it behind him.

Hartley immediately noticed the large bag of ice he held to his crotch. His eyes gleamed with mirth. "She decide to try out her sexdroid?"

Sabin grimaced as he dropped into a chair, stretching his legs as he got comfortable. "How did you guess?"

Hartley's lips tightened as though he were trying to refrain from smiling. "What happened? She didn't ... blow your cover, did she?"

Sabin narrowed his eyes, shifting the bag so it wouldn't weigh so heavily on his groin. "No. It was an accident. I ... pulled a muscle I think."

Hartley coughed and recovered. "We can get you some drugs, check you out, but you'll be out of *commission* for a while. At least a few days."

Sabin sighed. "What am I supposed to tell her? She thinks I'm getting repaired."

Hartley laughed. Laughed until tears came out of his eyes, and his face had turned red as though he were suffocating. Finally, the laughter subsided, and he took a shaky breath, looking at Sabin once more, hardly able to control his grin. "Think of something. It's what you're good at."

"I have to be reassigned. She's going to kill me," he enunciated each word for emphasis.

Hartley, sobered, studied him a moment. "You want me to hand your assignment over to another field agent?"

The question sent a jolt through Sabin, images immediately flooding his mind of Emily breaking in her newest toy. Mentally, he thumbed through every agent he was familiar with, but he knew there wasn't one of them he'd trust to keep his hands off of Emily. "You're right. We'd never be able to come up with a convincing cover story. It's just … I haven't had any sleep to speak of for days …"

The smile was back on Hartley's face, threatening to disintegrate into laughter. Sabin gritted his teeth. "… and I'm not sure how convincing I'm going to be as a droid when I can hardly move …"

Hartley stood, fighting a smile with hardened cheeks. "You have to do it ... for your country. Now go down to medical and they'll fix you up as best they can."

As he left the office, he heard the distinct sound of laughter ringing through the room.

\* \* \* \*

They'd patched him up as well as could be expected. He could walk without too much pain, thanks to the drugs they'd pumped in him. He hadn't sprained anything, but if anything like this happened again, he damned well wasn't going to a doctor and face that humiliation again. He frowned darkly just thinking about it.

The time he'd spent recovering at medics had allowed him to think up an excuse. He just hoped she bought it.

Emily was waiting when he got back. She gave him a once over, her eyes questioning. "Did they fix you up?"

Sabin swallowed. "They have to order a part."

Anger immediately darkened her eyes, and she frowned. "How dare they! They should be prepared. What am I going to do now?"

"You're angry," he said. It was an understatement. Despite his predicament, he was pleased that she was so pissed at not being able to use him as her love slave. It was gratifying to be so appreciated. Hell, he'd love to give her anything she wanted. He hadn't anticipated her being so ... disappointed.

She sighed. "I'm not angry at you. I'm mad at the manufacturer. Dammit! You're supposed to have a lifetime guarantee. What am I going to do now? I was just getting all worked up and ... and ... I'm going to call them and give them a piece of my mind!"

Sabin's eyes widened. He had to stop her from calling the manufacturer. It would blow everything. "I can still perform in other ways, Emily. And my parts should be ready in a few days," he added hastily hoping that would pacify her and head off a call that could be a lot more than embarrassing … for both of them.

She brightened, halting her tirade. "I hadn't thought about that. Good news!" She seemed to ponder it for several moments and he was just getting the uneasy feeling that she meant to try it out immediately, when she abruptly changed the subject.

"Hmm. Can you make dinner? I've made some real progress with my formula and I want to get back to it."

He nodded and she left. He nearly dropped from relief. It had been touch and go there for a few minutes, but he'd managed to muddle through. He frowned as he watched her departure, however, disconcerted that she'd dismissed 'the problem' that easily and turned her attention to other matters.

Dismissing it, he went into the kitchen and set to work. Time passed quickly in the kitchen. Despite all of his grumbling about being stuck with the task, he enjoyed cooking. She did not come though, drawn by the delicious smells or the rattle of cutlery. Finally, he sought her out. When he reached her office, he found her deeply absorbed in her work, so deeply she didn't notice him in the doorway.

Sabin left, went to the kitchen and returned to her office, bearing her dinner. She scarcely acknowledged him, mumbled a thank you, and he finally he left, knowing there was little else he could do to entice her away.

He lay in her bed for hours, staring up at the ceiling, torn between hoping she would come to bed so he could get on with his search, and hoping she would be tired enough when she did that she'd decide to forgo play. His groin still throbbed with pain.

He waited in vain, however, for she did not come to him that night at all. Exhaustion finally overcame him, but he slept fitfully in her bed, missing her for some unfathomable reason.

## Chapter Seven

The next day, she remained holed up in her office. She'd run her fingers through her hair until she looked like a mad woman, and the food he brought at breakfast and lunch remained untouched save for a few nibbling bites, barely noticeable.

He fed her cats, and they hissed at both him and Snoopy. Ungrateful beasts. Afterwards, he had nothing to do but wait. It was something he was used to in this line of work, but normally he had some way to entertain himself. He didn't dare interrupt her--he was just beginning to recover.

He was sitting in the living room when she finally emerged from her den. She hovered in the doorway, looking weary but smiling. "I did it," she said, almost breathless with excitement.

"Did what?" he asked, rising and walking to her. She threw her arms around his neck, hugging him fiercely.

"I just had to share it with someone special. I can't believe I didn't see it before," she said, muffled against his neck. She pulled back, looking him in the eyes. "I finally figured out the formula."

"That's wonderful." He returned her smile, feeling a desolation creep into his soul. Now was the time--to see if she were loyal to her country or not, if she'd betrayed them all to the UAN.

Emily bounded away. "Let's celebrate. I'm going to make some calls. I want you to go get something special for dinner tonight. Ooh. Filet mignons would be perfect."

She had to call her supervisors, he assured himself. Surely she couldn't be calling a contact other than someone with the project. Regardless, he had to go. If he didn't, he would never know the truth ... and might not now regardless. He felt sick at the thought of her betraying her country. Treason carried the death penalty.

He found he simply could not accept that Emily was a traitor. The problem was he wasn't so certain his judgment could be trusted anymore, or whether he truly didn't believe it, or just didn't want to.

Sabin left and sped down the metalway, fifteen miles over the speed limit. He dashed into the office, not even knocking before entering Hartley's domain. Hartley glanced up from his monitor.

"She's figured out the formula. Get ready to move on this one."

Hartley nodded. "We'll set two groups outside her house. We'll be ready."

"Good. And ... don't hurt her."

"If she's innocent, you have nothing to fear."

Satisfied, Sabin left to get the makings for a celebration dinner. When he finally managed to get back, he found her sleeping on the couch, her mouth open and one arm flung above her head. A desire to kiss her awake assailed him, and he was halfway across the living room before he curbed the urge. He had to maintain his distance. He couldn't afford to let any tender feelings distract him now.

The smell of steaks broiling awoke her some time later, and she came into the kitchen just as he was pulling them out of the broiler. She rubbed her eyes, smiling sleepily. "Smells wonderful."

"Go and get seated in the dining room. I'll bring them right out."

She nodded and left, and he loaded a tray down with his booty. She breathed deeply as he set the plate before her, and they stared at each other a brief moment across the table before beginning to eat.

"Who did you call?" he asked nonchalantly, cutting into his steak. He had to at least try. She seemed to trust him.

"Oh, Gramma, William, and the office. They were all so excited for me. And excited that the project can now be finished."

As they ate, she chatted about her formula, saying he was partially responsible for clearing her mind so well and relieving her stress. She blushed slightly as she said it, and he couldn't help but smile.

They'd just finished when he caught a glimpse of the ferret disappearing around the corner of the hall leading to her lab. Enlighten hit him. "Would you like dessert?" he asked, eager now, cursing his blindness for not seeing it before. He'd concentrated on her, as he'd been told.... Why had it never occurred to him before?

"Yes, please. Not too much though."

He stood and took their dishes, setting them quickly down in the kitchen, then darting through the kitchen back into the hall. Easing up quietly, he glanced around the door frame. Emily seemed absorbed in studying her hands. She wasn't watching the doorway, and he dashed past it. Hearing no accusing cry of discovery, he rushed to her office, moving as quietly as possible. He had a few minutes at best. It might be enough time.

Quietly, he opened the door and ducked inside, shutting it cautiously behind him. On the desk, the blue light from the monitor glowed faintly across the wooden surface and the striped fur of the ferret.

He was gratified to see his instincts hadn't failed him completely. It stood on its hind legs, scanning a paper pad, its nose twitching as it dipped and scooted back on the surface.

The door opened beside him, and Sabin grabbed Emily's arm, smothering her cry of surprise with his hand. "Shh. Look at your desk," he whispered, never taking his eyes off the ferret. He watched as it tore the sheet off with its teeth and bunched up the paper in its paws, folding and rolling the paper with unnatural precision.

He couldn't figure out how it had gotten inside. His question was answered as it hopped off the desk and bounded across the floor to an air conditioning vent. It worked its squirmy body under one loosened corner until it had escaped inside.

When it was gone, he freed Emily's mouth. "What was that all about? What are you doing? Snoopy just took my formula!" she whispered furiously.

He kissed her briefly. "I'll explain later."

He ducked out the door and caught the dark shape of the ferret disappearing down the hall. Quietly, he followed it until it disappeared through the small cat door leading outside. He couldn't let it get away--he had to follow it.

Waiting a brief moment, he followed it out. Outside, he caught the attention of two agents casing the back of the house. They followed his lead, keeping track of the ferret's movement.

It wasn't easy. Dusk settled over the sky, the light dwindling, making it difficult to see the ferret's slinky shape. Surely the animal couldn't travel far. And he knew by now Emily had no knowledge of what had been happening in her house. The damned rodent had been stealing pieces of her equations all along--that could be the only answer. He was amazed at how well it had been trained.

They didn't have to follow long. Down the trimmed lawn it went, past the edges of her yard, traveling down the road. It hid from passing cars, but he knew a second set of agents followed at a distance, rolling along in their vehicle with their lights out.

It scampered suddenly across the pavement, dashing for one darkened vehicle waiting at the end of the road. A door flung open as it approached, and it stood and climbed inside before the door slammed shut. The contact. It had made contact.

The car's engine rumbled to life, the headlights blinking on.

"Go, go!" Sabin yelled, running for the contact, pointing at the car. It was too late for subterfuge now. The trailing car revved its engine, racing down the road, roaring past him with a rush of wind.

The driver seemed to sense their approach before they could close in and pressed his foot to the carbon accelerator. He ran across a curb, metal grinding on the pavement.

The spy was going to get away. Sabin ran after him, his lungs choking for air, legs burning as he raced down the road. A second car cut across their path. The contact swerved, trying to go around, but missed. Tires squealed, metal screamed as it struck the government vehicle, and glass shattered from the impact.

Headlights flooded the area, banishing the dark. Agents swarmed the vehicle, guns targeted on the windows, ready to kill. One agent pulled someone out of the car--a man. He slammed the perp against the hood of the car just as Sabin reached the scene.

Sabin halted as he saw who it was. Never would he have suspected....

The agent roughly searched him, and another pulled out the ferret.

"It's a droid, sir," someone said, holding the thing up in the light. The formula drifted to the pavement, and Sabin snatched it up. A droid ... that explained everything, considering who its maker was.

An agent cuffed the man, pulling him up, turning him around for the charges. "William Forsythe, you're under arrest for the act of treason. You have the right to remain silent...."

## Chapter Eight

How could she have been such an idiot? Emily Shue, brilliant scientist and mathematician--complete moron who couldn't recognize a real man if he ... if he....

Emily blushed furiously, remembering everything he'd done, everything she'd begged him to do. It should have helped her feelings knowing she'd fallen for a real man and not some machine, but it didn't. She couldn't think about anything but the fact that he'd invaded her home and used her for some nefarious purpose. How dare he!

She would kill him. She would kill him if he *ever* darkened her door again.

A knock sounded on the front door. She'd locked the house up after he left. He would not be sneaking inside. Emily trudged to it, feeling her heart break with each step.

"Yes?" she called through the door.

"It's me ... Sabin."

How dare he come back!

Emily opened the door and glared at him, keeping her foot in front of it, refusing to open it enough he could come inside. "What do you want?"

He sighed, rubbed his eyes. He looked exhausted. Emily bit back the burgeoning pity she felt for him.

"To explain," he said after a long pause.

"About what? Your lies?"

"I work for the FBI. You were under investigation for treason. I had no choice. Do you understand me? It was treason, Emily. It was my job to find out who was responsible."

"So that's all I am? A job?"

He gave her an unreadable look, his voice strained as he said, "You know that's not true."

Emily felt overwhelmed by anger. "I don't. As far as I'm concerned, everything you've done and told me was a lie. God, I can't believe what an idiot I am." She slammed the door in his face and locked it, then pushed a heavy armchair in front of it for good measure.

He pounded on the door. "Emily! Open this door. Emily, please!"

Emily ignored him, running back to her room, locking that door as well. She dropped on the bed, smelled his scent on her pillow and flung it across the room before collapsing in a crying fit on the bed.

She had no doubts he'd laughed about it with his fellow agents, about how gullible she was, how she'd reacted to him, how many times he'd given *it* to her. And had he really been hurt, or did he just not want to sleep with her again?

She would never *ever* have sex again, so long as she lived. She was doomed to humiliation whenever she tried it. She couldn't trust anyone, no man--not even her ... her animals!

Only minutes after she vowed never to leave her room again, the phone rang, reverberating through the house.

Emily crawled out of bed and went to the kitchen, the ID revealed caller unknown. She knew she had to look a mess, with her hair tangled and her eyes red and swollen. Emily turned off video mode and answered it. "Hello?"

"Emily, don't cut me off--" Sabin's voice pleaded.

Emily immediately hung up, and ignored every call thereafter. It served him right. She couldn't help feeling childish and betrayed.

She stomped back to her room, determined to put him from her mind and get some much needed rest. She only prayed he would have the decency to recover her formula and turn it in to the project leaders. If not, she could work it out again. She had it committed to memory--what was she thinking? She couldn't trust he'd do anything right. Tomorrow, when she felt better, she'd turn over the formula and put this all behind her. Maybe she'd go on vacation a while....

Emily slipped into bed, calling the lights off, but she couldn't get comfortable, couldn't relax. Finally, she staggered out of bed, picked up Sabin's pillow and went back to bed, hugging it tightly to her chest.

She missed him, though she would never admit it, never out loud, and never to herself.

\* \* \* \*

Emily was officially cleared of all charges, and she was horrified to discover William had been stealing her work and passing it on to the UAN. It was further proof that she should never leave the house again--that no one could be trusted.

She was beginning to feel very paranoid and closed in, but she couldn't think of any way to get off her present course. It was hardly paranoia when everyone *had* been out to get her.

Eventually, Sabin's calls stopped. Rather than be thankful, it only increased her depression. She shouldn't have been so childish. She knew that now, but it was too late to do anything about it. She could never approach him at work, which was the only place she could locate him--not knowing his home address. Her face flamed just thinking about going to his office. He'd probably long since forgotten her anyway, as soon as he stopped calling.

It was illogical to think any differently, after all. She'd only been a case he'd been working on. They weren't supposed to get close or attached to the person they were watching. He'd probably only wanted to apologize to her, not anything else.

A week passed and then another. One day the phone rang. It had been a week since anyone called. No one bothered now that the dimensional jump formula had been perfected-- the project was underway and she wasn't needed any more.

Emily trotted into the kitchen and checked the ID. She smiled and answered the phone. "Hi Gramma!"

Gramma smiled back, lounging in her chair. "Hi honey! I've been meaning to call, but I have been in such a fret over what happened."

Emily sat down at the kitchen table, rubbing the back of her neck. She got a tension headache every time she thought about it--and Gramma didn't need to explain what she was referring to. "It's okay, really. You couldn't know any more than I did."

"I know, but I feel so bad you didn't get your birthday present."

Emily shrugged. "There's always next year." She laughed mirthlessly, feeling the years pile on.

Gramma chewed her nail, giving her a worried look. "I ... uh ... ordered you a replacement."

"What? NO! I don't want it. No more androids."

"Honey, I don't want you depressed. This will help you forget. He's just a domestic--not a sexdroid. And you've gotten so skinny with no one around to cook for you."

Emily shook her head. "No."

"For me? I worry about you. I don't want you being alone right now, and you know I can't travel down to see you. I've been so tired lately I can hardly leave the house."

Emily recognized this trick, and she was falling for it again. Gramma could lay the guilt on thick as any master manipulator. "Oh, all right. When does he arrive?"

"He should be there any time now. I lost track of the days...."

What she meant to say was she didn't want to give Emily a chance to say no. Emily knew her game, but she couldn't help smiling. "Thank you, Gramma. I love you. Now go get some rest."

"Will do. Bye!" She closed the connection.

Emily fixed herself something to drink as the sound of a car pulling up the drive reached her ears. She set her glass down and walked to the front door, stepping outside. A dark blue van sat on her drive in front of the garage. Across its side panel in bold lettering were the initials DATI: Domestic Android Technologies Incorporated, when life demands more.

The delivery man smiled a greeting, then went to the back as she watched and lifted up the rear door. He disappeared inside and came back with a loader carrying a box as long as he was tall.

He guided it down and around her walkway. "Where would you like me to put this?" he asked, tucking a clipboard under his arm.

"Inside, in the living room. I'll show you." She led him inside, and he guided the loader in, lowering the box to her floor.

"Sign here," he said, indicating the clear box on his clipboard.

Emily pressed her thumb against the screen, and it flashed and captured her signature.

"Thank you so much! Enjoy your new domestic," he said as Emily showed him out and shut the door behind him.

Returning to the living room, Emily looked the box over, trying to muster some enthusiasm. It was marked fragile, some assembly required. She didn't feel up to putting together some machine, but knew if she didn't do it now it would never get done. And really, how much work could it be?

Sighing, she went to the kitchen and came back with a box cutter, slicing the thick, nylon tape holding the box together. She ran it down, lengthwise, cutting away the remaining tape as she pulled the box flaps open.

She caught sight of a hand inside, and nearly jumped out of her skin when it flexed. She screamed as two hands grasped the edges of the box and a man hauled himself out of its depths.

Sabin.

Emily sunk down to a chair, her knees weak from surprise. "Wh-what are you doing here?" she asked, holding her heart as though she would faint or keel over.

Sabin blinked rapidly, rubbing the packing material off his body as he stepped out, spilling it across her floor.

"I came for you. To apologize for what I did. And to--" He broke off as she stood, narrowing her eyes at him.

She shook her head, rubbing her hands over her face, unable to believe he was truly here. "I can't believe you did this." She laughed, feeling suddenly buoyant and full of energy.

He looked at her warily. "Do you forgive me?"

She threw herself against him, and he closed his arms around her, hugging her tightly. "I can't stay mad at you," she said, her voice muffled against his neck.

"I was miserable without you."

She swatted his butt. "Good. You deserved all the punishment you got and more."

He pulled back, the laughter wiped away from his face, his eyes serious. "I love you, Emily. I don't know how it happened, I damned near lost my job because of it, and everyone ribbed me constantly at the office, including my boss, but nothing compares to the torture I've felt not being with you these past few weeks."

"Oh, Sabin!" She kissed him, his lips, his stubbled chin and cheeks, kissed him until her lips were swollen. He seemed to hold himself back, then, as if a dam broke inside, he crushed her against him and plumbed her mouth with his tongue, drinking her essence, the taste of her love.

Emily moaned, rubbing her body against his, reveling in the feel of his hardness pressing into her belly. He broke away, gasping for breath, breathing as hard as she. Her heart pounded in her chest, making her blood soar.

Emily met his smoky gaze, her excitement building. "I love you too, Sabin."

He smiled, his sexy dimples showing in his cheeks, and her body revved, hungry for him. She'd missed so much about him. Emily pulled away, walking toward the doorway.

"So ... are you repaired and ready to play?" Emily grinned mischievously. He growled and grabbed for her, missing as she dashed away and ran giggling down the hall--to the bedroom.

"The things I have to do for my country," he murmured, following her eagerly.


The End

# YAR AND THE ORGASMIZER9000

## By

## Marie Morin

## Chapter One

Serena became aware that her sex slave, Yar, was studying her carefully as she programmed the pod for her excursion to Las Vegas. It was forbidden to teach slaves. They knew everything they needed to know to pleasure their mistresses before they went on the market, and in any case, most women were far too busy to spend that much time with their toys.

On the other hand, it was also forbidden to visit Earth and she'd never let that bother her. It was an uncivilized, male dominated society for some unfathomable reason. Earth people were technological children beside her own world, but Serena had had a taste for souvenirs of Earth culture from the time she'd accidentally stumbled upon the planet decades ago during one of her first missions. More recently, she'd discovered a passion for the gambling and decadence available no where in the universe as it was in Las Vegas.

Instead of reprimanding him, therefore, she ignored him as she generally did. She liked his cleverness. She supposed that was probably the main reason she hadn't tired of him yet, even though she'd had him for several years and usually purchased a new sex toy yearly, or every other year at the very most.

When she'd finished programming the computer, she turned to him and patted him on the knee. "Be a good boy, now, and don't play with any of the buttons on the console while I'm gone."

"Will you be gone long, Mistress?"

"At least a few days. Maybe a week. You'll be fine. The ship's well hidden in this moon crater. If a patrol happens by, you are not, under any circumstances, to answer their hail. Understand? Otherwise, I'm liable to loose rank, and could end up in the brig, and you know what that means."

He frowned. "They'll sell me to cover your fine?"

Serena nodded.

"What am I to do while you're gone, Mistress?"

Serena raised her brows. "What do you usually do?"

He looked glum. "Nothing."

Serena smiled and patted his knee again. "Well, you can do what you usually do then."

Instead of looking relieved, he looked even more unhappy and Serena frowned. "Don't you enjoy doing nothing?" she asked curiously.

A number of emotions chased across his face as he battled an inner debate. Finally, he smiled vacuously. "I like to make love to you. Would you like for me to service you before you go?"

Serena grinned and patted his cheek. "Not this time, pretty fellow. I'm more interested in the gambling--If I need some sexual recreation, I'll probably just take an Earth male. They amuse me."

Yar reddened and Serena frowned, studying him suspiciously. "You're not jealous, are you?"

He turned pale. "No, Mistress."

"Good," Serena said, dismissing him. "You had me worried for a minute there. I thought I might need to send you off for reconditioning--run along now."

Yar withdrew from the pod and raced toward the air lock, knowing Serena was about to open the bay doors. He'd barely sealed it shut when the bay doors opened. He stood watching from the portal as she launched the pod from the belly of her ship.

After a moment, he thought of the viewer. He wasn't supposed to touch it, but Serena was gone. She'd never know the difference.

Turning, he raced along the gangway and climbed the ladder to the main operations room. Faking a feminine voice, he requested the computer turn on the viewer.

"Mistress Serena?"

"Yes?" Yar said in the same voice.

"You do not sound like Mistress Serena. I do not detect but one life form and it computes as the male slave, Yar."

Yar fought a round with irritation. "Yar is playing my recorded voice. I told him he could watch the viewing screen for entertainment while I was gone."

"Why did you not program me before you left?"

"I shall tell Mistress Serena you questioned her orders when she gets back. She'll reprogram you," Yar said.

The viewing screen blinked on. Relieved, Yar studied it and finally saw the pod, which was no more than a speck of moving light by now. "The pod's almost out of sight. Can you magnify?"

Obediently, the computer adjusted the viewing range and Yar watched as Serena's pod entered the Earth's atmosphere. It seemed to drop very rapidly toward the planet once it had left space. As he watched, four dark shapes, like a swarm of Barbron stinging insects, appeared on the screen and converged on the pod. Serena's pod suddenly began an odd sort of dance, zipping in first one direction and then another as the dark shapes trailed it. Yar frowned, wondering what Serena was doing.

Quite suddenly, two of the dark shapes collided, creating a ball of fire and light. Yar's heart skipped a beat. "Those barbarians! They're attacking Mistress Serena! Do something!" he exclaimed.

"I require orders," the computer responded.

"Do something!" Yar yelled again.

"You are a slave. You can not issue orders."

"Fire--before they strike her pod!"

"It is forbidden to carry out orders issued by a slave," the computer responded.

Frustrated, Yar looked around the ship, but he knew it was useless. He had never seen Mistress Serena fire a cannon. He had no idea how to fire one if the computer refused to do so. Helplessly, he watched Serena's pod as it continued to dance and loop circles around the dark shapes that trailed her pod as if attached by some invisible wire. Quite suddenly one slammed into the pod. A ball of fire and smoke arose. The other dark shape flew into the cloud and it, too, exploded.

Yar gasped, watching in horrified disbelief as Serena's pod began to drop toward the planet, trailing smoke. After several moments, it occurred to him that the pod seemed in tact and did not seem completely out of control.

"Closer, computer!"

Again, the computer magnified the view, and Yar watched in helpless fear as the pod skidded across the surface and disappeared finally in a cloud of earth and debris.

He began pacing then, wondering what he should do. Serena had said he was to do nothing, but she hadn't expected to be shot down by the barbarians. He thought she had landed the pod, but he didn't think she would be able to return to the ship with it.

If he could convince the computer to put out a distress call….

That wouldn't do. Serena would be furious. Someone would come, all right, but it was forbidden even to enter this solar system, and the penalty was worse for actually landing on the planet. He knew that much. He'd heard Serena's sisters….

"Computer, you must call Serena's sisters."

"I can not take orders from a slave."

After arguing with the computer for the better part of an hour, Yar's fear and frustration became purposeful anger. He began searching the console.

"What are you doing, slave Yar?"

"Looking for your memory chip."

"What will you do with my memory chip?"

"Remove it."

"You are not authorized to remove my memory chip, Yar."

Yar didn't respond.

"If you remove my memory chip, you will shut down life support, Yar."

"No I won't. I heard Mistress Serena talk about removing your memory chip. She has another one somewhere."

"I am calling Mistress Serena's sisters."

A sense of satisfaction settled over Yar and he sat down to wait for the computer to make contact, trying not to think what might become of him if Mistress Serena did not come back. It was possible her sisters might come to retrieve her ship and either take him as one of their own, or sell him. It was also possible they would not think retrieving the ship worth the risk of being jailed and fined.

He might spend the rest of his natural life trapped on this barren rock with no company but the computer.

He shuddered at the thought.

"I have managed to reach three of Mistress Serena's sisters. I can not get a response from the others."

"What did you tell them?"

"That Mistress Serena's slave, Yar, had become afflicted with space dementia."

Yar frowned. "Let me speak to them."

"They hear you. The channel is open."

"Mistress Serena's pod has been shot down by the Earth barbarians!" Yar exclaimed. "She needs help."

"What the hell is she doing on Earth? I forbade her to go back again. I told her she was going to keep risking it until she found herself kicking her heels in jail. Who is this?"

"Yar," he responded meekly.

"What the hell is a slave doing on communications? Did your mistress teach you this?"

"No, Mistress," he said, unable to identify the voice, though he suspected it must be Serena's oldest sister, Sylvia.

"What did Mistress Serena tell you when she left, Yar?"

"To do nothing."

"Then do nothing, damn it! And stay off communications before you're picked up, for Krone's Sake! She'll get herself out of whatever jam she's gotten into. She had no business even going to Earth! I'm sick of bailing that girl out of her jams."

"But … the pod crashed. How is she to get back?"

"Don't worry your pretty head over it, Yar. Mistress Serena can take care of herself," Serena's sister, Sadia responded, almost gently.

"But…."

"Close communications."

Yar stood listening to the silence for several moments and finally returned to the bed chamber and sat on his pallet, staring at Mistress Serena's bed. He was angry, confused and scared. It was all very well to say Serena could take care of herself. He knew under most circumstances, she could. She was an experienced ship's captain, and she'd fought in at least a dozen campaigns over the years that he knew about, and come out of the battles virtually unscathed.

This was different, though. She'd crashed the pod. He knew the Earth people were barbarians. He'd heard Serena call them that many times. He also knew that they did not have the technology the women of Barbron had. How would she repair her ship without anything to repair it?

He didn't know whether he felt better or worse about the fact that Serena had assured him the ship was well hidden.

No one was going to find him.

He could be here forever if she didn't come back.

After a while, it occurred to him that he should go after her. The idea paralyzed him for several moments. He wasn't supposed to fly a pod, and that was the only way he could go to help. He wasn't even supposed to consider doing anything he hadn't been specifically told he might do, or anything he'd been ordered to do.

If he rescued Serena, instead of being happy, she might send him for reconditioning.

She might sell him off.

After more consideration, however, he decided he'd rather be sold off or sent back for reconditioning than left on this rock. He stood up and began pacing, trying to decide what he would do once he reached Earth. He was fairly certain he could remember how Serena had programmed the pod. He thought he could get there, but what then? What if instead of just crashed and stranded without a way to repair the ship, he found that she was under attack? What if she had been captured by the barbarians that had fired on her ship?

Finally, he shook the thoughts off. He thought most everything Serena might need would be on the pod. Once he found her, she'd know what to do.

Then it occurred to him that the barbarians might shoot his pod down as they had Serena's. He didn't know how to fly it as Serena did. He only knew how to program the computer to fly it.

What if they captured him?

The thought shook him, but he decided he still preferred the idea of taking a chance to staying in the ship and dying of boredom, alone, with only Serena's onboard computer to talk to. He hated that computer.

Having made the decision, he grabbed his Orgasmizer9000. It was his only possession and he couldn't bear the thought of leaving it behind. Besides, it occurred to him that he might have to barter it for his mistress.

It didn't occur to Yar until he'd launched the pod that Serena's pod probably hadn't landed where she'd told it to land. Panic seized him when he realized it, because he only knew how to program the pod *exactly* as she had.

He realized suddenly, that he was going to have to look for his mistress and he had no idea how to do that.

He also realized, however, that he had no idea how to program the pod to return to the ship. He'd never seen Serena do that.

Unnerved, he settled back in his seat, watching as the pod took him, inevitably, toward the blue planet below him, trying to convince himself that, somehow, he'd figure out what to do once he got there.

Chapter Two

It was very dark when Yar landed. He stared out of the portal for many minutes, trying to decide whether to leave the pod or not. He could see nothing but rocks and a few scrubby looking plants. There didn't seem to be any threat from the barbarians, but he also didn't see any sign of his mistress' ship.

Finally, he grasped his Orgasmizer9000, opened the hatch and stepped out. The door closed behind him the moment he exited and he felt a moment of panic. With an effort, he dismissed it and looked around. Faintly, in the distance, he saw lights. His heart leapt with a combination of fear and relief as he realized it must be the fire from the crash and he scrambled over a rise for a better look.

To his dismay, he saw only scattered lights that he decided must be woman-made. They looked like the stars. It must be a city.

He stood indecisively, looking around, but he couldn't detect anything from where he stood that might indicate a crash site. Perhaps he should go back to the pod and ask the computer if it knew anything?

To his dismay, he found when he returned to the pod that it wouldn't open the hatch for him.

Finally, dispirited, he glanced toward the lights again. Maybe he could find a woman there who would be willing to help him find his mistress?

He would've been tempted to just settle by the pod and wait a while to see if Mistress Serena found him, but there were tiny things flying around him … tiny creatures that bit, and he had no protection from their persistent attacks.

He began walking toward the lights. It seemed to take a very long time before he began to see that the lights were coming from woman-made structures, and that there were some sort of strange vehicles moving along the strips of hardened rock he supposed had been made for them. Oddly enough, they seemed to be walking along the hard rock, or maybe rolling … part of them anyway.

Unnerved, he kept to the shadows, but kept moving, hoping he would see a woman that he could ask for help.

After wandering around for a while, he finally spotted a woman walking with her slave. He stared at them for several

moments, puzzled. The slave was walking right beside her
… and he was clothed.

Earth people certainly seemed to have strange customs. No
slave that he knew was given clothing. Maybe, though, they
needed them here because it was so barbaric and they had
the tiny biting creatures? And it was cold. He'd been trying
very hard not to think about how cold it was. He'd been
trying to ignore all the painful things on the ground that he
kept stepping on, but he was more miserable than he could
ever remember being in his life.

He waited until they neared him before he stepped out of
the shadows. It took him that long to decide whether to try it
or not, for the woman did not look like any woman he was
accustomed to seeing. She was so small. She looked … soft
and … helpless, not at all like a warrior should look. Perhaps
that was because she was very old, though?

When he stepped out of the shadows, the woman and the
man came to an abrupt halt and gaped at him.

"Mistress, could you help me please? My mistress' pod
crashed and I need to find her."

To his amazement, instead of answering him, the woman
opened her mouth and let loose a sound that vibrated his ear
drums and seemed to freeze the blood in his veins. When
she drew breath to let out another one, Yar covered his ears
and ran, certain any moment the vocal weapon the woman
was using on him was going to make his brain explode. He
was in such a panic to evade the weapon, he forgot all about
caution, running down the main stone path, dodging the
strange vehicles.

When he stopped at last to catch his breath, he discovered
to his horror that he was in the midst of a crowd of Earth
barbarians. All of them were gaping at him as if they knew
he was an abandoned slave. He stopped abruptly, realizing
he was surrounded, looking at the expressions on the Earth
barbarians' faces with fear. "I've lost my mistress," he
explained weakly.

"Tough call, buddy. Don't you just hate it when they toss
you out without your clothes?" a man said, and laughed.

"He's naked!" a woman shrieked.

"Do you see that?"

"My god what a hunk! Look at the cock on that man!"

"Someone call the police! He should be arrested!"

Yar's heart nearly stopped when he heard the word 'arrested'. They thought he was a runaway! It was the impetuous he needed to break through the crowd. He didn't stop running until he left the sounds of their voices far behind and reached an area where he was hidden in the dark once more.

He stopped, realizing they weren't chasing him, and stood in the middle of the rock path, trying to catch his breath. Finally, he looked around and discovered he was in a very different area of the city. The woman-made structures here looked more like individual habitats. There were not nearly as many lights either. He decided he must have left the commercial area behind. Perhaps he would have better luck here, he thought.

The idea had barely occurred to him, however, when he realized that most of the dwellings appeared dark inside. Either the occupants were not there or they were sleeping.

He began walking again, studying each dwelling he passed. Finally, he spotted one where many lights shone from inside and he hurried toward it. He had almost reached the portal to the dwelling when some small, hair covered beast leapt at him from the bushes. The sounds the beast was emitting were almost as frightening as the fact that it kept baring it's teeth at him and leaping toward him as if it would bite. Whirling, he fled.

Unlike the barbarians he'd met earlier, however, the savage beast chased after him. Yar could not believe the speed the beast was capable of, or the tenacity. The faster he ran, the faster the beast ran. He leapt over large plants, and the beast followed. He bounded over the barbarians' strange vehicles that had been left idle on the rock path and the beast merely ran around and met him on the other side. Finally, he saw ahead of him some sort of barricade, like the wall of a fort. It was very high and he wasn't certain he could scale it, but thought if he could manage it that perhaps the beast wouldn't be able to.

Taking a running jump, he managed to grasp the top of the barricade and haul himself over. He could still hear the beast, however, and since he wasn't convinced it couldn't get over, as well, he looked around for a high place in hopes he might escape it. There was some sort of ladder attached to the side of the two story dwelling in front of him, covered with a plant of some kind.

He ran to it and found a hand and foothold. The thing was strangely weak. He could feel it bending under his weight. Fearful that it would collapse any moment and deposit him on the ground so that the beast could savage him, he climbed faster, ignoring the sharp tines of the plant as he raced toward the portal just a few feet above it.

The portal was open, but not nearly far enough for him to climb through. After several frantic moments of clawing at it, he managed to push it open wide enough to climb through.

He found himself in a darkened bedchamber.

He didn't know whether to be relieved or more unnerved by the fact that the woman who owned the dwelling didn't appear to have a male slave. There was only one bed, no pallet for a male slave.

Hearing the sound of movement, Yar looked around in panic. Light shone from a crack around a solid portal on one wall that was large enough to be a hatch, though it didn't look like any hatch he was familiar with. Certain he did not want to face the female until he had time to figure out whether she would slay him for the intrusion or not, Yar looked around for a place to hide.

He could not bring himself to climb back through the portal. He could still hear the rampaging beast outside, just waiting to eat him.

As the hatch began to open, he leapt behind the heavy cloth that covered the portal he'd used to enter, trying very hard to hold his breath so that the woman wouldn't hear him.

* * * *

Adrianne had had an exhausting day and a very unpleasant evening. She had been thrilled when her boss had handed her the opportunity to entertain the potential new client, certain she could land the account and move up, finally, from junior exec at the company to the position she'd been angling for for well over three years.

Everything had seemed to be going really well when they had started the evening off. Tyrone Blanton had seemed such a gentleman, so open and friendly. She'd been smart enough not to jump right in and give him her spiel. She'd waited until they'd gotten their after dinner drinks, waiting until the moment seemed just right.

When he'd suggested they go up to his suite to discuss business, it hadn't occurred to her for a moment that she'd been set up … not until she got there, anyway. It was only after they'd reached his suite and she tried to steer the conversation toward business that she'd found out her boss had already landed the client. She had been sent as the main course for his entertainment.

She supposed she could have handled it better. It wouldn't have been the first time that she'd used her feminine charms to get what she wanted. The thing was, it was generally her idea, and she expected to be rewarded for being willing to go above and beyond the call. It had infuriated her when she discovered her boss had 'pimped' her out without even consulting her about whether she was willing or not. Even before she'd realized that, when she'd found out that the account had already been assigned to Harold Snodgrass, she'd lost all interest in seducing the client. She'd totally lost it when she realized she was the sign-on perk for the client.

She was going to be lucky if she wasn't fired.

Shrugging the dismal thoughts off, Adrianne finished drying off and wrapped the towel around her, tucking one corner in at the top to hold it in place. Despite her preoccupation, she thought she heard movement in her bedroom as she reached for the doorknob. She paused. After a moment, she opened the door a sliver and peered out, but she'd left the lights off in her bedroom. With the light behind her, she could see very little.

Opening the door wider, she looked around the room. Her heart stopped dead still in her chest when her gaze finally settled on the curtains by the window. A man was clearly outlined through the fabric.

Beneath the drapes, two huge, bare feet protruded.

Adrianne thought for several moments that she was going to hyperventilate and pass out where she stood. There was absolutely no point in looking around in the bathroom for a weapon. There was nothing in there that even came close to a weapons grade household object. Unfortunately, except for the lamp, which was all the way across the room, there also wasn't anything in her bedroom to use as a weapon.

Besides, the lamp was across the room. She knew if she walked past the man standing behind the curtain he would pounce on her.

After a moment, Adrianne backed into the bathroom and picked up the plunger. It wasn't much, but she thought maybe it beat trying to fight the man off barehanded. Holding it like a baseball bat, she crept toward the curtain. Finally, taking a deep breath, she grasped the fabric and snatched it back.

A wall of bare skin greeted her. Without thinking, Adrianne screamed like a banshee. The man yelped and thrust some strange looking object at her, more in the manner of an offering than in any way that was threatening. Thinking it must be a taser, Adrianne leapt back … too late. The object touched the skin near the bend of her elbow.

Something like fire shot through Adrianne, but it was not the fire of pain. Pleasure exploded inside of her like a nuclear bomb. All the strength went out of her body and she fell into an orgasmic puddle on the floor, every muscle in her body pulsing with the explosion of pleasure that saturated her.

Dimly, Adrianne realized the man was staring down at her, a look of panic on his face and a trace of uneasiness went through her as it occurred to her to wonder if the pleasure only proceeded an equally intense pain.

After a moment, he scooped her up and placed her gently on the bed. "Don't slay me, Mistress. I beg you. I did not mean to intrude. I was attacked by a beast and only trying to preserve my life."

It took an effort to open her eyes and look at him. Her body was still wracked by pleasurable quakes, her mind so awash with ecstasy she could barely think. "What was that?" she asked weakly when she managed to stop moaning long enough to speak.

"Some small hairy thing which emitted threatening sounds and kept baring its teeth. I believe it would have eaten me if I had not run faster."

Adrianne shook her head. She felt as if she'd had a whole year's worth of orgasms all at one time. "That thing in your hand."

The man looked down at it in surprise. "It was nothing but my Orgasmizer9000, mistress."

"Orgas…." Adrianne sat up, shaking off the lethargy from the aftermath of her climax with a supreme effort of will. "What the hell is an Orgasmizer9000?"

The man held the device protectively, as if he feared she would take it from him. Adrianne looked at him in surprise. The man must outweigh her by a hundred pounds … all muscle. He might have passed for that muscle bound, Austrian born movie actor, or a fullback for some professional football team, except he had long, flowing golden hair. "It's mine. Mistress Serena gave it to me." He reddened. "So I could pleasure her if my phallus failed or if she was bored with me. I am … not … a young slave."

"Mistress? Orgasmizer? What planet are you from?" Adrianne demanded, beginning to feel more like herself, although she doubted she could stand yet. Her legs felt like limp noodles. Her whole body felt weak and shaky.

"Barbron," he said promptly.

"Bar … you're kidding, right?"

He frowned. "I was not trained to amuse my mistress with clever wit."

This was becoming more and more bizarre … as if it hadn't started out that way to begin with, but Adrianne couldn't help but feel the man was no threat to her. He could have done anything to her, after all, when she'd been totally incapacitated by the wildest orgasm she'd every experienced in her life and all he'd done was very gently scoop her up and place her on the bed. He seemed afraid of what she might do to him, crazy as that sounded, which seemed to preclude that he had any intention of trying to harm her.

He didn't look crazy.

"Why are you walking around Las Vegas in your birthday suit?"

He looked puzzled.

"Without clothes? Where are your clothes?"

He still looked puzzled, but now he was looking at her like *she* was crazy. "Slaves are not allowed to own clothing."

"Slaves?" Adrianne said faintly. Finally, she stood up and moved to the lamp, flicking it on.

The man stood as she'd left him. He looked anxious, like a big teddy bear of a man--but he didn't seem to lack for intelligence. Adrianne smiled at him. "It's OK. Really."

He seemed to relax fractionally. After a moment, she moved toward him and walked around him, looking him over. He stood perfectly still, as if he was used to being examined in such a way. "So ... you're a slave?"

"Yes, mistress. Bred to serve."

"You were certainly bred," Adrianne commented, curbing the urge to check out his bulging muscles. Beautiful didn't begin to describe the man. He was the most flawless male, at least in appearance, that she'd ever laid eyes on. Which was one of the reasons, among many, that the idea of him being some sort of alien was impossible to grasp. He was clearly human. One absolutely stunningly beautiful male, but definitely built like every other human male she'd ever seen, except maybe better. His cock was a lovely instrument to behold and it was only semi-erect.

"Who do you belong to?"

"Mistress Serena."

"And where is Mistress Serena?"

He frowned. "I don't know. Her pod was fired upon by the bar--Earth people and it crashed. I came to help, but I don't know how to find her."

Adrianne studied him for several moments and finally moved back to the bed, sitting on the edge. She still felt more than a little weak kneed from her experience with his

Orgasmizer9000--which was positively the only thing about her experience tonight that made her wonder if there was, in fact, some truth to the strange man's very weird tale. As far as she knew, there was nothing like it on Earth--and it occurred to her, forcefully, that if there wasn't, there was a pure fortune to be made with the thing if she could only get her hands on it. She patted the bed beside her and smiled. "Here. Sit down. You look like you've had a very rough night."

He smiled gratefully and sat on the bed. "Thank you, mistress. Are you going to help me?"

Adrianne frowned. "Why don't you tell me the whole story from the beginning and then … we'll see, huh? What's your name, anyway?"

"Yar."

Adrianne's brows rose almost to her hairline. "Yar? That's … uh … different."

He frowned, but apparently decided the comment didn't warrant a response and launched into his tale, finishing with the comment, "Mistress Serena knows it is forbidden to come to this place, but she is the youngest in her family and considered to be wild … I'm not disparaging my mistress," he added hastily. "This is what her sisters say of her."

Adrianne mulled his story over for a few minutes. "Her sisters won't be coming to rescue her, then?"

Yar looked unhappy. He shook his head.

"And you decided to rescue her?"

"Mistress Serena told me I was to do nothing but wait for her return, but I was afraid she would not and I would be left there, on that rock, alone. Will you please help me, Mistress, so I can go home?"

Adrianne couldn't resist patting his knee. "Poor baby. You have had a bad night, haven't you?"

Instead of looking affronted, or lascivious, the gesture seemed to comfort him. "Yes. Earth people chased me. And that beast chased me. I have injured my feet and been attacked by tiny, biting creatures. I find this world very confusing."

He certainly sounded like a fish out of water, poor thing. Adrianne got up abruptly and began to pace the room, thinking.

Yar didn't move. He merely watched her, a hopeful, and expectant, look on his face. Briefly, Adrianne felt a rush of guilt. All she could really think about was the Orgasmizer9000 that he was clutching with a death grip. Apparently, it was the only thing he owned and he was reluctant to part with it. "I don't suppose you could pay for my help?"

Yar looked downcast for several moments, but then brightened. "I'm sure my mistress will reward you for your help."

"What about that?" Adrianne said, pointing. "Would you be willing to trade the Orgasmizer9000 for my help?"

Yar looked horrified but after a moment he nodded.

Adrianne grinned, firmly ignoring his downcast expression. "Great!" She began pacing again, trying to push the marketing ideas crowding into her mind aside so that she could formulate a plan to earn the 'reward'. Finally, she stopped, examining Yar critically. "The first thing we need to do is get some clothes for you. No way can we blend in with you running around naked as the day you were born."

Unfortunately, although she had a few cast-offs her ex-boyfriend had left behind when he'd moved out, David had been no more than medium in height and build. Yar would look like the Hulk if she even attempted dressing him in any of David's clothes.

A quick check of her clock told her there was little chance Darcy would still be up. It was going on 2:00 AM.

It occurred her then that as wound up with excitement as she was, she was also dead on her feet.

"We need to get some rest before we head out. I'm too tried to think straight right now. Where are you staying?"

Yar looked at her blankly. "Staying?"

"Sleeping," Adrianne said a little impatiently.

Yar looked a little taken aback. "Where ever you will allow me to sleep, Mistress."

Adrianne blew out an impatient breath, but on second thought realized she really didn't want him to get too far away from her while he was carrying the Orgasmizer9000. That ruled out the couch in the living room downstairs. What if he decided to sneak away while she was sleeping? She didn't think he would, but the poor thing was obviously disoriented … if he wasn't stark mad.

She shook that thought off. He was as tame as a kitten … big as all out doors, but sweet and gentle. "You can sleep with me. No funny stuff, though!" she added warningly.

He looked more than a little upset. "I have told you, I was not trained to perform amusements."

Adrianne shook her head. "No sex."

He looked relieved, which Adrianne couldn't help but find more than a little disconcerting. "It is not allowed unless my mistress orders me to pleasure her guests."

It took only that. It really had been a very bad day and her nerves, and her temper, were on edge. "Fine!" Adrianne snapped. "I wasn't going to offer it anyway. But, just so you know, until and unless we find your mistress, *I'm* your mistress. Now, get in bed and shut up."

## Chapter Three

If Adrianne hadn't been so irritated, she would have been amazed at how meekly Yar complied with her order. He crawled into her bed and laid down … on top of the covers. "Not there. That's my side. Get on the other side and get under the covers. This is the desert. It gets cold here at night, in case you hadn't noticed."

When he'd settled, Adrianne tossed her towel off and went to the dresser to find a nightgown. He was watching her, she saw, when she turned around.

"Is this an Earth custom?"

"Wearing nightclothes? Yes, for some of us, anyway. Some people sleep naked, though."

He frowned. "I meant about you being my new mistress."

"Oh," Adrianne looked away. She never had been very good about lying when she was looking directly at someone. "Possession is nine tenths of the law. If she isn't around to claim you, I can."

"Oh." He thought it over for several moments. "Should I sleep then? Or will you require me to service you?"

Taken aback, Adrianne couldn't think of anything to say for several moments. She considered the offer. There was no getting around the fact that the man was pure eye candy, and she couldn't help but be intrigued by the idea that he was a 'trained sex slave', wondering what sort of marvels he could perform. On the other hand, she'd been so thoroughly sexed by the Orgasmizer9000 that she was more inclined to sleep it off than to try for another orgasm tonight. Still, if he was willing, it might be her one and only chance to try out a sex slave. "Would you like to?" she asked curiously, willing to allow him to soothe her ruffled feathers after the earlier rejection.

He looked startled. "Yes, mistress?" he said after a slight hesitation.

Adrianne frowned. "You don't sound at all certain."

"This was not the answer you wanted, Mistress?"

Adrianne sighed gustily. "I asked what you wanted … never mind. Just go to sleep."

Yawning, Adrianne went to the phone and dialed her office, punched the buttons for her boss's voice mail and left him the message that she wouldn't be in for a few days because she was consulting with a lawyer, then hung up. Let the bastard stew on that one! If things didn't work out with Yar and the Orgasmizer9000, she was going to be looking for another job, but she wasn't going without a hell of a recommendation from that son-of-a-bitch. He'd be worrying about a lawsuit until she got back.

She dialed Darcy's number next and left a message on the answering machine. "Hi, Darcy! It's me, Adrianne. I need your help. Bring your sewing kit and anything you have in the shop in a man's size…." She broke off and thought about it for several moments. "I guess it would be tall, 44 or

46 in the chest. 34 or maybe 36 in the waist and at least a 35 or 36 inseam. Don't forget the sewing kit. You'll probably have to make some adjustments. Oh. Bring men's boxers, too. Thanks bunches, girlfriend. See you in the AM."

That done, she hung up, turned the light off and lay down.

As weary as she was, it was still difficult to ignore the huge mound of man lying beside her. Finally, however, weariness began to take the upper hand and Adrianne was just drifting to sleep when Yar spoke again.

"Did you mean what you said?"

Adrianne couldn't come up with a clue of what he was asking. "The clothes?"

"That I could say what I wanted?"

"Oh. Sure, sweety. Whatever," Adrianne responded, yawning again.

He was silent for several moments. "I … would like … to service you."

Adrianne's eyes popped open and she turned over. "What did you say?"

His eyes widened in alarm. "You said I was to say what I wanted."

She nodded. "I'm just curious to know why you changed your mind."

"I did not change my mind. I decided."

She couldn't help but smile. "And what made you decide you wanted to … uh … offer your services?"

Yar frowned, obviously thinking it over carefully. "Your are beautiful, and clever and kind. My body wants you. My head, too."

Adrianne stared at him blankly for several moments. "Why, Yar! That's just the sweetest thing anybody's ever said to me!"

He reddened.

She leaned over and kissed him on the lips, lightly. "Now, go to sleep. We've got a lot to do tomorrow."

He looked confused, but settled down and closed his eyes.

Adrianne settled as well. Her last thoughts as she drifted off was that she was going to have to try to teach Yar how to blend in a little better.

\* \* \* \*

Yar prepared their breakfast the following morning. Adrianne was alarmed when she woke and discovered that he was gone. Still more than a little groggy, she was trying to decide whether everything she remembered had actually happened, or if it was one of the most bizarre dreams she'd ever had--brought on, possibly, by the combination of seafood and her client's determined efforts to seduce her. How she could have exchanged the short, fat, balding Mr. Blanton with a man like Yar was a mystery, but she had to wonder.

When she woke enough to have her wits about her, however, she turned over. Sure enough, there was a very definite imprint in the bed beside her. Lifting the pillow, she sniffed. Immediately, a rush of warmth filled her. The man was a walking, talking aphrodisiac.

Panic shot through her and she sat bolt upright. Before she could launch herself from the bed and race out to find him, however, he tapped on the door and entered carrying a makeshift tray filled with plates of food. Adrianne stared at him blankly. "You cook?"

Yar was concentrating on balancing the tray. He said nothing until he'd carefully set it on the chest beside the bed. "Yes, Mistress."

"Adrianne."

"Mistress Adrianne."

Adrianne shook her head. "You can't go around calling me Mistress Adrianne. It'll attract too much attention. You must call me Adrianne."

He looked a little doubtful. "I will not be punished?"

Adrianne gaped at him for several moments before a surge of protectiveness went through her. She discarded the urge to cuddle him. "Oh course not, sweety! Here," she added, patting the bed beside her. "Sit down and eat with me."

He looked torn between pleasure and doubt. "I only prepared enough for you."

Adrianne gaped at the heaping plates. "Good God! I couldn't eat a tenth of that if my life depended upon it! Sit down and eat."

He looked at the bed but finally sat cross legged on the floor, took a plate and began eating. Adrianne picked up a piece of toast. "You seem very familiar with Earth food for somebody from another planet."

"My mis--Mistress Serena is very fond of Earth food. I learned to prepare it to please her."

"What else do you know how to do?"

He thought it over and finally shrugged. "Whatever must be done to keep a household running smoothly. Mistress Serena is a very important and busy woman. She does not have much time for me. She allows me to do whatever I like most of the time, as long as it is not forbidden."

"She is … kind to you?"

Yar nodded. "Much more than my other mistress' were. But she is not as kind as you. You are not a warrior, mistress?"

Adrianne almost choked on her toast. "A what?"

"Warrior?"

"Certainly not!" She thought about it for several moments. "I suppose, in a way … Business is a bit like battle. You just use different weapons to conquer."

He nodded. When he'd cleaned the plate and set it down, Adrianne handed him another one. After a moment's hesitation, he took it.

"I have a friend coming over in a little bit with clothing for you. I've been giving it some thought and I think the best way to introduce her to the Orgasmizer9000 is to give her a free sample. She'll never believe it, otherwise."

Yar looked at her curiously.

"I'm thinking … if all goes well and I get your mistress back, and you give me the Orgasmizer9000 … then Darcy would probably like being my partner marketing it. So this is what I want you to do when she gets here…."

When she was certain Yar understood what she had in mind, she led him downstairs, parked him in front of the TV and then handed him the remote and taught him how to use it. "What is the purpose of this, Mistress?" he asked curiously.

"Ordinarily, it's purely for entertainment. Right now, though, I want you to watch for news reports. If your mistress crashed anywhere around here, there'll be something about it on the news. They're not going to say a space ship crashed, mind you, or … What was it you called it? A pod? They might say a small plane crashed, but most likely they'll say something about a meteor. Or maybe they'll just call it a small explosion from some gas leak. Anyway, if they start talking about something like that, you need to listen very closely and remember the name of the place where they say it happened. OK?"

He nodded, staring so raptly at the TV screen Adrianne had to wonder if he'd remember what she'd said, or notice if there was a report. She decided they must not have TV where he was from.

Mentally, she shrugged. To her way of thinking TV was the least likely to offer up any clues. Taking her portable phone and the phone book, she flipped to the list of radio stations and began making calls. The doorbell rang while she was on her second call and she ended the conversation, hung up and turned to Yar. "It's probably Darcy. Remember what I told you?"

Yar nodded. "I'm very clever, Mistress. I never forget anything."

Adrianne looked at him a little doubtfully. "That must be nice. I'd forget my head if it wasn't attached."

Ignoring the curious look he gave her, she went to answer the door. Darcy stood on the stoop, her arms full of clothing, her eyes wide as saucers.

She was almost Adrianne's complete opposite--short, a little on the plump side, blond and shy. Not that *she* was tall, but she was at least average in height and poor Darcy was barely five feet tall-- and mostly boobs. Not that Adrianne would have minded having such an impressive 'bumper' herself, but on Darcy the boobs only made her look shorter and fatter.

"Did you hear the news this morning?" Darcy gasped excitedly.

"Missed it. I slept late."

"Somebody saw a UFO over Vegas last night!"

Adrianne suppressed a grin with an effort. "No! Really? Come on in. You'll have to tell me all about it, but first I want you to meet somebody."

Darcy followed her into the living room, chattering about the reported sightings. "Actually, I heard they sighted one …."

Darcy broke off and stared up at Yar when he stood up from the couch, slowly turning as red as a tomato. Adrianne grasped Darcy's shoulders. "This is my very best friend, Darcy. Darcy--this is Yar. He was flying in that UFO everybody saw last night."

She gave Darcy a little shove in Yar's direction.

Yar glanced at her, almost seemed to shrug, and held out the Orgasmizer.

Darcy, moving like a sleepwalker, her gaze fixed on Yar's face, held out her hand. The moment she touched the devise, she just sort of wilted to the floor in slow motion. Adrianne caught her friend and lowered her carefully to the couch, feeling more than a little concern as she watched Darcy twitch and moan. She frowned. "Is it supposed to be like this?"

Yar nodded.

"I looked like that?" Adrianne said, embarrassed and more than a little repulsed.

Yar shrugged. "Not exactly."

"You OK, Darcy?"

"Ohhhh," Darcy moaned.

"I think she's OK," Adrianne said, half to herself. "Maybe we should just give her a few minutes?"

Yar didn't take the hint and Adrianne reached for his arm and led him from the room. They waited outside the door for several minutes until Darcy's moaning seemed to subside. Finally, Adrianne peered into the room. Darcy was sitting up on the couch, looking around as if bewildered, her glasses cocked crazily on her face. "Better?"

Reaching up, Darcy straightened her glasses. "What was that … thing?"

Adrianne grinned and went back into the living room. "The Orgasmizer9000. Wasn't that just … the best?"

Darcy still looked more than a little confused. "The best what?"

"Orgasm. Wasn't that the best orgasm you ever had in your life?"

"*That's* what an orgasm feels like?" Darcy gasped.

Adrianne felt a moment of doubt. "It didn't feel like an orgasm to you?"

Darcy turned red. "Uh … well … I never had one before. *Is* that what it feels like?"

Adrianne didn't know whether to laugh or cry. "You poor thing! I'm so sorry, Darcy! I just wanted you to experience it so you'd believe me. I mean, it's just so fantastic I wouldn't have believed it myself if I hadn't.

Yar's promised to give it to me if we help him find his mistress. That's why I called you over … well, part of it. I needed some clothes for him so we can go looking. And I wanted to invite you to be my partner to market this … once it's ours, of course." Grabbing Darcy, she hugged her friend excitedly. "Can you just imagine the magnitude of this thing! We'll be rich!"

Darcy smiled a little hesitantly when Adrianne released her. "He's an alien?"

Adrianne nodded. "Come on back in here, Yar."

"He looks … dangerous," Darcy whispered, her eyes wide as saucers. "Are you sure he's … safe?"

Adrianne giggled. "Don't let his size fool you. He's tame as a kitten … like a big old teddy bear. Aren't you, Yar?"

Yar looked confused. "What is a teddy bear, Mistress?"

Adrianne frowned. "You can't go around calling me that. People will notice."

"Adrianne?"

"Never mind. It just means you're sweet and wouldn't hurt a fly."

"What is a fly, Mis … Adrianne?"

"Forget it. We need to get some clothes on you. Why don't you tell me what you heard about the UFOs while you're fitting him for clothes, Darcy?"

Darcy looked down at the mound of clothes she'd dropped on the floor. Grabbing them up, she held them toward Yar. When he reached for them, however, she released them and jumped back nervously. Yar managed to catch a shirt.

"That's good. Put that on and let's see how it fits," Adrianne suggested as she gathered up the rest of the clothing and deposited it on the couch.

Yar held it out, frowning as he turned it several times and finally put his arm in the wrong sleeve. Adrianne took it from him and helped him put it on. Unfortunately, the moment he shrugged his shoulders, the shoulder seams popped and a small tear appeared in the middle of the back. "Too small," Adrianne said and helped him out of it again.

"Uh, do you think you could put some … uh … shorts on him?"

Adrianne bit back a smile, but didn't turn to look at her friend. "Sure. I really hate covering up something that purdy, but I guess we have to, huh?"

"Pretty?" Darcy asked faintly.

Adrianne glanced at her but decided she'd teased her friend enough. "I think so, but you're right. Can't just leave him swinging in the breeze. Let's just hope the shorts you brought fit and his … uh … love muscle doesn't bust the seams."

The shorts fit, much to Darcy's relief. Once he was 'sheathed' she got up to help, but they discovered none of the shirts Darcy had brought fit him except the stretch knit and it couldn't really be said to have fit as it had been intended. The jeans fit him like a glove. Yar looked torn between happiness and discomfort once they had him dressed.

"I am overwhelmed with gratitude for your gifts, Mis … Adrianne. But I do not think I like Earth clothes. It is very hard to move."

Adrianne patted his arm. "You'll get used to it. Why don't you practice moving and sitting in them while me and Darcy discuss strategy?"

By the time Darcy had recounted the news reports, Adrianne was fairly certain she had a clear picture of the situation, and it wasn't good. "The FEDS have got her, sure as hell! Yar said he saw an explosion. They must have shot her down, in which case they were probably on top of it before she even landed.

"Sounds like she must have come down in Arizona, or maybe New Mexico. Which means they probably took her to that secret base close to Roswell that nobody's supposed to know about. Of course, from what Yar has said about her, she sounds like a pretty resourceful female, so she might have eluded them. We should take your van."

Darcy didn't look particularly happy about it. "But ... it's *new!*"

"Well we can't all squeeze into my little compact. Come on, Darcy. If we pull this off, we're going to be rich. It's the find of the century. Think about it."

Darcy looked glum. "And if we don't pull it off, my van's probably going to be full of bullet holes!"

Adrianne was taken aback. "You think they'll use guns?"

"You think they won't? Don't you think they'll think *they* have the find of the century? In which case, they're not going to want to give it up."

"Well, it isn't like we'll be trying for the ship ... the pod. We just need to break his mistress out."

"Just...!" Darcy exclaimed faintly.

Chapter Four

Adrianne had forgotten about shoes when she'd asked Darcy to bring over clothes for Yar. They stopped by a discount department store on their way out of town and bought him a pair of sneakers. He was pleased with them until he discovered he couldn't wiggle his toes.

Almost as an afterthought, Adrianne bought a backpack and every item she ran across that she thought might be helpful in a jailbreak. Unfortunately, explosives weren't readily available, so she purchased an assortment of tools she thought might be helpful in picking, or breaking, a lock, a set of wire cutters, lock cutters, rope in case they had to scale a wall or tie anybody up and flashlights.

It was mid afternoon when they reached the county in Arizona where the purported meteor had crashed. After getting rooms for the night, the three set out to grab a bite to eat and pump the locals for information. Adrianne decided a truck stop might be the best place to go for information so, although Darcy wasn't terribly happy about it, they drove around until they found what looked to be the most popular truck stop and pulled in.

A lull fell over the room as they reached the entrance to the restaurant. Yar seemed completely unaware of it, looking around with interest, but Adrianne and Darcy exchanged an uncomfortable glance, wondering if they should have put a little more effort into making Yar blend in. On the other hand, what could you do with a man well over six feet tall that was built like Conan the Barbarian?

Adrianne supposed they should have considered cutting his hair, but she hadn't been able to bring herself to suggest it. He had such beautiful hair!

The lull, thankfully, was short lived and everyone in the restaurant made a point thereafter of ignoring them. A booth would have been more comfortable, and far more private, but Adrianne opted for stools at the bar for the simple reason that she was more interested in information than food.

A waitress rushed over almost the moment they settled. "Can I get you folks some coffee?"

Adrianne preferred her caffeine in cola form and ordered one for herself and one for Yar. Darcy opted for the coffee. The waitress was back in a few minutes with their drinks. "You folks been traveling long?"

Adrianne smiled. "We're going to Florida. But we heard there was a meteor crash somewhere around here and decided to take a little detour to have a look at it."

"Where are ya'll from?"

"California," Adrianne lied promptly.

The woman had barely taken her eyes off of Yar since they'd sat down. At Adrianne's remark, a look of comprehension skated across her face, as if that explained everything. "Not much to see, from what I heard. What'll ya'll have?"

"What's good?"

"Everything," the waitress said promptly. "Our special tonight is the roast beef dinner."

"We'll take that."

The waitress glanced at Yar. He smiled at her and Adrianne thought for several moments the woman was going to drop her order pad. "Guess that's two," she managed to say, turning quickly to Darcy and lifting her brows.

"I'll have the same."

"I don't suppose you could give us directions to get out to the site?"

"Wouldn't do you any good," a young man seated just to Darcy's right muttered.

"Excuse me," the waitress muttered and took off.

Adrianne leaned forward, checking the guy out.

He looked to be in his early, or maybe mid-twenties. He was dressed more like a biker than a truck driver, his light brown hair straggling well past his shoulders.

Apparently feeling her gaze, he turned and looked first at Darcy for a long moment before his gaze skated past Darcy's bright red face to Adrianne's curious one. "Why wouldn't it do any good?"

"FEDS crawling all over the place. They've got the whole site barricaded off."

Excitement flooded through her. "Really? For a meteor?"

He made a derisive sound in his throat and returned his attention to the cup of coffee he held cradled in both hands. After a moment, Adrianne nudged Darcy and indicated with a jerk of her head that they should switch seats. Darcy looked happy to oblige and Adrianne wondered fleetingly if the young man had made her uneasy. She dismissed it, however, moving down to the bar stool Darcy had just vacated.

"I take it you've been out to the site?"

The young man glanced at her.

"My name's Adrianne," she said when he looked at her, then turned to introduce Yar and Darcy, discovering in the process that Yar had moved down a seat, as well, and that Darcy had been shuttled to the opposite end of the group. "This is … uh …." She shrugged. A more commonplace name didn't come immediately to mind. "Yar, and the lady at the end is my friend, Darcy."

"Chance," the young man said, leaning forward on his elbows until he could see Darcy, who barely glanced in his direction at the introduction. He grinned as her face lit up like a Christmas tree. "Darcy, huh?"

Adrianne hid a smile as she divided a glance between the two. After a few moments, Chance managed to pry his gaze from Darcy's breasts and glanced at Yar. He did a double take, then his eyes narrowed as he examined Yar more carefully. Finally, he looked at Adrianne again.

"Any particular reason you're looking for the … meteor?"

"Just curiosity," Adrianne lied promptly.

He nodded. "There's been a swarm of curious, but the Feds won't let anybody within miles of it. The locals I've talked to that happened to get a glimpse of it said it was huge … and it didn't look like any meteor."

"Maybe we could talk better if we moved to a quiet table in the back?" Adrianne suggested.

Chance shrugged. "I can't tell you much."

"I'd still like to talk."

He nodded and Adrianne summoned the waitress. "We're going to move to that back table over there."

The waitress didn't look too pleased, but pleasing the waitress wasn't high on Adrianne's agenda. When they'd settled again, the waitress brought their plates. As soon as the woman left, Adrianne leaned forward and said in a low voice, "It wasn't a meteor, was it?"

Chance shrugged, looked around, looked pointedly at Yar for several moments and finally said, "You tell me."

Adrianne's lips tightened in irritation. "We're not FEDS, so let's stop beating around the bush, shall we? It was a space ship that crashed, wasn't it?"

Chance scrubbed his face with his hands and sat back in his chair. "I haven't managed to get a look at it, but … yeah … I'm pretty sure it was a UFO. This place has been crawling with UFO enthusiasts. Most of them are camped out as close to the site as the FEDS will let them get, just a little north of here."

Adrianne frowned. "I suppose it would be useless to ask if anyone had seen … a stranger around here, then?"

"You mean besides him?" Chance asked.

"We're looking for a woman," Adrianne said bluntly.

"Gotta description?"

Adrianne turned to Yar. "Tell him what Mis… Serena looks like."

"She is beautiful," Yar said promptly.

Irritation washed over Adrianne, but it wasn't entirely because Yar's description was so unhelpful. "How tall?"

Yar held his hand just above the top of his head. "To here."

"That tall?"

Yar frowned, thinking it over, and nodded.

"Good God! Never mind. Her hair. What color is it?"

"I don't really think we need that," Darcy put it. "There can't be too many women over six feet running around the place."

Yar pointed to the table cloth.

"Red?"

"This color."

"So … you're looking for a red head somewhere in the neighborhood of six foot six? Did you file a missing persons?"

Adrianne gave Chance a look. "You know very well what I'm talking about."

"We could ask around, but from what I heard that thing came down pretty hard … NOT like a falling meteor, mind you, but it was definitely a crash. If she survived, I doubt she would have been in any condition to outrun the FEDS. They were here within minutes of the crash, from what I heard, and had cordoned off the area. The tale they're passing around is that it's a potential bio-hazard. Most everybody around here thinks it's a piece of space debris--satellite or something."

Adrianne threw a glance at Yar, wondering what he thought of the conversation. His expression told her he had followed the discussion well enough to realize that his mistress might be dead. She couldn't tell how he felt about it, but he had said she was kind to him and he'd been anxious enough about her to come looking for her. He must be feeling a good deal of distress over the possibility. She gave his hand a comforting squeeze.

"Could you give us directions to the site?"

Chance smiled faintly. "I can do better than that. I can show you a back way in."

\* \* \* \*

They'd been following Chance for over an hour before they reached a place where he signaled for them to pull over and stop. Chance, riding a motorcycle, led the way down a series of narrow dirt roads and finally along an overgrown track that didn't look as if it had been used in fifty years. They stopped beside a run down, abandoned shack.

Adrianne got out of the car and looked around. "I don't see anything," she muttered, wondering if she should have trusted the guy after all. It wasn't incomprehensible that he'd led them out in the boonies to rob them.

"I told you, the FEDS are crawling all over the place. We can't get within a mile of the site in broad daylight. We'll have to wait here for dark," Chance said as he parked his cycle and pulled his helmet off.

Darcy, who'd been driving and had come to join them, sent Adrianne a frightened look. "We're going on foot … in the dark? What if … what if we're spotted?"

"We'll have to run for it," Chance said cheerfully, moving to the rickety porch of the cabin and taking a seat. "But we'll have a better chance of *not* being spotted if we wait till dark."

Darcy glanced from Chance to Adrianne. "I think I'll stay with the van … if it's all the same to you. Someone ought to stay and make sure nobody messes with the van. And, if they do chase you, I could start it up and be ready to make a quick getaway."

"Good thinking, Darcy!" Adrianne said, beaming at her.

"What about the little fellow?" Chance asked, pointing at Yar, who'd climbed out of the van and was looking around curiously.

Adrianne turned to look at Yar, frowning. "He should probably stay with Darcy. He's … uh … not used to this sort of thing."

"And you are?"

Adrianne glared at him. "Let's just say I'm better at thinking on my feet."

Chance hooked a jaw in Yar's direction. "What about it? You going to let her tell you what to do?"

Yar looked at him as if he'd lost his mind, then looked at Adrianne. "I do not think I understand the slave's question."

"Slave!" Chance snapped, jumping to his feet. "Did he call me a slave?"

Adrianne put her hand out. "There's no sense in getting all pissed off at him. He doesn't understand."

"Well, maybe I'll explain it to him," Chance said belligerently, stomping over to Yar and giving him a shove … at least, Adrianne assumed that was what he'd intended to do. Yar didn't so much as budge.

He sent her a helpless look. Adrianne set her jaw, stalked over to the two of them and wedged herself between them, giving Chance a push. "Leave him alone, Chance. I told you, he doesn't understand. On his world, men are bred to be slaves. He assumed you were. He just doesn't understand our customs."

Chance took a step back. "He's an alien?"

"I thought you'd figured that out by now. He described the *other* alien, remember?"

"Yeah, but I thought … well, he doesn't look like an Alien."

"We're trying to help him find his mistress so he can go home."

Chance looked excited, but then something apparently occurred to him because he frowned, and looked Yar over again carefully. "You *want* to go back to being a slave? Why don't you just stay here and be a free man?"

Adrianne glanced up at Yar. She'd been too wrapped up in trying to fulfill her part of the bargain to give much thought to Yar's situation. He'd said he wanted to find Serena so he could go home and it hadn't occurred to her to question whether that was what he really wanted or not … or if that was what was best for him.

"*Is* that what you want, Yar?"

Yar looked both scared and confused. "I could … decide?"

"I suppose you could. You said it was forbidden to come to Earth. If they won't come here, then you wouldn't have to worry about being captured, would you? What do they do with runaway slaves, anyway?"

Unconsciously, Yar put his hand protectively over his groin.

Chance paled. "Aw man! No wonder you didn't think about it."

Adrianne studied Yar a long moment and finally took his hand and led him over to the rickety porch and told him to sit down. "If you think there's any chance you could get in trouble, don't think about it, OK?"

"But … I could decide?"

Adrianne sat down beside him. "It's against the law to have slaves here. If you decided you wanted to stay, you would be free. If we can't find Serena, or we do and we don't manage to release her, you would be a free man."

Yar frowned. "But … you said …."

Adrianne felt a blush rise to her cheeks. "I didn't mean it. I was just … I could see you expected to be ordered to do things and it was easier than trying to explain that you didn't have to do anything you didn't want to do." She thought it over. "Well, actually, everybody has to do things they don't really want to do. Even when they're free. But you have a choice. You can do it, or you can face the consequences.

"Like what my boss did to me. I could've done it and kept my job. But I decided I didn't want to do it, so now I have to look for another job. See what I mean?"

"What did your boss tell you to do?" Yar asked curiously.

"He wanted me to please a client … sexually. It totally pissed me off when I realized that was what I'd been sent to do, so I left. *Not* that I'm worried about it, mind you. I wouldn't work for that bastard again if he gave me the raise I thought I was going to get!"

Yar thought that over. "You get to decide if you want sex?"

Adrianne nodded. "The men too. Thing is, you have to ask and if they don't want to then you don't get to even if you want to. That's how choice works. Everybody decides whether they want to or not and sometimes you choose them, but they don't choose you."

He frowned. "You do not want me?"

"I hadn't really thought about it," Adrianne lied. "You said you wanted to find Serena and go home."

He lowered his voice, as if he was afraid someone would over hear, although Chance and Darcy were too far away to hear even a normal tone and, from what Adrianne could see, too caught up in flirting to notice anything less subtle than a freight train. Chance was, at any rate. Darcy was wearing her scared rabbit look, as if she'd just discovered herself in the clutches of Jack the Ripper. "If I stayed?"

Adrianne studied him. She'd been too focused on getting her hands on the Orgasmizer9000 to think about anything else, at least consciously. On a sexual level, she found Yar a definite 10 and a half. She couldn't help but wonder if that was something that had been bred into him--a severely potent masculine appeal--but, in the end, did it really matter? Natural or not, it was definitely there.

Strangely enough, he also brought out almost a … motherly instinct in her to want to take care of him. She supposed, in a way, most women wanted to feel needed, but she had avoided men that were too needy. She enjoyed being completely independent. She didn't want the responsibility of having anyone dependent on her … or she never had before.

She wasn't so certain she felt that way when it came to Yar.

Not that that mattered. The chances were strong, in her opinion, that once Yar got his 'land legs' so to speak, he wouldn't be needing her, or anyone, to take care of him. It might take him a while to get used to the way things were on Earth, but he'd already taken the first step toward independence by deciding to come after his mistress in what he perceived as a hostile environment. He was smart enough to have learned English, just from observations, as Serena had, she supposed. He was intelligent enough to have figured out how to get the pod down to the planet just from watching Serena program it. He didn't say much, but there was every indication that that was from caution, and probably training, than because he was slow.

She patted his knee. "We'll see when ... and if ... the time comes, OK?"

Yar frowned. Briefly he looked distressed, but in a moment he had his 'impassive mask' firmly in place, the expression he wore when he didn't want anyone to know what he was thinking. "This means no?"

"It does *not* mean no. It means ... when you've had time to figure out what you really want, *then* we'll talk about it. I'm not going to take unfair advantage of your innocence."

## Chapter Five

Yar exerted his newfound independence by refusing to stay with Darcy at the van while Adrianne and Chance went to check out the site. His stated reason was that she was his mistress and he should stay with her, but she couldn't help but wonder if it was because he was so anxious to be reunited with Serena.

She didn't like leaving Darcy alone. Chance showed every indication that he would've been happy to stay and protect her, but they couldn't very well leave him when he was the only one that knew the way.

And this was her show. She wasn't about to be left behind.

"Keep the keys in the ignition and if we're running when we head back this way," she told Darcy as they left, "make sure the van's ready to roll the minute we get in."

Chance had told her they were about a mile from the site. It seemed like further. The terrain was rough and although the sky was clear enough to shed plenty of light so that they could see each other, it was still too dark to keep them from stumbling over rocks and scrubby bushes.

When Adrianne finally reached the point where she thought she was going to have to beg for a breather, Yar simply scooped her into his arms and kept going, as if she was light as a feather--which she knew she wasn't. Her ass alone … but she didn't want to think about that. She was trying hard not to think about how heavy she must feel to Yar.

After her first yelp of surprise when he picked her up, and a half hearted demand to be put down, she subsided when he insisted that she was tired and needed to be carried, looped her arms around his neck and enjoyed herself. By the time she decided she was rested enough to walk again, Chance had halted them with a sharp whisper and flattened himself on the ground. Adrianne did likewise when Yar set her on her feet. They'd been peering down at the activity for several moments before it occurred to her that Yar was standing as she'd left him. She turned to look up at him in surprise and irritation.

"Get down!"

He knelt beside her. "I will soil my clothing," he objected reasonably.

"It'll wash … if we get the chance. If they see you, we might not!"

Reluctantly, he lay down beside her.

The whole area below them was bathed in light from the floodlight towers that had been set up around the crash site. There must have been a dozen men and women wearing civilian clothing milling around--probably scientists. There were at least three times that many soldiers. The center of attention was the wreckage that was being carefully secured with heavy cables. Nearby stood an empty flatbed truck.

Three men stood on the empty bed, busily assembling a huge wooden crate.

Adrianne frowned. "Looks like they're about to move the ship. I don't understand why they'd assemble the crate first, though."

"Because it isn't going into the crate." Chance pointed to a huge helicopter off to one side that Adrianne had assumed had been used to bring in the scientists. "They're going to air lift it out of here across the desert. The flatbed and the crate are just a diversion. They know the UFO people are camped out all around here and there's no way they'll get it out on any of the roads without being spotted."

"Figures. I don't see any sign of a tent where they might be keeping Serena."

"Alive or dead, they probably took her out long since."

Adrianne frowned. "But where?" She thought about it for several minutes. "Somebody is going to have to risk getting close enough to overhear their conversations."

Chance glanced at her. "I'll volunteer."

"You think you can get close enough without being spotted?"

He shrugged. "I've got as good a chance as you have … better than the mountain over there."

Adrianne frowned. He was always making wise cracks about Yar and she found it very irritating. Now didn't seem the time to argue about it, however. "They've probably taken her to that secret government facility that nobody's supposed to know about near Roswell, but we should try to be sure before we waste time going there."

Chance nodded and began to move toward the activity below them. To Adrianne's relief, he managed to reach the semi without being spotted and crawled under it, hiding behind the wheels. She shifted, trying to get into a comfortable position so that she could keep an eye on the movements below.

After several moments, she noticed a guard pacing the perimeter on the other side of the lights. Her heart skipped a beat, and she pushed herself up a little higher and looked around. After several nerve wracking moments, she spotted the guard that had been posted on their side. He had taken a seat on a rock maybe twenty or thirty feet from where they lay on the ground.

Her first instinct was to move. She quelled it with the thought that Chance would expect to find them in the same place when he came back. Shifting toward Yar, she put her lips near his ear. "See that man over there with the very big gun?"

A shiver went through Yar as her warm breath caressed his ear, but he turned and looked in the direction she indicated and nodded his head. "Watch him. If he moves, tell me."

Deciding that was taken care of, Adrianne returned her attention to Chance and trying to think of what they might do to create a distraction if they discovered it was necessary. She discovered, however, that she couldn't see Chance. Looking around a little frantically, she discovered that he'd moved to another vehicle and was crouched beside it, obviously listening to the two soldiers on the other side.

Panic seized her. If she could see him, the guard might be able to if he decided to look toward the camp instead of out over the desert.

After several agonizing minutes, Chance made his way carefully back to the semi, looked around and began to make his way back toward them. At almost the same moment, Yar leaned toward her and whispered in her ear. "He is walking."

Adrianne whipped her head around so fast she butted noses with him. Craning upward, she saw to her horror that although the guard hadn't spotted Chance, he was moving directly into an intersecting path with him.

She looked at Chance again, wondering if he would spot the guard and relieve her of the necessity of having to draw the guard's attention, but it was obvious from the quickness of his movements that Chance hadn't noticed the guard. She put her lips to Yar's ear again. "Get ready to run like hell."

When she looked for Chance again, it was just in time to see him collide with the guard. Leaping to her feet, Adrianne took a running jump and landed on the guard's back, grabbing his rifle with both hands. Fortunately, Chance recovered more quickly from his surprise than the guard did.

He planted a fist on the man's jaw that was hard enough it rocked his head back on his shoulders. Adrianne didn't duck quite fast enough. The back of the guard's head cracked against her cheek hard enough to make her bite her tongue, and she released the man even as he fell to the ground.

Scrambling to her feet, Adrianne whirled to run, looking around for Yar. He was standing where she'd left him, gaping at her and Chance as they stampeded toward him. "Run!" Adrianne whispered loudly as she passed him, expecting any moment to hear the whiz of bullets past her head.

She doubted very much that the punch Chance had thrown at the man had actually knocked him out. It had obviously stunned him, but that wouldn't give them more than a few minutes head start.

Hearing the pounding of running feet behind her, Adrianne ran faster. Quite suddenly, an arm snaked around her waist and jerked her off her feet. It jolted the breath from her lungs. When she finally managed to catch her breath, she discovered that Yar had snatched her up under one arm and was running with her, like a quarterback with the ball under one arm. Gritting her teeth to keep the jarring impact from making her bite her tongue, Adrianne twisted to see how close their pursuit was. Chance was several yards behind them. Behind him, the guard choked out a cry of alarm and scrambled to his feet.

"Run faster!" Adrianne exclaimed as she caught a glimpse of the guard leveling his gun in their direction. She squeezed her eyes shut, expecting any moment to feel a bullet in her ass, knowing the way Yar was carrying her it must be the biggest target on the range.

At her shout, however, Yar put on more speed and within moments they'd run down a dip in the ground that, she hoped, took her out of sight, if not out of range, of the soldier.

The trip back to the van didn't take nearly as long as the trip from the van to the crash site. Yar covered it in less than ten minutes, with her under one arm. She thought, later, that he'd probably broken more than one record.

"St…art the v..v.. an," she shouted the moment she was within shouting range of Darcy.

Even as she shouted, however, the van took off in a billow of dust, pulled a wild arc and headed straight for them. Darcy skidded to a halt beside them and Yar snatched the door open and tossed her in, leaping in behind her. A few moments later, Chance dove through the door. "Go! Go!" he shouted even before he'd slammed the door.

Darcy's eyes widened as a wall of soldiers erupted over the rise. Slamming the van into reverse, she shot backwards, whipped the wheel around, shoved the van into drive and shot rocks and dirt about ten feet in the air with the wheels as the van shot forward.

Despite the wall of dirt Darcy had thrown up as a smoke screen, several bullets smacked into the van. Adrianne screamed and threw herself toward the floor.

"Oh my God!" Darcy screamed.

"Darcy! Are you hurt?" Chance gasped.

"They hit my van! They shot my brand new van!" Darcy sobbed, scooting further down in the seat until she was looking at the road through the space on the steering wheel above the horn.

Adrianne scrambled up on the seat when the sound of firing grew distant. "Anybody hit?"

Darcy sniffed. "My van!"

"Are you hurt?"

"No."

"Yar?" She peered at him in the dimness, but could see no sign of injury. "Chance?"

"I'm OK."

"You think they'll follow us?" Adrianne asked.

He shrugged. "I doubt it. I think they were mostly just trying to chase us off."

Adrianne gave him an indignant look.

"They *shot* the van!" Adrianne and Darcy said almost in unison.

"But they chased us on foot. If they'd meant business, they would've brought one of the vehicles, don't you think?"

"Maybe they figured since we were on foot they could catch us. That doesn't mean they won't go back for a vehicle."

To their relief, they saw no signs that they were being followed, even after they reached the highway once more. Deciding to take no chances, they returned to the hotel, collected their bags and left town.

It wasn't until they'd tossed the bags into the van that it occurred to Adrianne that they'd abandoned Chance's bike at the old cabin when they'd made their escape. "What are you going to do about your bike?"

Chance shrugged. "Wasn't mine."

Darcy gaped at him. "You *stole* it?"

He reddened. "Borrowed," he said uncomfortably.

"From who?"

He shrugged. "I didn't catch his name," he said evasively.

"Well," Adrianne said philosophically. "At least they won't be able to trace it back to you."

Darcy's eyes widened. "Is that *all* you can say? He just admitted to stealing the bike!"

"I did not." Chance said irritably. "I told you. I borrowed it. Mine's in the shop."

"He is obviously not a very reputable person," Darcy said stiffly.

He sent her a faint smile. "But you like me anyway, don't you?"

Darcy gaped at him. Her lips moved, but she couldn't seem to make words. Chance seized the opportunity and kissed her soundly on the mouth. Darcy struggled for a moment and finally went limp against him.

Grinning, Adrianne exchanged a look with Yar. "I think she likes him," she whispered.

Yar turned to study the pair for several moments and then looked at Adrianne again. "Why?"

"She didn't knee him in the balls." She waited until they were finished, unwilling to interrupt. After all, as shy as Darcy was, she rarely dated … and to Adrianne's certain knowledge, Chance was the first 'younger' man she'd ever shown the least interest in.

"Can we drop you somewhere?"

Chance studied Darcy a moment longer before he glanced at Adrianne. "I could always come along for the ride."

"What do you think, Darcy?"

"Huh?" Darcy asked vaguely.

"Never mind. Sure. We can take you to your place and grab a bag."

Chance shook his head. "I think we ought to shake the dust from this place as quick as we can. I'll manage."

Adrianne shrugged. "I'll drive. I think Darcy's a little too shook up." She took the keys from Darcy's limp hand and climbed into the driver's seat. After a moment, Yar got into the front seat beside her and Chance and Darcy climbed in the back.

"So … where are we headed?" Adrianne said as she started the van.

"I think your guess is probably right on target. I didn't hear anybody say where they'd taken her, but they definitely caught her and she's definitely alive … at least she was when they took her."

Adrianne turned out of the hotel parking lot and caught the highway heading east. "It's not on any map," she muttered thoughtfully.

"No, but I'll bet money there'll be somebody around Roswell that could give us a good idea of where to look."

\* \* \* \*

They drove for a hundred miles before Adrianne decided they'd put enough distance between them an the angry FEDS and began looking for a hotel. Adrianne rented two adjoining rooms, but they met up with a serious problem when they got to the rooms.

"No offense, buddy," Chance said, looking at Yar, "but I don't plan on sharing a room with you, much less a bed."

"There's two beds in each room," Adrianne said firmly as she handed him one of the keys and went to unlock the door to her room. "Women in one room, men in the other."

"I will stay with you," Yar said, following her into her room, carrying the bags.

"There is no way I'm staying in the same room with you and Yar!" Darcy snapped.

Chance grinned. "I knew you liked me."

Darcy glared at him. "I meant Yar will have to stay in the room with you."

Adrianne glanced from one to the other, but decided she didn't feel like mediating an argument over the sleeping arrangements. "Hey. I'm dead on my feet. And I'm filthy from crawling around on the ground. You three slug it out. I'm going to take a shower," she finished, grabbing her bag and heading for the bathroom.

She'd just stepped under the shower head to rinse the soap from her hair when she felt a chilly breeze. Wiping the water from her eyes, she squinted toward the curtain. Yar was standing outside the shower, holding the curtain back. Behind him, she saw the door she thought she'd locked stood ajar.

Adrianne let out a yelp of surprise. "Yar! You scared the pee out of me. Talk about visions of Psycho! Go!" She made a shooing motion. "You're going to have to wait your turn."

Yar looked puzzled. "I came to assist you."

Adrianne studied him a long moment. Tomorrow, if they were really lucky, they would help Serena escape. Once she did, she would take Yar with her and Adrianne realized quite suddenly that she would be very sorry to see him go. It went without saying that she'd never met anyone quite like him, and it was unlikely she ever would again. She smiled. "Take your clothes off."

## Chapter Six

Smiling, Yar stripped his clothes off, stepped into the shower with her and looked around. "This is nice."

Adrianne soaped a cloth and rubbed it over his chest. "Yes it is. Very."

Yar went 'Indian' faced as she swirled the washcloth over his chest and down his belly and Adrianne couldn't tell whether he liked it or not. "You don't like this?"

Confusion flickered across his features. "Yes."

Adrianne smiled. "What's wrong, then?"

"I came to assist you."

Adrianne studied him a long moment. "Then you can wash me when I'm done washing you."

He smiled, but he looked as if he was in pain when she wrapped one soapy hand around his cock and began massaging it. "Where are Darcy and Chance?"

"Darcy went into the other room to take a shower. Chance followed. He said he had caught her and locked the portal between this room and the other one."

Adrianne repressed the urge to giggle, wondering if Chance had decided to wash Darcy's back and how Darcy was going to react to that. After a moment, she dismissed it. If Darcy hadn't booted him out of the room by the time they were through in the shower it seemed unlikely she was going to.

She moved a little closer to Yar. "This is a very nice … tool you have here."

"Thank you," Yar said a little breathlessly.

Reaching a little lower, she cupped his testicles and began massaging them. Yar jumped, bending forward slightly, as if someone had punched him in the stomach, and Adrianne looped her free arm around his neck, pulling him down and brushing her lips against his in invitation.

He took the hint and opened his mouth over hers, thrusting his tongue into her mouth like a ravishing conqueror instead of the captive. Fire danced along Adrianne's veins and nerve endings, culminating in her sex and bringing her instantly to dew point as his tongue skated along hers, entwined, stroked, explored every inch of her mouth. Dropping the washcloth, she pressed herself fully against him, locking her other arm around his neck as his kiss took the strength out of her knees.

They were both breathing heavily when he broke the kiss at last. "Would you like for me to service you?" he murmured huskily.

"Mmmm. Show me everything you know," Adrianne responded.

He promptly scooped her into his arms, stepped out of the shower and moved through the doorway into the main room. Dimly, it occurred to her that Darcy might come storming through the connecting door at any moment, but she dismissed the thought almost at once, knowing Darcy would retreat instantly.

They were both dripping wet, and soapy. Adrianne shivered slightly in the chill but in a moment Yar covered her with his own body. Grasping her arms, he pushed them over her head and held them there as he kissed her into mindless oblivion, then proceeded to nibble his way along her cheek to her neck, then down. Releasing her hands, he cupped a breast in each hand and finessed first one and then the other, stimulating her nipples with his mouth and tongue until she was moving restlessly beneath him, gasping for air.

Her body, thrumming with the pleasurable sensations of heightened sensitivity, began to sense overload and demand release. Her sex was wet with want, her muscles in her belly convulsing rhythmically as if kneading his cock already.

She reached down, grasped his cock and tried to urge him to join with her. He pulled her hand loose and thrust it to the bed. "I haven't shown you everything yet," he murmured huskily.

The comment alone almost sent her over the edge. She clutched the sheets, gasping as he made his way down her belly. Pressing her legs tightly together, he parted the folds of flesh around her sex with one hand and placed his mouth over her clit, sucking on it. She bucked, tried to part her legs as a bolt of pleasure went through her that was so exquisite her belly clenched.

She moaned, gasping in little breaths of air as she felt her body moving closer and closer to release as he teased her clit with his tongue, nudging the center of her pleasure with quick, hard strokes. Her fingers, where she gripped the sheets, began to cramp as she struggled to hold her climax at bay just a moment longer, just a few moments longer until she reached a point where she began to struggle to grasp it.

A jolt of dismay went through her as he stopped abruptly. As he moved up and over her, however, she opened her eyes, certain he meant to thrust his cock inside of her. Instead, he began to suckle her breasts again, teasing her nipples until her body began to skate the edge of pain--the pleasure had become so intense.

When he moved down her belly again and pressed his knees against the outside of her thighs, Adrianne grasped two fistfuls of his hair, knowing she couldn't stand to be teased any longer. He ignored the tug, teasing her clit once more until she thought she would scream. She did scream when her climax hit her as abruptly as a freight train, hard and fast.

She was still gasping and trying to catch her breath when he moved down her body, spread her thighs and began nibbling the inside of her thighs. Too weak to fight him off, she tried to ignore the tiny ripples of pleasure that made her belly clench. He continued downward until he reached her feet. Adrianne tried to jerk her foot from his grasp, but he held onto it, massaging it. When she relaxed, he began sucking her toes.

Expecting it to tickle, Adrianne was surprised to discover the ripples of pleasure growing stronger once more. When he'd thoroughly finessed her toes, he worked his way back up her thighs with nibbling kisses. Adrianne held her breath as he reached the apex of her thighs, hoping he would kiss her pussy again, afraid that he would. She cried out when he fastened his mouth over her clit once more and suckled, convulsing upward, gripping his hair. He disentangled her fingers, pressing her hands against the bed again, then moved upward and caressed her breasts with his mouth.

Within moments, Adrianne felt her body climbing toward release once more. She could barely catch her breath, could barely think, but she was certain of one thing, she wanted Yar inside of her this time. Clutching his shoulders, she wrapped her legs around his waist, lifting her hips. To her relief, he obliged, aligning the head of his cock with her sex and thrusting. As wet as she was, it took a moment for her body to adjust to the girth of his cock. She pushed against him until finally she felt him sliding fully inside of her. He allowed her to set the rhythm, thrusting and withdrawing in direct counterpoint to her own movements. When she began the little gasping breaths that proceeded her climax, he rolled onto his back, bringing her to a sitting position above him. She moved over him, searching for just the right angle that would give her the most pleasure, opening her eyes to watch him.

His face was tense with concentration as he held her hips to steady her. It was all she needed to send her over the edge once more into ultimate bliss. He gripped her hips as her climax took her, continuing to thrust as her climax hit her so explosively it sapped all the strength from her limbs.

Finally, she collapsed weakly against him, fighting for breath. It was several moments before she realized the heartbeat thundering in her ears was his, not her own, and several moments more before she realized that she had climaxed, explosively, twice, and he had not.

Disappointment flooded her. "You didn't come."

Yar's expression was one of confusion.

Weakly, Adrianne slid off of him. "You didn't … enjoy it?"

"It is not allowed," he said hoarsely.

Adrianne stared at him in dismay. "Not … but…."

"You are … satisfied?"

"Thoroughly," Adrianne gasped weakly.

"May I go now?"

Adrianne stared at him. He looked as if he was in pain and suddenly it dawned on her why he was so anxious to leave. "You may not."

He looked dismayed.

"This is Earth," Adrianne murmured, leaning toward him. "We share the pleasure. You give me pleasure and I give you pleasure." She kissed him lingeringly on the lips, then pulled back to look at him.

He was studying her, as if he wasn't certain she had meant it. "I can … take pleasure?"

Adrianne smiled. "I insist."

He pushed her to the bed and rolled over her. His cock was hard as a rock as he pushed inside of her. Having climaxed twice already, Adrianne was a little stunned at the shock waves of pleasure that went through her the moment he entered her. Her body convulsed around his hard flesh, gripping it like a massaging hand. Digging her heels into the bed, she thrust against him as he began to move. He held himself slightly above her, supporting his weight on his elbows and Adrianne caressed his chest as he moved inside of her, marveling at the feel of his skin and muscles against her palms.

She looked up at him. "I love the way you feel inside of me," she whispered huskily.

He stiffened at her words, his face contorting almost as if he was in pain. With a hoarse gasp, he began to move again, faster and harder, driving into her hard enough she began to slide upwards on the bed. She gripped him more tightly, gasping as she felt her body tensing on the verge of release.

She cried out as her body exploded with intense pleasure. With a hoarse cry that sounded as if he was dying, Yar's body jerked convulsively as he, too, found release at last. He collapsed bonelessly on top of her as if too weak to hold himself up, his body still shuddering with release.

Adrianne struggled for breath, stroking his back lovingly. Finally, he gathered himself and rolled off of her, much to her relief. Dragging in a deep, much needed breath of air, she rolled over to face him, smiling at the expression of relaxed repletion on his face. Finally, she reached up and caressed his cheek. He opened his eyes. "It was wonderful … every time. But the last was the very best."

He pulled her close, hugging her tightly. "Thank you."

Something warm and almost painful filled Adrianne's chest until she had to struggle to breathe. She stroked his soft hair. "It was my pleasure," she murmured.

\* \* \* \*

Yar woke her a few hours later and made love to her again. Exhaustion claimed them afterwards and they slept until nearly dawn, when Adrianne was once more wakened by the skate of Yar's hand over her hip. She smiled sleepily.

"I've created a monster," she muttered, but she realized after a moment that she would have all the time in the world to catch up on her sleep after Yar was gone. She didn't want to waste a moment while he was with her.

She didn't think of the Orgasmizer9000 once while Yar was making love to her. As wonderful as the device was, Yar put it to shame.

Finally, they showered and dressed and Adrianne knocked on the connecting door. After several moments, Darcy, looking as thoroughly fucked as she no doubt did, opened the door. Her hair was standing on end, her mouth, neck and chest reddened from whisker burn, and her eyes blurry and unfocused.

"Ready?" Adrianne asked with forced cheerfulness.

Darcy merely stared at her blankly for several moments before enlightenment dawned. She nodded. "Gimme a minute," she slurred and slammed the door once more.

They stopped for breakfast before leaving town. Adrianne was torn between happiness for her friend and jealousy as she watched Chance and Darcy bill and coo at each other over their breakfast plates.

Yar was quieter than usual, if possible, frowning as he ate, and Adrianne wondered if it seemed as tasteless to him as it did to her. No doubt he was thinking about the fact that this would probably be his last Earth breakfast.

She was tempted to ask him if he'd rather just turn around and go back home with her. Somehow, the idea of getting rich off of the Orgasmizer9000 had lost it's glow. None of the things she'd planned to buy once she was rolling in money, nor any of the things she'd planned to do seemed nearly as exciting when she thought about the fact that she would only have Darcy to share the thrill with. Of course, if she had lots and lots of money, she would have many opportunities to meet all sorts of men.

None of them would be Yar, though, she thought glumly.

Resolutely, she dismissed it as they paid for their meals and left, heading toward Roswell.

They were in no particular hurry since they were within a few hundred miles of their goal now. They could not attempt a rescue before it was good dark. Serena was being held on a base, which would be guarded, and it would be all too easy to see them during daylight.

Arriving at last in the late afternoon, they found a hotel first, renting two rooms again, although Adrianne was fairly certain she wouldn't be sharing a room with Yar that night.

It occurred to her that they could just surveil the place and then work out a plan and try for Serena's release the following night, but it also occurred to her that the scientists that had been brought in to study her might be more interested in studying her corpse than talking to Serena. For that matter, who knew if she could survive the FEDS' debriefing? It was all very well to talk about the Geneva Convention, but she doubted the FEDS would consider an alien's rights to be the equivalent of human rights.

It was only right to move as quickly as they were able to.

When they'd settled in their rooms, Chance left to see what information he could glean. He returned a couple of hours later with a local youth who'd offered to act as guide.

As Chance had done when he'd shown them the crash site, the youth led them down winding, overgrown tracks that wandered in first one direction and then another. After a couple of hours of driving around endlessly, he showed them a place to park the van.

Darcy decided to join them. Adrianne wasn't so sure it was a good idea. Darcy and Chance were so wrapped up in each other neither of them were paying a lot of attention to what was happening around them. Besides, they'd had to make a quick getaway before. They might have to again.

Darcy and Chance both insisted, however, so the four of them, led by the youth, made their way cautiously toward the base until they were close enough to see. Except for the dangerous looking guards at the gates, the place looked deserted. There wasn't a soul in sight or even a vehicle.

Stealthily, they made their way around the base, checking each building for any sign of occupancy. Finally, they struck pay dirt when they reached the hangars. Several vehicles were parked outside and guards were stationed in front of the hangar doors.

Adrianne looked around, trying to decide if they would be able to drive a little closer after dark. "What do you think, guys? Do you think the van could make it across the desert here?"

The young man glanced at her. "They'd hear you miles before you got here. Sound carries, even if they didn't see you."

"Shit! No way could we run that far with the soldiers behind us. The van must be two miles from here, at least."

The youth looked startled. "Why would the soldiers be chasing you?"

Chance gave her a look. "She meant if they saw us."

The youth accepted the comment without remark. "If you had a couple of horses, you could muffle their hooves and probably get a lot closer. Of course the horses would probably be nickering, but there's still a few wild horses around here. They might not think anything of it."

"Unfortunately, I don't ride," Adrianne said. "What about you, Chance?"

He shrugged. "I have. Can't say I'm great with horses, but the horses they rent out for trail rides are usually pretty manageable."

Adrianne glanced around again. It seemed likely that the FEDS had transported the ship to the hangar, but would they be holding Serena there? Somehow, she doubted it. Of course, the building was large enough to put several houses in it, so it was possible. "Let's look around some more ... see if any of the other buildings are occupied."

There were more guards at the back of the hangar, but Adrianne spotted a walk-in door about halfway down one side ... probably locked, but she made a mental note of it. As they made a circuit of the base, they discovered a smaller building that also appeared to be occupied. Two guards stood outside. "I wonder what that building is," Adrianne muttered out loud.

"I think it's the brig," the young man volunteered. "They must have somebody in there or they wouldn't be guarding it."

Chance and Adrianne exchanged a glance. "You think so?" Adrianne asked.

The boy shrugged. "The place was deserted for a while … or mostly--only a couple of guards at the main gate that we saw. Me and a couple of my buddies came out here once to check it out. I'm pretty sure that's the brig."

They made the long walk back to the van, drove back to town and dropped the boy off. "I'm not too keen about the horse idea, but I honestly don't see another way. We can't get close enough to the base to have much of a chance of escape otherwise."

Since no one else seemed to have a better idea, they located a stable and arranged to rent horses for a trail ride. Adrianne didn't feel up to the task of trying to load the horses in a horse trailer, and, in any case, Darcy didn't have a trailer hitch, so she told the man they were 'camping out' in the van and asked if he'd deliver them to a designated spot so that they could get an early start the next morning.

It meant sitting out in the desert while they awaited delivery, but she couldn't think of a better alternative. The man looked at her a little strangely, but agreed readily enough that he could deliver the horses after he closed the stables for the evening.

They had nothing to do then but kick their heels for several hours. Adrianne found she was a nervous wreck. She knew she'd be climbing the walls if they stayed in the motel waiting. So she suggested instead that they go out to eat and then go to a club for a drink.

It was obvious from Yar's expression that he had no idea what she was talking about, but he never disagreed with any of her suggestions. Chance perked up at the proposal, which made Adrianne a little uneasy. "Three drink limit," she said firmly.

"I'm not driving," Chance said indignantly.

"You'll be riding, though. If you fall off your horse, I'll be alone."

"Yar's coming, isn't he?"

"I seriously doubt if he knows any more about horses than I do, but it'd probably be a good idea to have him with us when … if we get Serena," Adrianne said, glancing at Yar. "Are you coming with us?"

He nodded.

## Chapter Seven

The bar was hot with the crush of bodies and the music almost overwhelming as the four of them made their way inside. Adrianne caught a glimpse of a table near the back that was empty and started toward it. Like most bars, she felt like salmon swimming upstream as she struggled through the tangle of gyrating bodies with Yar, Darcy, and Chance trailing behind.

A waitress buzzed by when they were seated, collected their orders and vanished. Adrianne wasn't particularly fond of country music, which seemed the flavor of the day in the bar--probably the flavor of every day from the looks of the patrons. She was far more interested in getting a drink to soothe her nerves anyway, particularly when she noticed two men that stuck out like a sore thumb.

The 'small' one was about Yar's size, and white. He was almost dwarfed by the other man, who was a very light skinned man of African descent.

She'd noticed the two men twice before, once when they stopped for lunch the day before and then again earlier today. Three times was no coincidence.

They might as well have been wearing a placard that read 'FEDS'.

Adrianne took a gulp of her drink when it arrived, almost choking on it.

Leaning forward when she caught her breath, she asked, "Do you see those two men over there?"

Chance was busy chugging his beer. Yar and Darcy glanced around cautiously.

"Which two men?" Darcy asked dryly.

"The two men that have been following us that look like federal agents," Adrianne said tartly.

Chance strangled on a mouth full of beer. He coughed for five minutes. By the time he was able to catch his breath, the two men had vanished. "Where?"

Adrianne looked around. "They're gone now."

"What makes you think they're following us?" Darcy asked in a scared voice.

"This is the third time I've seen them since Arizona. Don't you think it's a hell of a coincidence that they've shown up at the same place we were three times in a row?"

"But … how could they follow us? *Why* would they follow us?"

"Maybe they've figured out we're up to something? Maybe we didn't get clean away like we thought we did back there at the crash site?"

Darcy took a long swig of her drink. "I'd like to go now."

Adrianne shook her head. "They're probably waiting outside for us. We'll have to figure out a way to lose them before we leave."

Yar took an experimental sip of the beer Adrianne had bought him and made a face. Despite her anxiety, or maybe because she was so tense, Adrianne chuckled. "I don't like it either, but men seem to."

Chance made a snorting noise and Adrianne glanced at him suspiciously. "What?"

Her eyes narrowed. Obviously, he felt intimidated by Yar. He seized every opportunity to make cutting remarks. Thankfully, Yar ignored him … or maybe he didn't understand their language and customs well enough to realize Chance was being an asshole? In any case, she was relieved, whether it was ignorance or just Yar's good nature that kept him from clobbering Chance. "You know. Cut it out."

Chance shrugged and turned to look at the dancers.

"We need to work out a game plan," Adrianne said. "Or maybe I should say, work on the details."

Again, Chance shrugged. "We take the horses as close as we can get, sneak in, break this alien female out, ride off into the sunset."

Adrianne glared at him, but before she could demand to know what they were supposed to do about the guards, a woman came up to the table.

"Mind if I borrow your man for a dance?"

Adrianne looked the woman over. The woman had spoken to her, but she hadn't taken her eyes off of Yar and Adrianne didn't like the way she was looking at Yar ... at all. Unfortunately, Yar wasn't hers. She shrugged. "You want to dance, Yar?"

He smiled. "I love to dance."

"Have at it," Adrianne said tightly, focusing on the drink in her hands.

When Yar rose and left, she turned to watch the two wind their way through the crowd to the dance floor and finally, resolutely, turned her back on the pair.

"What are we going to do about the guards?"

"I think, between me and Yar, we can handle them," Chance said cockily, sending Darcy a smoldering look.

"We're not going to have time for you guys to 'have fun'. We need to get in and get out."

Chance shrugged. "Got any pepper gas?"

Adrianne frowned as it occurred to her to wonder how Yar's Orgasmizer would work on a man. If it worked the same way on men as it worked on women all they had to do was give the guards a jolt and they'd be incapacitated long enough for them to tie the men up. A smile curled her lips, and she turned to look in the direction that Yar had gone.

She could no longer see him. A crowd had closed around Yar and the woman.

He must be a pretty good dancer if the crowd was any indication. Even as she turned, the women in the group began to stamp their feet and scream encouragement. Curious, she craned her neck to see what was going on.

She still couldn't see anything and finally stood up. Just as she did so, Yar leapt on top of a table. He was nude from the waist up, gyrating his hips while he slipped the T-shirt back and forth between his legs--like a male stripper. Adrianne's jaw dropped as he reached for the snap of his jeans.

"Oh my God!"

"What?" Chance said, responding to the horror in her voice by leaping to his feet.

At just that moment, a very male roar interrupted the feminine whoops of appreciation, and the table Yar was dancing on shuddered, as if from a blow.

"Yar's in trouble!" Adrianne yelled, surging forward.

The crowd ringing Yar parted abruptly as Adrianne approached ... not to allow her access, but to avoid the very large body that came skittering across the floor toward her. Adrianne looked down in stunned surprise at Yar then up at the bull of a man that was advancing toward them. "Get up! Quick!"

Yar leapt to his feet, looking around just in time to receive the fist the bouncer threw at him. Adrianne didn't think. Grabbing the heavy glass her drink had been served in, she heaved it at the man, catching him right between the eyes. The man staggered back a couple of steps, shook his head, and started toward her with a look in his eyes Adrianne didn't like at all. Adrianne clutched Yar's arm. "Don't just stand there! Do something!"

"What?" Yar asked.

"Hit him!"

Yar swung at the man, but it was obvious even to Adrianne that Yar had never been in a fight in his life. He clipped the guy on the jaw purely by accident. Fortunately, Yar had about sixty pounds of solid meat packed into the punch and a good bit of momentum. The guy hit the floor and skidded backwards.

The crowd, which had seemed too stunned to react up until that moment, broke into a free-for-all as two men leapt out of the way, spilling their beer on the man and woman standing next to them. The two who'd been drenched in beer leapt to their feet. The woman slapped one of the 'culprits'. The man with her punched the other guy in the face. Within seconds the bar was a heaving mass of struggling bodies, swinging fists, flying bottles and smashed chairs. Screaming women were running in every direction or throwing everything they could lay hand to.

The two federal agents burst through the front entrance just as all hell broke loose and were almost instantly absorbed into the general fray.

Seeing them, Adrianne realized they had 'lucked' into the perfect distraction for an escape. Grabbing Chance by the back of his shirt, she yanked on it to get his attention. The guy he'd been about to clobber seized on Chance's distraction and jacked his jaw sideways. As Chance's head snapped in her direction, Adrianne shouted. "We have to go now. Cut it out."

Looking around, she discovered that Darcy was already halfway to the door.

Yar, she discovered, was on the floor again.

Grabbing a beer bottle, she cold cocked the guy standing over him. "Get up. We have to go."

Yar scrambled to his feet, but before she could guide him to the door, he'd slugged the guy that had put him on the floor.

She'd say one thing for him. He was a fast learner.

He was grinning from ear to ear as he went for the next man.

Just like a man!

"You can beat somebody up later. I promise. Right now, we have to go. The cops'll be here any minute to arrest everybody in the place."

That got his attention. Grabbing her hand, he plowed the way through the bar to the entrance, belting everyone that stepped in his path on the way out.

They were racing toward the van when Chance came out the door as if he'd been pitched out, executing a belly flop in the parking lot.

"Quit screwing around, Chance!"

Shaking his head, he managed to drag himself to his feet, looked around in confusion for several moments and finally staggered toward the van.

They were almost a block away before they caught the first glimpse of flashing blue lights.

\* \* \* \*

Under the circumstances, they decided to stop by the hotel room long enough to allow Chance and Yar to clean up. Yar was upset that he'd lost his shirt in the fray and Adrianne wouldn't allow him to go back for it. After the two men had cleaned up, they headed out once more, stopping at a discount store to buy Yar another shirt. The man was leaving with the horses when they finally arrived at the appointed spot. They had to flag him down and Adrianne's stomach tightened another notch when she realized how closely they'd come to completely demolishing their plans. The mixed drink had helped, but that went the way of the wind when the fight had broken out and they had such a close call with the cops.

Once they'd picketed the horses, they waved the man off, promising to have the horses waiting for him when he came back for them the following evening. Adrianne hoped the horses would be waiting for him and not corralled on a federal reserve.

As soon as the man was out of sight, Adrianne and Yar mounted one horse, while Chance mounted the other. Darcy had been designated as lookout once more, to stay with the van. Adrianne had brought her backpack filled with her 'break-in' tools and made certain Yar had the Orgasmizer. She needn't have worried. Yar kept a close watch on it. And who could blame him? It was the only thing he owned. She felt like a total bitch for coming up with the idea of taking it in exchange for her help.

Despite the fact that they'd covered the horses' hooves to muffle the sound, they didn't dare take the horses too close to the base. When they were within a half a mile of the base, they dismounted, tied the horses securely and made the remainder of the trek on foot.

It was pitch black. Only a smattering of stars could be seen overhead, most of them having been obscured by a heavy cloud covering. It was a blessing and a curse rolled into one. They could barely see, and they didn't dare use flashlights, but at least they had the comfort of knowing they probably couldn't be seen either.

Unless the guards were using those night vision glasses.

Adrianne shook the thought off, but she breathed a sigh of relief when they managed to reach the fence without incident. Dropping her back pack, Adrianne dug out the heavy wire cutters.

"Wait!" Chance cautioned. "It might be electrified."

Adrianne swallowed a gulp of fear. "If it is, we're screwed."

"It probably isn't, but it would be a good idea to check before we try to cut into it. You got a screwdriver with a rubber handle?"

She dug around and finally produced the screwdriver she'd bought. Chance peered at it for several moments and finally cautioned them to get back. Gingerly, he touched the tip to the wire. To everyone's relief, nothing happened.

"Now we use the cutters." Tossing her the screwdriver, he clipped one long line up the fence, then one across.

"You're not going to cut it out?" Adrianne asked a little doubtfully.

"I'm hoping it won't be noticeable if we leave it like this."

She nodded and they slipped through the small opening one at the time, then scurried across the open area to the nearest building, flattening themselves against the side of it.

Peering around the corner of the building, Adrianne saw that two guards were stationed outside the brig, just as they had been earlier. She ducked back. "They're standing squarely in front of the door. It was too much to hope, I guess, that they'd be walking around the building and give us a chance to sneak inside."

"I think me and Yar could sneak up on either side of the building and take them."

"You'd probably have a fight on your hands, in which case everybody that was anywhere around would come running." She glanced at Yar. "How does that thing of yours work on men?"

Yar looked taken aback, then revolted. "My ... tool? I can not!"

Adrianne bit back a chuckle. "The Orgasmizer."

He looked relieved and then uncertain. "It was designed for women. I do not know."

Adrianne shrugged. "My guess is, pretty much the same. Anyway, we're about to find out.

They crept around to the back side of the building, then divided up. Adrianne took the Orgasmizer and sent Yar and Chance around the other side to make sure they subdued the guard on that side while she took the other one out. When she reached the front of the building, she waited for several moments to make sure Yar and Chance had had time to get into place, then made a psst noise.

The guard stiffened and turned slowly to look behind him. As he turned, Adrianne touched his hand with the Orgasmizer. He jerked, as if he'd been electrocuted, his eyes rolled back in his head and he crumpled at her feet, jerking. Leaving him, Adrianne rushed around the front of the building. Yar and Chance each had hold of one of the other guard's arms. Chance had his hand clamped firmly over the man's mouth. Adrianne held out the Orgasmizer and advanced until she was within inches of him.

"I'd let go of him if I were you."

The moment Yar and Chance released the man, Adrianne stuck the business end of the Orgasmizer to him. As the other guard had, he jerked as if a bolt of electricity had gone through him and collapsed in a writhing heap on the ground.

"She-it," Chance exclaimed. "What is that thing, some kind of stun gun?"

"Oh, it's stunning," Adrianne said with a chuckle, "but it probably won't hold them long. We need to get them tied and gagged and get moving before somebody notices the guards are missing."

Yar and Adrianne left Chance binding the guards and moved cautiously inside. There was only one man on the inside. Adrianne caught him with the Orgasmizer as he rose from his chair. A quick search of the desk the man had been sitting at produced the keys to the cell behind him.

Serena lay sprawled on the third bunk to the right. She didn't stir when they approached. More than half expecting it to be a trap, Adrianne approached the woman cautiously.

She discovered, however, that it was no trick. Serena was conscious, barely, but her eyes were glazed. "Damn it! They've drugged her."

Yar nodded. "She is a great warrior. They would not have captured her otherwise."

"What'll we do now?"

"I will carry her."

Adrianne frowned, looking doubtfully at the amazonian proportions of the woman. "Can you?"

"I must." He sat on the edge of the bunk and pulled Serena upright. She stared at him blankly a moment before a drunken smile curled her lips. "Zat you, Yar?"

"Yes, Mistress Serena."

She patted him on the cheek … actually it was more of a slap, though Yar didn't flinch. "Good boy," she murmured before her eyes rolled back in her head.

Placing his shoulder under her belly, Yar stood, shifting her until he had her balanced. Chance met them in the outer room. "God almighty! You weren't kidding, were you?"

He whirled then and led the way out. They were still struggling to get through the cut in the fence when the alarms went off. Yar had to put Serena down and drag her through the opening. By the time Adrianne managed to get through, he'd pulled Serena across his shoulders again. Instead of running, however, he turned to help her.

"Go! You've got enough to worry about. I can take care of myself."

He kept pace with her as she ran, however, and she had the feeling that he was holding back on her account, rather than because of his burden. When they reached the horses, he carefully placed Serena across the horse Chance had ridden, then grabbed her around the waist and tossed her onto the other one, climbing up behind her.

They kicked the horses into a gallop just as a search light caught them in its beam.

Adrianne was glad they had brought the van as close as they dared. It seemed doubtful they would have out run the soldiers otherwise, for they weren't hampered with the need to be quiet. Before they had covered more than half the distance between the base and the van, the very distinct sounds of a military vehicle reached their ears.

Adrianne craned around for a look back and her heart leapt into her throat. They weren't going to make it. The horses were willing, but they were no match for the horses under the hoods of the trucks.

The trucks were barely a quarter of a mile from them by the time the van came into view, and closing fast. "Darcy! Start the van!" Adrianne shouted.

To her consternation, nothing happened. "Darcy! For God's sake! They're right behind us!" she screamed.

Darcy stepped out from behind the van at just that moment, caught in the high beams of the military trucks that were right behind them. Even from a distance, Adrianne could see that Darcy's eyes were wide with fright. What she couldn't understand was why Darcy was just standing at the end of the van, looking frightened, instead of jumping into the driver's seat. In the next moment, she discovered why. Two men stepped from behind the van.

It was the FEDS.

Adrianne felt sick. They had the military behind them and the FEDS in front and nothing but two tired horses.

Turning in Yar's arms, she kissed him quickly. "Put me down and go! You and Serena might still be able to make it."

He looked surprised for a moment, and then his jaw set. "No."

"The horse can run faster without two people on it. Chance can help you and Serena find the way back to the pod."

As she was struggling to slide off the horse, a blinding light caught them abruptly.

Stunned, Adrianne looked around, and then up, wondering how she could have failed to hear a helicopter.

It wasn't a helicopter above them, however. It was a sleek, silver cigar. The military vehicles came to a screeching halt as the vessel settled near the ground and ten of the biggest women Adrianne had ever seen in her life leapt from the portal that opened near the bottom of the craft. Screaming like wild Indians, they fired light bursts from some sort of guns that disintegrated the military vehicles to dust even as men dove from the trucks in every direction like rats off a sinking ship, throwing their guns down and running back toward the base as fast as their legs could carry them.

"Serena's sisters," Yar said, a note of resignation in his voice.

## Chapter Eight

Serena was still a little groggy, but had recovered enough to get off the horse and stand. "Sylvia?" she said a little doubtfully as the tallest of the women approached her.

Sylvia smiled wryly. "It is a good thing for you, Serena, that these Earth barbarians were stupid enough to hold you in the same place as your ship. Without the tracking chip, we could not have found you. For that matter, it is a good thing that you are the baby. Otherwise we would not have come to look for you."

Serena grinned and threw her arms around her oldest sister, hugging her tightly.

"As always, your timing is perfect."

Apparently oblivious of the Earth barbarians, the sisters shared a round of hugs and excited conversation for several moments, but, to Adrianne's dismay, they had not forgotten the situation. They simply saw none of the Earth barbarians as a threat.

After they'd reacquainted themselves, they turned to study the Earthlings.

Chance was still seated on his horse, staring at the women with his mouth at half cock. Unnerved by the women, Adrianne inched a little closer to Yar. To her surprise Yar placed an arm around her protectively.

Serena didn't miss the movement, or its implications. Her eyes narrowed for several moments. After a moment, she approached them, stopping a few feet away and placing her hands on her hips. Yar stared at her a long moment and finally released Adrianne and went down on one knee, bowing his head. "I rejoice that you are freed, Mistress Serena."

Serena smiled thinly, patted the top of his bent head, and turned her attention to Adrianne. "You helped me to escape."

"I did."

"Why?"

Adrianne blushed in spite of all she could do. "I made a bargain with Yar to help free you in exchange for the Orgasmizer9000. We don't have anything like that. It would make me rich."

To Adrianne's surprise, Serena looked her over with a touch of respect. She smiled faintly. "I am forever amazed at how puny Earth women are, but you have potential."

Adrianne smiled. "I'm pretty amazed myself at the women of Barbron."

Serena chuckled.

"These others--they helped also?"

Adrianne looked around. "Chance, over on the horse … and my friend, Darcy. The two men are Federal Agents. They came to stop us."

Serena jerked her head in some sort of signal and her sisters moved, surrounding the two federal agents.

"You and your friends may go."

Adrianne glanced at Yar. "What about Yar?"

"My slave?"

Adrianne's lips tightened, but she held her temper in check. It was obvious from Serena's reception to her previous comment that Serena was a business woman. "I will barter for him."

Yar glanced at her sharply, but Adrianne ignored him.

A gleam of interest entered Serena's eyes. "What?"

"Those two men over there."

Serena threw back her head and laughed. "They are not yours to barter."

Adrianne couldn't help but smile back. "It was worth a try."

"What about the machine there?"

Adrianne glanced at the van. "It's not mine. I have a car, though … it's back in Vegas. But you'll have to go there anyway to get the pod Yar used," she added hastily.

"Done!" Serena held out her hand and although Adrianne was a little surprised at the very human gesture, she shook hands with the woman.

Serena smiled. "I've always had a fondness for things from Earth."

Adrianne looked around. "I'll take us a while to get back."

Serena shook her head. "You'll go with us. I get the car, then you get my slave."

"What about those two?" Adrianne said, jerking her head in the direction of the agents. "They're not just going to let us leave."

Serena turned, studied the two men for several moments and finally walked over to them. After studying them for several moments, she faced the black man. "I'll take this one."

"I think not!" he said in a deep, melodious voice and threw a punch at her. Serena was far quicker however, and apparently just as powerful. She knocked him flat, then leaned over, pulled him up and threw him over one shoulder, patting his ass. "Nice."

The other agent made a dash for it, but was quickly subdued and one of Serena's sisters tossed him over her shoulder and started back toward the craft.

Adrianne turned to Darcy. "I'll see you back in Vegas."

"You trust them?" Darcy whispered worriedly.

"Not especially. But it's the only chance I have to get Yar. I can't very well fight for him."

Darcy chewed her lip. "Adrianne … is it really worth the risk?"

Adrianne turned to look at Yar. "He is."

\* \* \* \*

The trip from Roswell to Las Vegas, that had taken them almost twelve hours to drive, took less than thirty minutes in the Barbron craft. To be on the safe side, they set the craft down near the pod, well outside the city and hailed the first cab they saw upon reaching the city limits. Adrianne was more than a little anxious that Serena might change her mind about their bargain when she saw the car. It was only a couple of years old, and a sports model, but nothing at all like the van Serena had wanted. To her relief, Serena was thrilled. Adrianne demonstrated the workings of the vehicle, then held on for dear life as Serena careened around the neighborhood several times, trying it out.

"It uses gasoline. You might have a problem with fuel," Adrianne felt compelled to tell her.

Serena shrugged. "There is always fuel of one kind or another to be had."

It took an effort to stand once Serena stopped the car and let her out again. Her knees were so weak, she had to lock them to keep from wilting to the sidewalk. To her surprise and alarm, Serena got out of the car and summoned Yar, who'd waited for them on the front walk. Yar approached her and knelt, bowing his head.

"The Earth woman has changed you," she said thoughtfully. Yar threw her a startled look and Serena smiled. "You were never quite as a slave should be, Yar. It's one of the reasons I was always so fond of you." She was silent for several moments. "I would have freed you for helping me to escape even if the woman had not bartered for you, but I see no reason not to take what was offered.

"Go …with my blessing. Breed fine daughters on your Earth woman. The women of this world need a better root stock. The women here are too puny."

Yar looked at her with a mixture of confusion and hopefulness. "I am a slave. I can not breed."

Serena chuckled, shaking her head. "Of course you can. Few of the women of Barbron can afford the time or the luxury of breeding their young themselves. We transfer our hatchlings to those who can."

Yar frowned. "But I have not."

"You have. I will tell her her father is a free man of Earth. Perhaps one day she will come to see you."

Dismissing him, she climbed back into the car, shifted it into gear and floored the gas pedal.

"I hope she manages to make it out of Vegas without the police pulling her over," Adrianne murmured as Serena tore off down the street with a squeal of tires. "What did she say to you?"

"That you are mine," Yar said, smiling a little doubtfully. "Are you?"

"If you want me," Adrianne said cautiously.

He wrapped his arms around her and pulled her close. "I want you. But I am not sure I will be useful to you. I do not know Earth ways very well. I must take care of you, yes?"

Adrianne grinned against his chest. "Between you and the Orgasmizer9000, I think we'll do just fine."

The End

Check out other NCP titles in Trade Paperback from these talented authors:

## ANGELIQUE ANJOU:

Tears of the Dragon

## JAIDE FOX:

The Shadowmere Trilogy
Intergalactic Bad Boys Book One and Two
His Wicked Ways/Winter Thaw
The Fallen (Anthology with Marie Morin, Celeste Anwar, and Kimberly Zant)
Ultimate Warriors (Anthology with Brenna Lyons, Joy Nash, Michelle M. Pillow)

## MARIE MORIN:

The Atalantium Trilogy
Supernatural Lovers (Anthology with JC Grey and Mandy M. Roth)
The Fallen (Anthology with Jaide Fox, Celeste Anwar, and Kimberly Zant)

Printed in the United States
63820LVS00003B/424-456